THE DWELLING OF ALL SOULS

THE DWELLING OF ALL SOULS

BY BRANDANN R. HILL-MANN

BOOK III OF THE HOLE IN THE WORLD

For my husband, Chi
Thanks for being my partner on this wacky ride.

CHAPTER ONE

INNES

"Give it some thought, Cameron." Innes' advisor, Dr. Alvarado, stood, offering him a firm handshake across his oak desk. "I think it's a good fit for you and should give you a leg up in choosing a medical school."

"Agreed." Innes squeezed his hand back, letting a half-cocked grin turn up. He had no reason to be humble. He had fantastic grades, promising skills, and a work ethic he was frequently praised for. He would have his choice of medical schools; even without an impressive list of extracurricular activities and even considering the small school where he would soon complete his undergraduate work. But this was not just any opportunity: a chance to do some real good, being the hero for a change in a way that was healing, not destroying. "I'll let you know, sir."

"That's a good grip you have there," Dr. Alvarado noted. "You work out?"

Now the bashfulness crept up in a flush on his neck and cheeks. "Weight training. It's a recent hobby." Which was a funny way to describe something he did almost compulsively to keep the nightmares of being nearly killed at bay. "Can't go around being a damsel. I'm way too handsome. And I cook."

Dr. Alvarado laughed, then picked up a stack of essays and tapped them on the desk. Innes recognized it for the dismissal it was and left without another word.

A chance to travel. A chance to see parts of the country or maybe the world and maybe have a positive influence. No, not as some savior, but as someone who could use his skills to help. People needed medicine, and he needed practice.

He shouldered his backpack, what his best friend Kahrin would describe as "nerd-sized" and made his way to the parking lot, aware that his were the only steps on the concrete and it was after dark.

No, he wasn't scared of the dark. And he wasn't going to pretend that there was any fault in being afraid of something, for even the greatest heroes knew fear in the face of dragons. The past few years had taught him something important: that he could not always trust what he saw to be truth, and that he was vulnerable in a world behind a veil he was never meant to cross.

His heart thumped in his throat, and his keys were in his hand long before he climbed the steps to the level where he'd left his Prius. Moments like this were when he could remember most vividly—when the silvery crescent scar at his throat throbbed with phantom pain—and he remained hyperaware of every goosebump or feeling of static charged air. He'd grown up dreaming of magic being real, of knowing it was, of thinking he needed it to be, only to be mostly let down by the realities of the way it was twisted.

Safe in his car, he drove through the relatively quiet city streets, to the gym near where he and Kahrin lived. He had enough time to work through a complete circuit of training before he needed to be home to wash for his date. His first date in a while that wasn't in the middle of the day or a very public place. Lizzie had proven to be as harmless as he could determine without introducing her to Kahrin, and it was not yet time to jump from that bridge into that rushing river of whitecaps. Not that his best friend would be jealous, beyond her normal way, but she would definitely over-question the woman until she was sure she was no magical threat.

Dating had been difficult since Evangeline, the stunning redhead who had lived across from him in his first apartment building. He'd thought she was just an intense woman with a very pronounced crush. Actually, she'd been an empousa, a seductive part-demon who had been determined to have the magically blessed blood that flowed in his veins. She'd nearly killed him, and they hadn't even really been dating.

He used the way his memories of Evangeline chilled him to drive him as he lifted and pushed himself to increase the weight in his sets. He let the burn in his muscles remind him of the life still flowing in his veins, and every hard breath out was an appreciation.

"Need a spotter?" Carbry had joined them in the city after finishing his first term in community college back in their sleepy farm town.

Innes couldn't say he hated having the guy around again. "Actually, yeah." He laid back on the bench and let Carbry set the weight. "Add another plate to each side?"

"How come Quirke isn't here spotting?" Carbry had been a common friend between he and Kahrin since high school, and something of a paramour of Kahrin's off and on after. More off than on, but the arrangement seemed mutually agreeable. And none of his business.

"Working." Innes breathed deeply and waited until Carbry's hands were floating above the bar before he took it off the stand and let it press against his muscles.

"Which job?"

"She quit the night club." A hard breath out. "Mostly catering now." When his arms wobbled to failure, Carbry caught it and helped him reset it in place. "I thought you'd know."

He laughed. "Nah. I haven't seen her in a couple of weeks. And not like you're implying in a while. How's she doing?"

She really hadn't mentioned Carbry lately. In fact, she'd not really mentioned anyone lately. Not since Jude, but that was months ago. Weird. Innes sat up, planting his feet on the rubberized floor, and slapping his palms on his lap.

"Same as always." He paused. That wasn't quite true. She'd been, well tame wasn't a word he'd use out loud, but her usual summer storm nature seemed a little more subdued lately. "Guess she's just reprioritizing. I'll tell her you asked about her."

Carbry chuckled and gave him a look that said Innes was missing something. "Nah, bro. Just say hi for me. And good luck."

"Will do." He slung his towel over his shoulder and retrieved the cleaner for the bench, wiping it down thoroughly before leaving.

The many oddities of Kahrin didn't register much other than his needing to have their version of a check-in with her. But she was at work, and he needed to hurry if he was going to pick Lizzie up on time. And he couldn't have anyone thinking his hair ever looked like this!

Lizzie was lovely. Petite, dark with dark hair, round in many places that made her nice to hug. Which was as far as they'd gone, other than a brief peck to the cheek. He couldn't tell if it was him holding back, or her. He decided he was going to give it an honest try tonight. Which he did. He showed up with flowers, a daring bouquet of roses which she immediately arranged in water as he wandered her apartment for the first time. He'd picked a nice restaurant on Emilia's recommendation—once he verified that "moderately priced" meant the same thing to him and his dear, older friend and kinky fairy godmother of a sort. Lizzie had ordered a moderately priced meal and he did the same, and they shared a less moderate bottle of wine. The conversation flowed easily but remained shallow. In a moment of boldness, he'd kissed her when they walked back to his car and invited her over.

She accepted.

That went moderate too, and when she fell asleep heavily beside him, he laid awake and stared at the ceiling, wondering if he'd ever lie comfortably in a bed with someone else again. Well, other than Kahrin. But that was different, wasn't it?

Speaking of Kahrin, he came back from the en-suite bathroom with a glass of water to swallow an aspirin to a soft tapping on the glass of his second story window. Something between a sigh and a chuckle escaped him in a breath and he set his glass down and quickly crossed the room before she woke up his guest.

"To what do I owe this surprise? Did you forget what side of the house you live in?" He knew very well why she was here, and it likely had to do with her keys and phone downstairs on the breakfast bar in his kitchen. That had required some answers to questions of Lizzie's.

She rolled her eyes, her hair down in waves after being braided up for her shift. "Hilarious. Let me in, I'm freezing."

"Why didn't you use the door?" He grinned, leaning against the frame. "Also, I'm not alone."

"I knew it." She chewed her lip and peered past him, or would have if he hadn't shifted to block her view. Nosy! "Is it Linda?"

"Lizzie."

"Right. I forgot you went regency this time." Something flitted through her expression before she flashed her eyeteeth to him again. "Anyway, the faster you let me in, the faster I leave."

Would normal people be annoyed? He couldn't help but wonder, because he and Kahrin, both individually and in their relationship, were anything but. Whether it was normal or not, seeing Kahrin now was more exciting than his whole night with Lizzie. That was probably not a good sign.

"Hurry."

She climbed in and he sheep-dogged her past the sleeping woman in his bed and down the stairs. "I put them on the counter for you. How did you go all the way to work and back without your keys and phone?"

"Public transportation." She shrugged as she bounced down the stairs on light toes. She stopped by the door and held up a black shoe. "Prada. Nice. You got a fancy lady."

"She wore Louboutins when we went to brunch." He couldn't let Kahrin think he was entirely uneducated, especially since she wasn't exactly a designer label person.

"Right." She shrugged. "I'm off."

"Oh, no." He shook his head and pointed at the stairs.

"Uh, that's a new kink even for us. Sorry. Hard pass." She sucked air between her teeth. She was teasing and he knew it. While he saw nothing wrong with it, simultaneous multiple partners was not their preference.

"No. Out the way you came in."

"You're joking!"

He lifted both his brows to give her the answer she already knew. Funnily, he wasn't even sure why. It would have been so much faster to let her go out the door and across the hallway. "Maybe you'll learn to keep better track of your belongings."

Her nose wrinkled, no doubt a few choice words on her tongue, but they remained unsaid when they were interrupted.

"Innes?" Lizzie stood at the top of the stairs, robed in his dress shirt. He'd not exactly offered it to her, but he pushed past that fact. She'd been in a dress; it was only polite. "Is someone here?"

He sighed; sure this was his payback. "Lizzie, this is my best friend, Kahrin."

Lizzie blinked, bleary-eyed, as if she was trying to put together what he just said as a serious answer. "Oh. She's a she."

"Yep." He jerked his chin to the stairs. "And she was just leaving."

Kahrin huffed, and again he asked himself why he was beholden to this course. Kahrin climbed the stairs, stomping on each one as she went. "Fine."

"I don't understand. Does she live here?"

"I live next door." Kahrin breezed past her into the bedroom, and he heard the window open again. He jogged up the stairs, grateful he'd put boxer briefs on when he'd gotten up. Brr!

"Oh," Lizzie said. That was the only thing she said as Kahrin slung a leg over the windowsill.

"See you for breakfast?"

He scrubbed his eyes. "I thought you were having brunch with Emilia." Something about a party dress and how wearing Band-Aids under it was a crime, according to the older woman.

"Yeah, after my run."

Oh, of course. Silly of him.

"Good night, dear."

"Night." She leaned to peck a kiss and he leaned to accept, but she decided against it, glancing to Lizzie and scampering away. Why did that disappoint him?

He turned around to find Lizzie searching out her clothes. "Oh, you don't have to go."

"I think it's best I do." She gave him a pretty smile, her even white teeth bright in the moonlight against her black skin. "Innes, I like you," the words formed a sort of frost in his belly, "but I think I know why you're so unavailable."

He blinked. "I'm not un... I'm very available." He thumbed over his shoulder to indicate Kahrin. "You mean this? She does this all the time."

"I get that." She sighed, but not derisively. "I'm not interested in some kind of package deal."

Right. He probably should have seen that one coming. "Look, you should sleep. I'll go down on the couch."

"Can you just take me home, please?"

"Of course." He hustled down the stairs. "Let me get some clothes, and my—" Keys. Kahrin's keys sat on the counter, the keychain, carved out of shell by her father, gleaming in the dark, and his were missing from the dish. "Give me a minute, and I'll get you right home."

CHAPTER TWO
KAHRIN

"Kahrin."

"What?" She paused, a piece of previously frozen strawberry staining a wedge of equally previously frozen honeydew on her fork mid-air.

Emilia's expression was amused as she watched Kahrin over the top of her Bloody Mary. "You know what." The rings on the older woman's fingers clinked softly as she set the glass down, making that distinct thunk that only comes from glass against glass. "Of course that poor dear was upset. What woman wouldn't be put out by a beautiful woman climbing in the window of her beau's bedroom?"

"Who says 'beau' anymore?" She was avoiding the question. She'd known when she went in the window she was taking a risk, but she really hadn't cared. "That's not, um," she trailed off and studied the scalloped edge of her glass fruit plate.

"What, dear?" Emilia tilted her head though her eyes never left Kahrin's. The sensible bob of her silver hair swayed ever-so-slightly, as if it had been trained to always behave exactly as Emilia wished it to. Knowing Emilia as she did, that was not as unlikely as one might think. "You're safe to speak your mind with me, you know."

"I know." Kahrin huffed, no longer wanting the inferior strawberry that was so large it tasted mostly like water. Not at all like the wild ones that Da sometimes took her out to pick when she'd lived at home. "It's not Linda—"

"Lizzie."

"It's not Lizzie's feelings that are throwing me." She pursed her lips and wrinkled her nose.

Emilia folded her hands in front of her, the twinkle in her eye taking on an understanding that Kahrin had foreseen. She'd hoped she was wrong. "You have to tell him."

"Tell him what?"

She knew when she'd said it that it wasn't going to fool Emilia to play stupid. Even if Kahrin hadn't said it out loud, their fairy godmother of sorts knew them better than she had any right to.

"You're jealous."

How did she do that? Somehow Emilia could make the most absurd two words sound so normal. "No."

"Kahrin, my dear. No one benefits when we're not clear and honest about our wants and needs." She reached across the table and rested her hands over Kahrin's. "I can see it. Feelings wear so clearly on youth. More so on you."

"So I love him? Big deal." That was not news to anyone. She and Innes had shared a special bond since they were young and catching fireflies in jars in the south field.

"You know that's not what I mean." She tipped Kahrin's chin up so she could meet her eyes. "Perhaps it wears the same name, but it is not the same feeling."

Kahrin let out a hard breath, tucking a strand of hair back from her face. "It'll pass. It's another impulse. Another flit from thing to thing."

"Do you think that's true?"

Dammit. Emilia was too smart, but that's why Kahrin sought her out. It wasn't just the serious business of pasties and gel inserts for pumps that caused her to ask for this date. "Would you believe me if I said yes?" Emilia simply maintained her gaze. At least she knew whatever magic the woman wielded was not going to affect her, even if she worked mostly in charms. Kahrin was immune to magic. No, not immune, she did not exist to magic. "Fine. It's not like the other stuff."

The "stuff" she meant was the way she'd been happy to blow through lovers and flirtations in rapid succession. She changed jobs more frequently than she washed underwear, and she was usually pressed to buy new underwear every paycheck because of her disdain of doing laundry.

She flopped back in her chair, but a lift of one of Emilia's silver eyebrows had her sitting up straight again. "I want him."

"You want him?" Now a clever twist turned Emilia's lips. "That's not new. He's spectacularly handsome and endowed with many fine features."

Yes. Endowed indeed, but that wasn't what had her twisted up in knots lately, whenever Innes mentioned another date. "Not in a sex way." Well, yes, in a sex way, and she laughed because they both knew better. "Not just in a sex way. I want," she struggled to get the next words out, "my best friend to be more than my best friend."

"I don't think that is necessarily more. Perhaps it's simply a natural part of what has always been." She paused while the server arrived to refill Kahrin's coffee from a silver pot with a fancy spout. It was conversations like this that made Kahrin wish she didn't have to wait until midnight for her first legal drink. "He loves you, my dear."

Kahrin's feet bounced beneath the table. "What if he says no?"

"Then you've lost nothing." Kahrin wasn't sure that was strictly true. She and Innes had never been like that, even when they'd become physical in their friendship. "What are you afraid of?"

"Of losing the most important person in my life. After everything we've been through, he's the only one who knows everything. He's my family." She felt a heat crawl over her nose. "He's my hero." In a real-life way. In a fairy tale way. And now she wanted him in a weird romance novel way that was supposed to end with everyone getting what they want.

"You know that's all he's ever wanted to be."

"How do I tell him that? That I want to just change everything?"

"Just like you told me." Emilia smiled. "And there's nothing like a fancy party to give you the chance. I find these things are less awkward when in the arms of a dashing young lover and being spun in a dance."

She meant the joint birthday party Emilia insisted on throwing for both of them tonight. Only two weeks between her birthday and Innes', this year they had opted to wait until the eve of hers so she could toast with her first legal drink. Not that Kahrin had a great number of not-legal drinks in her history.

"He'll be bringing Linda."

"Lizzie."

"Right. Whatever." Not that Kahrin held any ill will to the woman. She seemed like a lovely woman from their short meeting. "I can't tell him I want to…" she trailed off again.

"Be with him."

Kahrin swallowed hard and powered through. "That I want to be with him. Not while his girlfriend is there."

"As someone who loves Innes dearly," Emilia started, and she was the only person Kahrin would accept loved him even close to as much as she did herself, "I think you do him a disservice by not telling him. How can he make an informed decision if you keep back some of the information?"

That wasn't fair. This wasn't negotiating the realms of very kinky and somewhat taboo sex. At least not yet. She and Innes had shelved that not long after the ordeal with Evangeline and André. She certainly did not bring that proclivity of hers up on her series of first dates. "That's not the same thing."

"Isn't it?" Emilia picked up the check that had been discretely laid on the table during their conversation. They had a dress fitting to get to, at Emilia's insistence. Kahrin had never paid so much for a dress in her life, and her kinky fairy godmother was adamant that it fit to perfection. "If you hold back the truth, one or both of you could be hurt. Some hurts do not heal with balm and gentle aftercare." Emilia was the expert.

Kahrin looked at her hands. "I think about sharing anything I share with him with anyone else and it just feels so wrong. I got a phone number from a very full of himself man last night and I just threw it away." Usually, she was in a hurry to assign them a shallow descriptor in her phone and call them as soon as possible. "I know you're right." If she loved Innes as much as she said she did, and she did, she couldn't keep something like this from him. She breathed deep and looked up to Emilia with a slightly more playful smile. "We can probably cancel that appointment at the lingerie store, then. I won't be needing any fancy panties."

Emilia laughed, the sound a glorious tinkle that seemed to brighten the sunny dining room.

CHAPTER THREE
INNES

Big news was best shared with your best friend. Innes found almost no pleasure in being excited alone and decided the second worst torment in his life was not driving with Kahrin so he could tell her all about it on the ride to Emilia's gallery for their party.

All the better, since he got to tell his very single best friend about his newly single status and career news while dressed in a tux and tails. He was counting on her being so distracted by the cut of his trousers that she wouldn't even focus on the downside, which was the not insignificant amount of time this opportunity would keep them apart.

Perhaps he had more than one motive for the trousers, then.

He found Kahrin parked where any new twenty-one-year-old who wasn't abstaining from alcohol would be: holding up the bar with one of her elbows and chattering with the bartender with a smile painted a distracting shade of red. She was hard to miss, easily the prettiest girl in the room, which he'd always believed, and always remembered not to say to any of the women he dated. How she stood upright with the full weight of her hip-long hair in an up-do, he would maybe never understand.

He slid up behind Kahrin, the bright pretty eyes of the bartender giving him away before he could surprise her. He slid an arm around her waist.

"I think I like you better on this side of the bar," he said into her shoulder, dropping a kiss there like it was something he did all the time. Because it was. Such had always been the way of their friendship.

"Yes but being on the other side is how I pay the rent."

"It's not rent when you own the building," he pointed out as the bartender slid a martini glass with something bright pink in it to her. "I'll have what she's having," he said to the other woman.

"Brave man," she said with a chuckle, scooping ice into a shaker. "You don't even know what it is."

"You say that like it's my first day as her best friend."

Drink in a gloved hand, Kahrin turned about in his arm and grinned up at him. Her mouth twitched like she might tug at her lip with her teeth, and then seemed to remember her lipstick and refrained. "I was looking all over for you."

He bumped his nose against hers. "By all over, do you mean you stopped at the bar and waited for me to find you?"

"Da always says that if you get lost you should stay in one place."

He picked up his drink and dropped a few bills into the tip jar. He took a sniff and almost flinched. It was bright pink and smelled vaguely like orange and lime-flavored gasoline.

"Which is it? You were looking everywhere, or waiting for me to look for you?"

"Those aren't really mutually exclusive things."

She had a point, at least one in the little world of their relationship. He clinked his glass to hers. "Happy birthday, Kahrin."

"Thank you." She took a hefty sip of her drink, eyes widening a little. He followed suit and could see why. It was stronger than the color had suggested. "No Lizzie tonight?"

"Funny." He took another drink and decided it was too early in the night and the conversation to let the alcohol go to his head. "Strangely, she was not enthusiastic about our open-door friendship policy."

She twitched a shoulder. "Technically, open window."

How did she do that? Pretending she was just an innocent victim of happenstance? As if she hadn't needed to scale the front of the house and shimmy along the trim to tap on his closed window. "You forgot your phone and keys on purpose."

Scoffing, Kahrin protested. "I would never!" She tilted the glass to her lips once more with a giggle.

He let her get half a sip before whisking both their glasses away and setting them on a passing tray. "You're right. That doesn't sound like you at all." He moved backward toward the dance area, tugging her by the hand in a way that gave her no question that he wanted her to follow. "You deprived me of my date, so now you have to fill in for her."

The fleeting misery of losing her drink was quickly replaced by a vulpine grin on her full mouth. "This is supposed to be my night off."

"Hilarious." He spun her about and let his hand fall to her waist as they moved into the music. "In a way, you did me a favor."

"How so?"

They swayed without talking for several beats of the music. Emilia really had gone all out, booking a string ensemble and everything. "I didn't see her being the long-term sort." It was as true as anything. Honestly, he wouldn't say it out loud, but he'd been—

"Bored?" She did it for him. "I'm sure she's fun for a Jane Austen book club."

"Is that judgment I hear?" She wasn't wrong. Lizzie was sweet, funny, and happy to please him. A little too happy to please him. The sex had been fine—vanilla, but fine—and if that was all he wanted everything would have been, well, fine. But fine left him strangely unfulfilled. Still, he couldn't let Kahrin off the hook that easily.

"Just honesty."

"You're not even sorry, are you?"

"Should I be?"

He answered by way of a smile and turned her about into a playful dip. "As it happens, I have something I want to tell you."

She righted herself, light brown face dusted with a flush. "I have something to tell you, too."

Interesting. "Did you throw this whole party and get dolled up just to tell me something you could have sent in a text?" He was teasing her, and she obviously knew it, judging by the roll of her eyes. Still, he feigned confusion.

"This is Emilia's party." A statement of the obvious if ever one had been made. "But you know I'd never turn down an opportunity to wear a matching bra and panty set."

This time his puzzlement was genuine, and he frowned. "You're not wearing a bra." As if to reinforce that fact, he tickled his fingers over the full expanse of her naked back, the cut of her dress stopping just short of the curve of her rear.

She shivered, and it only seemed to bolster her apparent mischief. "I know."

His mouth went dry instantly and he swallowed. Oh, she was good. Was that how it was going to be? It hadn't been part of the plan for the evening, but he was just a man at the end of the day with only enough blood to stretch so far.

"You're on dangerous ground, you know," he growled into her ear, ghosting his nose over the soft skin of her cheek.

"Am I?" How she managed it without a giggle was a question for the ages.

"You know you are." He let the light scent of powder and the coconut oil of her hair product fill his senses, deciding that his announcement could wait just a little longer. He gripped his guiding hand firmly into her waist, drawing a little gasp she tried to hide. His lips twitched their approval, and he pulled her possessively tight against him. Their respective relationships, such as they were, had ended with convenient timing, it seemed. Very convenient.

"Belated happy birthday to you, too, Pretty Mouth."

"You agreed no gifts this year."

"I lied." Her wide eyes locked with his. The physical relationship between them came and went over the years, never a given, and never a demand, making it a delightful surprise when they fell into it as easy as breathing. He realized that the thing he'd been missing in his last relationship was the promise she relayed in her mismatched hazel eyes. Something she offered to him and no one else, and something he took from no other. Not even Emilia, in all the exciting things she'd taught him in their own peculiar friendship. That dalliance had been another type of fun, while it lasted.

"Good." He dipped his head the good foot and more between them, taking the slight pout of her full mouth as invitation, and teased a kiss, exaggerating that he did not want to smudge her lipstick. "You know I despise lying."

She lifted her chin. "I do."

It was definitely a challenge, the sort only she could pose. It made heat lance through him as if it had only been days ago they'd been holed up in that little cabin at the lake, and not nearly a year. "You know I won't correct you in public," he murmured.

"I do."

Suddenly nothing in the room mattered beyond the hitch in the rise and fall of her chest, or the way he could feel the heat of her pulse in the scant space between his mouth and the join of her ear and jaw. "You also know the rules."

"They don't cover everything."

A fair point well made.

Innes darted a glance to the other end of the gallery, calculating the fastest exit. He'd never make it home. This required a plan B. "Come," he ordered, catching her hand and marching her quickly to the hallway leading to the rooms where he was sure she and Emilia had dressed. He tried, and failed, to look casual as they wound around the various guests and catering staff along the way.

He made it as far as the bend in the hallway before he lost his resolve, ensuring they were out of line of sight before crushing her between himself and the wall. He kissed her again, this time with the ferocity of a starved animal at a fresh kill. Her fingers gripped the lapels of his jacket, and he just could not allow that. He slid his hands down her arms until he could clutch her wrists and pinned them to the wall on either side of her head. She let a soft whimper and grew more insistent in returning his kisses. He shifted one wrist until he held both in one hand, letting his other grope downward to verify that, yes, her panties did match her bra.

"You're not playing fair tonight." Oh, there was no pretending his need wasn't at its peak.

She tilted her chin to invite him to explore her neck, which he did, gladly. "Love and war, and all that."

"Which is this?" He pulled back enough to ensure she would answer.

"You tell me."

Whatever it was they wanted to talk about was going to have to wait. He lifted her from the floor enough to find the handle of a door and spilled them into the room.

CHAPTER FOUR
KAHRIN

Kahrin couldn't say this was the reaction she expected, but she couldn't say it wasn't, either. More that it was the one she wanted and hadn't been sure about.

Their physical relationship dropped off sharply in the aftermath of their retreat to the lake when Evangeline had bewitched André and tried to kill her on the way to drinking Innes' magical blood. The closeness, the nights cuddled up together, the rest of their friendship had remained intact, because of course it had. They had never been like that even when it was like that. She couldn't say she hadn't thought about it a few times, on the rare nights they didn't see one another. And thoughts led to less thought-y things. She'd never asked if that worked for him as well.

Innes barely remembered to close the door to the little dressing room behind him as he moved them into more privacy. He dropped her into one of the large stuffed chairs and balanced with a knee on either side of her.

"Wicked woman," he chuckled, so low she could feel it in the deepest parts of her. "You planned this."

She looked up at him as he pushed his jacket off, his expression darkening. "It does have my fingerprints all over it."

He pushed her dress up, hands smoothing along her legs until they reached the seam of her hips. "You know we can't do anything yet. You know the rule."

Yes, yes, not until they got a clean bill of health from the clinic. No one wanted to spread rashes or worse. "There are other things we can do in the meantime. It's not an either/or situation, here."

"Has anyone ever called you a genius?"

"Not everyone can see brilliance like you can." She laughed as he squeezed her leg where he knew it would tickle. She lifted her bum off the chair to allow him to follow through on the line of thinking that led to his nails dragging over the soft flesh there. It quaked through her, ending in a needy whimper against his mouth. "I want you."

"You shouldn't be so subtle." He scored lines over the insides of her thighs and tugged at the skin over her pulse points with his teeth.

Across the room, tucked in her purse, Kahrin's phone buzzed.

"Leave it," he ordered. She'd missed that particular tone of his voice, that commanding way that he reserved for her. She nodded, lifting her chin so he didn't decide to stop chasing his thoughts across her throat.

So, it wasn't exactly the way Emilia had suggested she discuss it, but at least she was getting her point across. Or was she? It occurred to her that this was not unusual behavior, and that she was giving him no reason to think this was anything other than one of their casual trysts or venting urges. She pulled her head back, out of reach of his kiss, and caught his dark gaze.

She struggled to get the words out through her stuttering breaths. "No, Innes. I want you."

He paused, his brow creasing in apparent confusion. A moment later she could see the dawning of what she was saying in his expression, and he softened, withdrawing his hands to cup her face. "Kahrin, what are you—"

"Now, where on Earth could they be?" Emilia's voice pitched with exaggeration as she clearly announced her impending arrival. Even with her warning issued, giving them time to climb off one another, she pretended to struggle with the door handle.

By the time she finally entered the room, Kahrin sat wide-eyed and flushed in the chair, with Innes behind her, his jacket somehow back on and buttoned. He leaned his weight on his arms over the back of the chair.

"There you two are. Missing your own party." She tutted playfully, her expression knowing.

"Hello, dear," Innes greeted her.

Emilia smiled; her lips pursed as if she had a canary held in her mouth. "I hope I'm not interrupting. The guests are waiting to meet you." She knew full well what she'd walked in on, and likely anticipated it when she'd sent Kahrin in Innes' direction with her advice that night. Wordlessly, she pulled a handkerchief from her sleeve and wiped carefully at Innes' face. When she pulled it back it had smears of red which were familiar to Kahrin.

"That's supposed to be smudge proof!" she grumbled as she got up to rush to the mirror. Her legs wobbled as if her bones were jelly as she retrieved the tube from her bag to touch up.

"I don't think their testing is as rigorous as you think." Innes straightened his collar and ensured that his face was relatively lipstick-free. "We're right behind you, dear," he reassured Emilia, who swept out of the room in a cloud of perfume and fluttering silk.

"I'm coming back if you are not out there in three minutes."

Kahrin groaned, which quickly melted into a laugh as the door latched behind Emilia. "Well, I could run ten miles right now."

Innes laughed and she let him draw her into his arms. He sobered, tilting his head down. "What you said just before," he jerked his head toward the door to indicate the certainly intentional interruption.

"It's gonna have to wait." She hopped up and pecked his jaw, making sure to aim behind the bare patch of skin where his stubble would not grow—Yelena's kiss. "It needs more than a minute to explain. What did you want to tell me?"

There was a pause. She didn't like a pause. A pause meant he had to think about what he was saying to her. That meant it was serious. Her sternum became a solid rod of ice, and she tried so very hard not to show the twinge of panic she felt.

"It also needs more than a minute," he finally answered. "Especially after," he gestured vaguely around the room as if she needed a reminder that wasn't a pulsing below her belly of what they had been doing only moments ago. "At home. After. Okay?" That pretty mouth of his pulled into a smile she recognized, one that was just hers, full of affection and amusement.

The ice in her chest thawed just a little at the way his eyes searched her face. She wished for just that moment she could read his thoughts. Or better yet, that he would just tell them to her.

"Okay. After." She brushed the front of her dress to smooth wrinkles that did not exist.

He caught her elbow before she could leave the room. "Stay the night with me."

"I was going to anyway." She tried her hardest to seem nonchalant, but Innes was not a person she could ever hide her feelings from. "For tomorrow's clinic slash breakfast date. It saves time."

He shook his head, his fingers playing over the apple of his own throat, and his eyes intent on hers. "No, I mean stay the night. With me."

The way he emphasized the last two words sent a jolt through her belly. They'd spent countless nights sleeping over since childhood. They'd shared a bed in their adult life in more than just a physical situation. This felt different. An invitation to something. A reassurance.

She felt herself nodding before she could even get her lips to cooperate. The breath caught in her throat over her softly spoken, "Okay."

Her cheeks ached as a smile climbed over her face. She stood pointed toward the wall until she thought he'd left. "Wow," she whispered. She knew nothing much could happen, but the shift of gravity between them made it feel less urgent.

"Kahrin?"

She turned to see him holding out a hand to her. "Emilia doesn't bluff." He tilted his head with a small chuckle. "Well, not about this."

She wound her arm into the crook of his and returned to the party at his side, like it was the most normal thing she had ever done in her life.

CHAPTER FIVE
INNES

The center of Innes' gravity had shifted, and it was never more plain to him than when he opened his eyes that morning. Finding Kahrin in his bed was not unusual, not even bundled up in sleep clothes, and especially not hogging the blankets. Waking up before she did was. It was a little indulgence he would keep for himself, watching her in repose, entire body relaxed in rest. His chest squeezed with a small ache, but a good one, a welcomed one.

Where had last night come from?

Best friends, since forever. Ten years old, a skinned knee, ice cream, and they'd never looked back. No one was surprised when they began sleeping together, not even when they always insisted they weren't like that. They'd never laid a claim to one another, even after exploring darker urges between them, the kind that made her choose a high-neck sweater instead of a loose shirt and required her to rest quietly while he murmured reassurances to her. They came and went as they chose, never pried into each other's romantic lives, even after André and Evangeline, without invitation. Was she trying to lay a claim now? What changed?

More importantly, why did it not feel like a change at all, but instead a natural progression?

She'd fallen asleep on the ride home, and they didn't talk like they'd planned. For the better, really, as he now needed to rethink his plan. Kahrin was always a factor in his life plans, especially after magic made them dependent upon one another, but her lusty confession in the gallery green room added a weight to it he'd not expected. A welcomed one.

She stirred, her eyes fluttering open. "Hey, Pretty Mouth."

He gazed down from his position; chin propped up by his fist on his elbow. Words wouldn't come to his lips, so they just kept one another's gaze. A silent conversation that said more than voices could have.

"You're quiet."

"Just enjoying this," she answered.

He chuckled. "I hope so, or you have a weird system for punishing yourself several nights a week."

"You know that's not my particular kink."

That stirred something low below his stomach, something he couldn't get distracted by just now. "Lucky for me."

"We should go. Get there early." Her tongue wet just the pad of her lower lip before her teeth bit into the soft flesh. Most people would not believe her capable of this sort of calm shyness. To him it was a special side she reserved only for him. He'd just taken it as a facet of their friendship. It still was, but in just a handful of hours, he was starting to see things with a different light.

"To get there early." He brushed a bit of hair from her face and lowered his mouth to leave a light kiss on her brow. "Kahrin—"

She sat up and spun her legs away from him and out of the bed. "After, okay?"

"After." They kept saying after. Like they were dancing around the final rise of the road in a journey and afraid to travel over it. This felt like it should have been the easiest step ever, especially hand in hand. What were they afraid of? And it was definitely they, as if a connecting line allowed the sensation to travel from her heart to his.

Leaving his room and getting around broke the quiet bubble of the morning, but not in a bad way. Anything that had felt uneasy melted as they joked and laughed and fought over the last of the coffee creamer. They raced to the car, bickering over who got to pick the music and who was going to choose breakfast before they got to the clinic.

The local free clinic was usually empty early in the morning. They were no strangers to its waiting room, taking their respective health seriously even when they weren't entangled physically with one another. Naturally, Kahrin demonstrated that she'd never been in public before by tossing a few flavored condoms at him from a free basket. Also, apparently Ma never taught her how to sit in a chair, evident by the way she draped her legs over the armrest and into his lap as she sorted their mail between them. Honestly, why did they even have two separate boxes?

She sifted through it, putting the relevant stuff in her lap, including anything accidentally left in her box instead of his, and the junk in another pile. His lap. The task passed quickly, and when she'd finished that, she tore open a fancy envelope addressed to her.

She frowned, the furrow between her brows so deep that it was a permanent fixture when she was relaxed. "Ew."

"Hm?" Innes leaned over to see what had provoked that response. Could have been anything, from raisins to an open and gutted corpse in a horror movie. Seeing as he'd kept his pain au raisin hermetically sealed from her plain bagel, this one was less clear.

"Is that Seth Fisher?" It was an unnecessary question; they'd both gone to high school with this would-be sweetheart of hers.

"One and the same." Her nose wrinkled. He was the grandson of one of the farmers adjacent to the Quirke farms. "I guess that's his wife? In the squeeze chute."

Wait, what? He looked again, certain he'd heard her wrong, or that this was more of her Kahrin-specific hyperbole. It could have gone either way, and he was sorry to find out it was neither. "Ew. Is that a baby announcement?"

"Ew," she drew out longer. "Yes." The woman in the picture was pinned inside the contraption meant for holding animals still for certain procedures, her head out the front. Beside her stood one Seth Fisher, who had once had eyes for no one but Kahrin, wearing elbow-length rubber gloves and proudly displaying a sign that read "SUCCESS" in large, printed letters.

"Is it supposed to be funny?"

"It's barbaric," she muttered. "I can't believe I cried over him."

He leaned over and nudged her cheek with his nose. "I feel like I've heard someone say that before." He dodged out of the path of her elbow before she could pay retribution for his version of 'I told you so.'

"Joke's on him. It's been almost a decade and I'm still not having babies."

Innes snorted. The Fisher family sprawled through generations of conservative values, including very strident beliefs about sex and procreation. Seth once fancied the idea that Kahrin would be suited to a life of churning out another round of Fishers to farm their land. After a few dates, the discovery that Kahrin's moral compass worked differently than his caused an irreparable rift between them. One that had hurt Kahrin deeply. In fact, while he knew she wouldn't admit it out loud, it had started her down a spiral of doubting herself, letting words like "slutty" and "immoral" poke wounds she still licked.

He put his arm around her, bumping his head against hers. There were times to coddle her feelings and times to make her laugh. Innes knew which was which almost without fail. "Can you imagine all the incredible sex you're probably missing?" Probably an unfair comment, considering their interruption last night.

She wrinkled her nose and huffed a laugh. "You know I love me a good missionary position."

"I bet he leaves his socks on."

"Well, yes. Feet are weird." Her chuckle came more like popcorn now. "Lights always off."

"You wouldn't want to make eye contact while doing the Lord's work." He faked a shudder. "That would be awkward and then you might never complete the task at hand."

"Well, you shouldn't be using hands anyway."

She tore the photo in half, much to his relief. It was best they didn't dwell on it.

"I still wish you'd let me punch him." Seth Fisher's rejection of her had sent Innes into something of an incandescent rage. And not just because it had been Innes who, supposedly, had "soiled" her.

"I think you've punched enough of my beaus." She gave him a pointed look.

"Who says "beau" anymore? Besides, André hardly counts." He'd been bewitched. Not that Innes had known when he'd thrown the haymaker. Or that it changed the things her former professor said to her.

"Hey, give me your phone. Da called a few days ago." Not unlike her to put off calling people back.

"It's in the car." He shrugged, and she mirrored it. Clearly not a pressing need.

They quieted down, the waiting area no longer theirs alone as a pair of young women entered and sat a few seats away. From the look on their faces and the noise which had preceded their entrance, Innes could guess they were here under less enjoyable circumstances. Kahrin offered them a friendly smile but didn't get to offer any other comfort when her name was called.

To say things were in, out, and done would have been underselling the experience. Worth it, though, to keep them both safe. He met up with her in the waiting room and slipped an arm around her back as they left. She threw a lewd gesture to some of the protestors some feet away but paid them no more attention than that. He hoped they got frostbite.

Settled and buckled into the car, he guided the car onto the main highway through town. A quiet hung between them that didn't feel quite like the comfortable ease that usually existed there.

"They said I should have my results by midday."

"Yeah, same," she added, her eyes focused out the window, the tip of her thumb between her teeth.

"So," he drummed his fingers on the steering wheel as she started digging around in the glove box. "Did you want to talk?"

"Have you seen my charging cord?"

"Just use mine." He knew it wasn't worn through from her constantly winding it around her fingers. "It looks like your ma called me while we were inside."

"Probably about my birthday." She plugged her phone in and dropped it in the cupholder. Her eyes slid to him but flicked back to the road.

"Kahrin?"

"I do. I do want to talk." She chewed her lip. "It's just," she hesitated, "I'm scared."

His fair-to-middling self-preservation instinct meant he knew better than to press too hard before she was ready to talk. It had taken her years to openly say things like "I love you," and he wasn't about to push her now. Not with something they both knew was huge.

"I can go first, if you want," he offered, breaking his own promise.

She brightened. "If you want."

"I've been offered a—"

Her phone apparently gained enough power to explode with notifications.

"How long has that been dead?" he asked.

"I don't know." She shrugged. "I only just remembered I left it in here."

He tutted with affection, but she wasn't paying attention; her eyes glued to the screen, that crease in her brow returned. She tapped a notification that started a call. "Brecken?"

Brecken? Wasn't her eldest brother up north, working? He thought he remembered that he and Alec, Kahrin's middle brother, had both moved together.

Brecken ranted indiscernibly on the other end. "Yelling at me isn't going to— no, I didn't listen to—" She huffed her aggravation. "I called as soon as I saw you called a hundred times."

She rolled her eyes to Innes, who met them with a sympathetic look. It wasn't unusual that she and Brecken bickered, both having that particular Quirke belligerence. But this felt especially heated.

"Shut your trap and tell me where you are."

Silence.

She hung up and dropped the phone into her lap and stared at nothing ahead of them.

"Kahrin?" When she didn't answer, he reached over and squeezed her hand. She turned it palm up and wound her fingers with his. She looked to him; eyes glassy with tears.

"Da's in the hospital."

"Oh."

He threw on his blinker and cut across two lanes of traffic to turn the car around.

CHAPTER SIX
KAHRIN

Nothing seemed real. Not Innes' hand at her back as he guided her through the morass of hallways in the hospital. Not the sound of their boots squelching on the linoleum tile. Not the looming entrance to hell that was the door to Da's room, or the blips and beeps and whirring of various machines inside.

Innes murmured things she couldn't comprehend, but was sure were all very fine sentiments. He wasn't one to be trite.

An eerie pall encompassed the room, like it was already a tomb. Lights were dimmed, save a corona above the head of the bed where the monitors and machines hung. Kahrin had seen too many walls of monitors detecting signs of life in dimly lit, too-quiet rooms over the last few years.

Da looked... small. So small. Her father was not a large man, something she and her brothers had inherited, with only Alec and Ma standing taller. Da always had a large presence, and people respected him. He could make things grow with his brain and maybe kill a person with a half-hearted glare, though she didn't know for sure.

The man in the bed, draped with the stringy-weave blankets of hospitals, did not appear capable of any of those things.

"Kahrin, Innes." Ma rose from the one comfortable-looking chair and gathered them in her arms. Unsure what she expected, it surprised her to see Ma so collected. Other than papery, purple circles beneath her eyes, and her hair obviously unwashed, she was the only familiar thing about the room.

"What happened?" Innes asked before Kahrin could organize her words to do the same. For the moment, she let him speak for her, because he would know the right questions to ask while she floundered under emotions she couldn't yet name.

"I don't know." Ma stepped back, pausing with her hands on Kahrin's cheeks. "When he left for the big barn, he was fine. When he didn't come back for lunch, I took lunch to him, thinking he was caught up with that stubborn new buck." Their youngest male goat had come to the farm not long after Kahrin moved out, which hardly made him new, but that seemed an odd thing for her to bring up right now.

Ma continued, "When I got there, he was on the ground, and that blasted animal was chewing his coat."

"Oh." Finally! A word she could manage that made a semblance of a response. Her head bobbed to reinforce her brilliant contribution.

"He wasn't breathing. We don't know for how long."

"Well look who could finally be bothered."

Kahrin pinched the bridge of her nose, bracing for a confrontation with her equally acerbic eldest sibling. He entered the room, followed closely by their middle brother who carried a traveler tray of coffee.

"Hey Kahrin, Innes." Alec nodded to each in turn, as if the gesture had the power to undo Brecken's abrasive greeting.

Not even Brecken, who made the new buck look compliant, could stay angry at a time like this, at least not until hugs were exchanged. When he withdrew from the embrace, Kahrin could see that his temper was born of impotence. No Quirke brooked helplessness well, and the patriarch of their family being in such a state left them with plenty of that feeling to spare.

Once Alec released her from his hug, Kahrin approached the bed, stopping short by a few steps. She held the air in her lungs, as if releasing it would scatter him to ashes. His chest rose and fell just out of time with the rhythm of the machine, forcing his lungs to move, and his golden-brown skin dulled with a chalky pallor. She turned into Innes' arms and released her stuttering breath against his chest.

She let the safe circle of his hold on her create a shelter, just for a moment while she gathered her strength to face this. She had to.

"How long have you been here?" Innes' voice rumbled in his chest and buzzed in her ears.

"Ma's been here since yesterday," Brecken answered. "It would have been nice to give her a break while she waited for us to drive down."

"Brecken," Ma warned, proving no Quirke was too old for a scolding. She sighed. "I should go home and shower."

"And maybe eat something," Alec added.

"And rest," Innes reminded, because they all knew she would fight it until her body gave up.

Kahrin let him hold her out at arm's length to look at her, and she was ashamed of herself for not having been available sooner.

"We've got this, hm?"

That single syllable held so much weight between them. It wasn't a question asked, but a point made: between the two of them, they could handle this. Was that not how this new arrangement went? An extension of what already existed?

She smiled, strained and weak, but nodded, before she turned back to face Da.

"Can he hear me?" With all the time she'd spent unconscious, it seemed she should know that answer.

"It doesn't hurt anything to talk to him, either way," Ma told her as the rest of the family gathered their things. Ma rested a hand on Kahrin's arm. "Maybe you can reach him. You've always had a special bond."

So, okay. No pressure.

"Iskandar," Ma cooed as she leaned over Da's bed. "I'll be back as soon as possible, okay?" She pressed a kiss to his forehead, remaining still for a moment before whispering, "I need you to fight. We still need you."

Never in her life had Kahrin seen Da fail to obey a direct order from Ma.

Kahrin reached for Da's hand, hesitating, still convinced he was fragile and would crumble in her grip. Slowly, she gripped it more firmly as the weighted hospital door whooshed and clicked softly behind them.

Da wheezed. It was subtle at first; she almost missed it. Then he gagged, fighting against the tube in his throat. Her eyes went wide and she dropped his hand, colliding with Innes at her back. Da wheezed one more time, a wet, crackling sound gurgling in his throat, then went still again with only the machine pumping air into and out of his lungs.

"Innes, go get a nurse." She lunged for the call button, but Innes caught her around the waist.

"We can't"

"What?" He couldn't be serious! "Why not?"

"Grab his hand again."

Kahrin opened her mouth to argue, but he didn't give her a chance. "Just do it, okay? Trust me?"

She did, so she did.

CHAPTER SEVEN
INNES

Innes had no explanation for what he was seeing. Even given his medical studies and volunteering at the hospital, Da Quirke appeared odd when they'd come in. There had been some smudgy quality to his face, almost blurry, like when Innes looked up from studying too long and his eyes needed to refocus. He'd attributed it to fatigue and hospital lighting and hadn't questioned it.

Until Kahrin had taken her father's hand in hers.

It was hard to tell what happened. The blurriness snapped into sharpness, though not really. As if a single moment ceased to exist, he first saw one thing, and then the next, but his brain couldn't comprehend that transitional instant. When Kahrin had let go, startled by Da's labored breathing sounds, the same happened in reverse. Scientifically speaking, it made sense to have her try it again to see if the whole thing could be replicated. Scientifically.

"Why can't we just get the doctor?" She asked while she did as he directed. If there was ever a time for her to not argue with him, this was it, but it occurred to him that she might not be able to see what he was seeing.

He did not like that thought.

Like it or not, he'd guessed right. "Look." As soon as her hand met Da's, the same reaction happened. "What are we going to tell them?"

"You're saying this is magic." He didn't need to answer, and didn't have a chance to, as Da started grunting and gurgling again. "He's choking!"

"He's fighting the breathing tube."

"You have to do something!" She managed to whisper and pitch her voice high at once.

"I'm not a doctor, Kahrin." Why did he need to keep reminding people he was still an undergrad?

"Either get one or act like one!"

Da started thrashing, trying to talk around the tube. Innes hated it, but Kahrin was right.

"Don't let go of him," Innes directed as he assessed his options. "I've only seen an extubation." Because he'd never been allowed to do one, being that he was not yet a doctor. But what were his other options? Explain a magical illness his best friend could un-magically cure?

Kahrin wrapped her arms around Da's before finally climbing up onto the narrow bed beside him. Thank goodness they were both made of the same diminutive stature.

"Da," she crooned close to his ear. "Innes is trying to help you, but you have to stay calm."

Innes paused as many machines as he dared and took a cleansing breath. He'd seen it done. He'd read about it. Had it explained. There were steps. If he kept to the steps, he could do this. But the steps couldn't stop his chest tingling, or his pulse blasting in his ears.

Tape first. Deflate the balloon. It took him a couple of fumbling tries but he found it. His hands shook, and he scolded himself for it. Some doctor he'd make! He looked to Kahrin and back to his hands, then began repeating the steps out loud again and again.

"I— I need you to breathe out, sir," he hastily added as if he was still a child playing stick ball in the Quirke's yard. Da obeyed, and Innes pulled. Da coughed, the sound weak and crackling.

Kahrin flopped forward, sniffling with the first unleash of tears she'd allowed. "Don't let go of me, Da."

He wheezed, his throat raw from the tube and dry from the air. Innes found little lollipop shaped, wetted sponges, and cracked a pack open. He swabbed out the inside of Da's mouth so he could swallow. "Do you remember what happened?"

Da shook his head, shuddering at the apparent bitterness of the swab. "Couldn't move," he rasped. He squeezed his eyes tight. "Grainne?"

"She went home," Innes answered. "She didn't see any of this."

Da's eyes found Kahrin, the pieces clicking together in his expression, if slowly. "Magic."

Innes clenched his jaw. Not again. This could not be happening again. This could not be the magic he'd championed, longed to see his entire life. Not the force of wonder he believed in with such ardent fervor that he'd dragged his best friend, incapable of experiencing it, into his determined hopes. Evan Greves. Evangeline. The bewitching of André. All the time they'd been in this very hospital, clinging to their lives. He wasn't naïve, he knew that all things light also had a dark, but nearly all he'd seen of magic so far, save Yelena, was cruel. Wicked. Ruinous.

As if on cue, Yelena's kiss on his jaw tingled, reminding him that even that immortal's token of affection came with its own darkness.

"It seems so, sir." He hoped that magic realized it owed them. If Da's illness was magical in nature, perhaps magic could undo it.

"I damned well know it is," Da groused, his words hoarse.

The malady may have been magical, but the toll on Da's body was very much not. If he'd truly only been here a couple of days, and Innes had no reason to believe Ma, Brecken, and Alec were lying, he was deteriorating rapidly. His face seemed sunken, his hazel eyes dim, and his frame and muscles overly defined from fatigue and dehydration.

"Da," Kahrin's voice warbled, "who would do this to you?"

Despite what Innes thought was a reasonable question, Da remained quiet, the upsetting wet squelch in his throat and lungs dominating the room. He closed his eyes, the usual serene expression of his deep thought too accurately mimicking death when paired with the occasional stillness of his chest.

Innes cursed himself while they waited for an answer, looking at the web of veins woven over the backs of his hands. He was too early in his education to really be helpful.

"Da?" Kahrin repeated, "did you hear me?"

Innes must have zoned out. He glanced up to ask Kahrin to give her Da a moment to answer and noticed by the clock that more than a few minutes had passed.

Da Quirke nodded, and had they not both been watching him they would have missed it. Evidently, that would be all the answer they would get on it.

"You have to tell us what you know," Innes added, needlessly in his opinion. "We can't help if we don't know."

"My debt, Makoons," Da coughed.

Innes frowned, but Kahrin was less quiet in her confusion. "What does that mean? What debt?"

Da blinked, then opened his eyes, clouded and watery where they were once bright and hazel. Or perhaps they were tears to match expressions around the room. He lifted a hand to brush Kahrin's cheek, which broke enough tears to cause an ache in Innes' chest.

"Go," Da pushed out with a shuddering breath, and closed his eyes once more. He used what looked to be the rest of his strength to pull his hand free of Kahrin's grasp, then strained to roll his back to them. He immediately began convulsing as the magical illness settled on him once more, the strange blurring shading his face once more.

"No!" The single word rolled, guttural and choked from Kahrin's throat. "Da, don't do this!"

As the machines started reacting with alarms and beeps, Innes wrapped his arms around her waist and pulled her away from the bed. He was back barely a foot when she kicked free and flung herself over her father's form again. "Da!" she repeated, each iteration climbing in shrill pitch.

The window rattled, and the blood in Innes' veins seemed to effervesce against his skin. The air around him seemed to suck inward, making him feel like he might unravel from the lack of pressure.

"Kahrin," he said, needing her attention, and there wasn't much time. She flailed against him, and he heard footsteps approaching. "Kahrin, stop. I don't know what you're doing, but you have to stop. We don't have time."

"I can't do anything!" she shrieked. If she were referring to the whatever that was happening, the machines blipping and pausing only to stagger to a start again, he wasn't sure that was true. He had no idea what it was, but she was the cause.

He dragged her away again and spun her about to force her to face him. "Focus on my eyes. You have to stay calm."

She slapped a hand over her mouth before reaching up to touch his upper lip. She pulled her fingers back, smeared with crimson, and she went still. The oddness of the room stopped as quickly as it had started. But there was no time to talk about whatever had just happened.

"We are on our own with this." He pulled her tight to him, crushing his arms around her and let her sob against his chest as the cacophony of beeps and ringing continued.

CHAPTER EIGHT
KAHRIN

Kahrin's shoulders shook, though she was not crying. The weight of her head rested in her palms, supported by elbows on her knees. She couldn't—no wouldn't—cry again. That would be admitting the possibility of an end of her father's life–possibly by his own choice. That had not happened. For now, he was stable, though reportedly in a coma. If not for Innes' quick thinking to explain the scene discovered by the ICU staff, one or both of them might be sitting in a jail cell and not a waiting room. The lie that Da had pulled his own tube out sold easily enough, and given his convulsions, he wasn't available to blow their story.

Lies did not sit well with either of them, and lies about Da's health sat particularly bad with Kahrin.

Innes returned from the nurse's station with pity coffee—what the nurses offered bereft family members from their own coffee pot—and handed one to her.

"I added milk."

"Thanks."

"He's stable," he reassured her.

"He's in a coma, Innes." She couldn't manage the bite she wanted her words to have, which was just as well. Innes did not deserve her lashing out at him. He was hurting, too.

"But stable." He sighed, his shoulders drooping in defeat, as if any of this were his fault. "Several systems are strained, and he may need blood."

"I'm not a match." They'd already checked, and she couldn't even offer that to help her own father, but he didn't want her help, did he? He'd made that crystal clear. She scrubbed her eyes with the heels of her hands.

"But I am."

Wait, what? Kahrin sat bolt upright, eyes locked on his. "Since when?"

He shrugged. "At least since I had them test me."

That was impossible. Innes' recovery after the attack by Evangeline had been touch and go and the hospital's blood stores low, so the doctor, while boggled, had dismissed the lack of a match for Innes as a fluke, some antibody thing that their small city lab couldn't isolate. While Kahrin and Innes both knew it was one of the effects of a unicorn's kiss, marking him as a True Believer, that was hardly information they could share with anyone else. Touched though she was that he'd been tested anyway, she couldn't push her mind past Innes' blood being a match when not so long ago, Da's had not been a match for him.

"What does that mean?"

"At the very least, that I am going to donate before we go home. Would you mind driving?"

She shook her head. "Whatever gets us there faster." She looked toward the elevators. "Ma should be here soon, and I'll fill her in. Well, on what I can."

Worse than lying about Da's health was lying to Ma, who had an uncanny knack for knowing when one of her children was not being honest.

Innes crouched in front of her and tipped her chin with a crooked finger. He placed a peck on her lips, leaving her wanting more, if just to have something else to think about.

"I'll only be gone as long as I need to be." He stole another fleeting kiss. "Check your email. You could use some good news, hm?"

This third kiss he offered was followed by a familiar heat, and for that brief span of time, everything bad fell away, and only the two of them existed. As if she could draw a new reality based on the feeling of his lips playing over hers.

The clearing of Brecken's throat shattered the moment. It took all of Kahrin's self-control not to snap at him.

"Time and place, you two. Geesh."

"Says the grown man who says geesh." Kahrin stood to face her brother. "You don't have to comment on everything."

"Says the grown woman who can't keep her mouth shut about anything," Brecken retorted.

"Enough," Ma scolded. Dark gouges scored the pale skin under her eyes. The grease and errant flakes in her hair made it clear that she never got that shower she went home for. "What happened?"

Innes squeezed her hand. "Catch her up. I'll be back as soon as I can."

She explained what she could, and artfully dodged what she could not, thanks to Innes practicing it with her again and again. And just where was her Emmy for best performance in a drama? Truly, she was under-appreciated.

Ma pulled her into a tight hug, dipping her head to rest it against the side of Kahrin's. "Thank you for being here."

Alec came from the elevators, brushing snow from his toque and fleece-lined Mackinaw coat shoulders, after his walk from the parking lot. "Where's Innes?"

"Donating blood. Just in case." Kahrin shrugged, but Ma's twitched brow seemed to ask a question no one else thought to. She'd been as good as a mother to Innes, and clearly, she recalled the blood situation.

"It's good to see you two closer these days." Ma stroked Kahrin's cheek.

"Ma, if we were any closer, they'd need nuclear fission to get us apart."

"You should go sit with him," Alec suggested. He looked different than the last she'd seen him. He wore his hair longer now, the top and sides pulled back from his more angular face. "Da's not going anywhere, and we got Ma."

Brecken snorted, clearly having an opinion. Ma stymied any further comment with a hand on his arm. Brecken would chew glass before he defied Ma, and Ma would ensure those were his options.

What was Brecken's sudden problem with Innes?

"I'll call if anything changes," Alec promised.

"I don't mind staying with you," she offered. It sounded half-hearted, even though she meant it.

"We can't all stay." Ma's tone settled the matter. "You and Innes go home."

Kahrin took the stairs instead of the elevator, the thought of staying still making her legs twitch. Besides, it gave her a chance to check her email. She scrolled with her thumb to find the new one from the clinic, and a forwarded one from Innes. Both of their tests results! All clear!

He was right. That was a bit of a pick-me-up, all things considered. She grinned, hands resting on the push bar to the first floor where the lab was located.

"Kahr!" The stairwell echoed as Alec chased after her, his steps telling her he was taking them two at a time. He swung over the rail, skipping the last few. His brown face flushed with exertion. "Look, Breck doesn't know, so keep it to yourself, but--" he looked up at the stairs above them, "there's a false bottom in Ma's hope chest."

Kahrin gave him a quizzical look. How could he know that?

"I was a sneaky little shit," he explained. "Bet you're glad."

"Less so when you read my diary." Brothers.

"Look in there as soon as you two can make it out to the farm." He wrapped her in a hug. "And say hi to Pickle." He let go of her and ran back up the stairs, two at a time, just as he'd come down.

CHAPTER NINE
KAHRIN

"Your brothers know?" Innes shook his head, the straw of his second juice box caught in the corner of his mouth giving him a boyish look to go along with his surprise.

"I guess?" She still didn't believe it herself. "Or at least Alec does, enough to set us on a path. Maybe he doesn't know about all of the--," she waved her hands around, "this."

She focused again on the road to keep her mind from giving in to the dizzying reality that her family had more secrets than she'd realized. Given Ma and Da's emphasis on honesty in their upbringing, she always assumed they were all open with one another. The irony of the fact that she and Innes kept secrets the last few years was not lost on her. Lying was the worst punishable offense in the Quirke home.

Innes slurped the dregs of his juice box, the uneven staccato providing an odd rhythm to the song of evening traffic and the blinking of lights turning on as dusk settled. She hated driving at the best of times, and this time of day hardly qualified. It set her teeth on edge, and her knuckles whitened as she gripped the wheel.

"Do you want to go to the farm tonight? Maybe answers will help."

He meant well, as he always did with her, so she smiled tightly instead of biting his head off. Figuratively, not the way Evangeline had tried.

"It could also beg more questions."

"And send you spiraling." It was like he was in her head sometimes. "Besides, we have enough to keep us busy tonight."

Kahrin's eyes flicked to him. She changed lanes to turn into their cul-de-sac. Not like him to go from serious to that so fast, but she was not going to complain. Itches needed scratching even in times of trouble, and distractions were more than welcome. Specifically sexy, well-endowed distractions. She pulled the car into their shared driveway and turned to face him, tucking a leg under herself. She could see her grin reflected in his bistre eyes in the light from the sunset.

"You've got dirty in your eyes, Pretty Mouth."

"What?"

She unbuckled her seatbelt, and then his, leaning in close to catch his mouth as she switched from her seat to his lap. "I checked my email."

The crease in his brow let her know she'd completely misread the moment, though his grin caught up with hers a moment later, taking on a salacious slant. "Not what I meant, but good to know."

Oh. "What did you mean, then?"

"I mean, we should discuss what happened back there in your Da's room, and maybe tackle that long list of all the other things we wanted to talk about." He rubbed the back of his head.

She took a deep breath to buy a moment and slow her thoughts. Truth was that very topic had been chasing itself around her mind, and she'd been working very hard to ignore it.

"Probably whatever was hurting Da bouncing back after I let go." After Innes had pulled her away, but who had time for semantics when she was dodging a question?

She pulled the latch to open his door and slid from his lap, marking that she was done with this discussion.

Innes had other ideas. "I don't think that's it." He followed her to the stairs up to their twin townhouses and reached the outer door before she did. Damn his long legs! He stepped between it and her. "You did something in there. Something big."

She looked up and down their sleepy little street, then back at him. "We know that's not possible."

"Do we?"

"I can't do magic, or see it, or touch it. Let alone make all of," she waved her arms about, "that happen."

"How do we know?"

She blinked, befuddled by his apparent lapse in memory of the last few years.

"What?"

"Well, we don't—" He stopped himself, as if only now recognizing how exposed they were. He unlocked and opened the door, ushering her quickly through it and up to what was his half of the townhouse. "We never had a chance to find out what it means that you're a Hole in the World."

"Yes, we do! Evan Greves—"

"Died, after only telling you what he needed you for. Hardly reliable."

He had a point, which she grudgingly conceded. "Da would have told us."

"How could he?" He reached for her hand, pulling her to his favorite reading chair. She didn't stop him, deeming his lap a much better place for this conversation. "When is the last time someone like you lived to adulthood?"

He had her there. Both Evan Greves and Da had told her she would have been killed in infancy, or as soon as she'd been discovered, in normal circumstances. Both men had their reasons for sparing her. One lost his life for it. Would the other follow? She felt some kind of way about that, which was as specific as her mind could manage at the moment.

"So, you're saying they were wrong?"

Innes shook his head. "Not wrong. Ignorant, with not enough evidence to know otherwise."

"So, you think I have some non-magical magic power?" She felt some kind of way about that, too, only this time like she was feeling it from elsewhere in the room, or just a moment behind herself. She liked being special, but this wasn't the same as being the hottest girl showing goats at the State 4-H livestock competition. This kind of special kept both of their lives in a precarious balance on a knife-edged fulcrum.

Also, she liked life better when she knew who and what she was, even if she didn't know what she was doing.

"Maybe." The single word pulled her back into the moment. "Something happened back at the hospital, and I think it's tied to your emotions."

Fantastic. Because those were so predictable.

"And tied to Da's illness. What did he mean about debts?"

"Maybe because he kept you alive?"

She made a harsh snort that stopped up mid-sinus and invoked her gag reflex. "Shit deal for him."

"Hey." The rebuke in Innes' voice was a little less convincing when paired with the sadness in his warm eyes. "Don't do that. None of this is your fault."

"I didn't say it was."

His lips twitched. "You thought it though. Hard." Apparently so hard he could hear it. He lifted his dark brows which still held onto the brown his hair had abandoned when they were teens.

"Okay, fine, but can you blame me? Everyone I love is hurt by my existing."

"Kahrin." He bumped their heads together lightly. "We love you. That's why you're here."

"Knowing you're obligated doesn't give me the warm fuzzies you might expect."

He blinked. "Kahrin, what's wrong?"

"Uh, my Da's in the ICU and it's all my fault?"

"No." He shifted her about so he could see her face. "I don't think that's it."

She slipped from his lap, and he stayed put, as if sensing she needed the physical space to work through whatever it was she was working through. He watched her travel in a circuit, like a boat in a canal that could only go back and forth. She sighed. There was no lying to Innes. "I don't like people sacrificing themselves out of obligation to me."

"No one's doing that, Kahrin."

"Da's my father. He has to love and care for me."

"Mine didn't."

She stopped to see the sharp downturn of his mouth and winced. "That's not what I mean."

"What do you mean?"

She grunted, kicked her socked foot at some invisible offense on the rug. "I don't want to be anyone's obligation." There. She said it. That wasn't so bad, right? Except it felt like all her entrails were becoming extrails. Especially since the concept she knew as time seemed to dissipate as she waited for him to say something.

He stood, drawing a hand over his styled-to-not-look-styled hair. "Your Da chose to save you. To protect you. Even now he won't let whoever is doing this to him take you."

She hated that he was right. She hated that she already knew that truth but still needed to hear it.

"And what about you?"

"What about me?"

"Do you feel obligated to stay with me? To protect me?"

Innes crossed his arms over his chest, resting his mouth between thumb and forefinger. She held her breath, waiting for him to respond as if the only other option was passing out. He sighed. "Well, you of all people should know the answer to that."

Because of Evangeline. Because of Evan and Yelena. Because only she knew the full of their secrets, and that they were safer together.

"Because," he continued just before he rushed her and caught her in a hug, trapping her arms at her sides and growling into her neck. "I apparently have a kink for being driven half out of my mind at all times."

She squealed as his fingers found her most ticklish places. When she couldn't twist away, she dropped her legs out and caused them both to fall to the floor at the sudden shift of weight. He continued, merciless until neither of them could breathe from laughing, and they lay on the floor gasping.

He turned so that their eyes met, and he sobered, the flush of their struggle adding a softness to his face. "I choose to be here, you know."

She flushed. "But what if you meet someone?"

"I meet lots of people," he teased.

She rolled her eyes. "Ha. Ha."

He tugged her arm until she wrapped herself around him. "Kahrin, do you know why I'm not married?"

That was quite the swerve in topic. "Because your last girlfriend wanted to suck you dry in a not fun way?"

"She wasn't my girlfriend."

"Weird how she wasn't as caught up over semantics as you."

Now he rolled his eyes and pretended to be exasperated. "Okay, why we're not married?"

She froze, as if moving would represent words and words were bait for a trap. "Because…" the word hummed out in a hesitating couple of syllables, "we're not like that?"

"Because I don't want to be with someone out of obligation."

"Oh." Her cheeks ached as she felt the smile dominate her face. "Me neither."

"You're loved, and people make sacrifices for love." He grinned. "Like Prince Lír."

"Like Prince Lír." Who, in Innes' opinion, was the epitome of a hero. In her mind his comparing himself to Peter S. Beagle's hero felt apt.

"Also," he added, his voice going to almost a whisper, about to invite her to share a secret. "We're a little like that, aren't we?" He chuckled as her eyes went wide, clearly pleased that he'd figured her out. "I choose you, Kahrin. Every day that I'm here."

Her eyes fluttered to hold back a fresh round of tears. "Okay."

"Did I ruin the fun of you springing this on me with your talk?"

She wound her fingers with his and nodded. "How did you know?"

"I know you, and I know us."

"And you can't spell 'us' without 'me.'"

His mouth puckered in disapproval. "That is not how the song goes."

"That's how I heard it." She pushed up from the floor.

"How you choose to hear it!" He sprang up from the floor to chase her, and despite all that they did not know, she felt lighter, because she knew this one truth: They were choosing each other. Like that.

CHAPTER TEN
INNES

Innes was getting used to this secret pleasure of waking up before Kahrin, and her newfound emotional vulnerability, combined with the circumstances of her father's illness meant she was sleeping earlier and waking later. Given the assurances that had arrived in their respective emails, he was surprised that she'd dozed before sex could ever have come up.

Her eyes fluttered open as the sun filtered in between the curtains, painting the peaks of her visage with gold and peach light. A muzzy smile lit her face.

"Morning, you," he murmured.

"You're still here, I see."

She was, of course, referring to their talk of choices, but he chose a different angle in response. "Well, this is my house."

She wrinkled her nose. "You don't know that."

"I'm pretty sure."

"Go get the deed."

"Then I'd have to get up."

"We have to get up anyway."

She had a point, but he wasn't ready to concede the battle just yet. "But it's cold," he whined in a very non-heroic manner.

"Ah! The mighty Achilles shall fall victim to the Paris that is his miserly use of the thermostat." Not that she was any more generous with the heat on her side of the house.

As if her taunts were insufficient, she planted her feet against his stomach and pushed with all the strength gained of her daily runs, which likely would have succeeded in dislodging him from the bed. In the name of theatrics, however, he rolled onto the floor with a dramatic wail.

"Curse you, wicked woman!"

For a moment it seemed he landed on his arm wrong as an odd, sharp tingle shot from elbow to wrist, leaving a burning sensation along the skin there. If he had, it was jarred back as Kahrin flopped from the bed. Small she might be, but also muscular and solid, and she knocked a winded laugh from him upon impact.

"It is cold out here!" As if this was a surprise. She dropped a kiss to his lips and sprang to her feet before he could even register it happening. Such was the way with her, a perfect storm leaving rubble before you knew it landed. "Dibs on first shower!" She disappeared into the en-suite and he moaned as he heard the water running immediately.

"Save me a little hot water!" No, his begging was not going to get him his way, he was sure.

She popped her head out, dangling a leg from the knee just around the corner. "You know this shower is big enough for both of us, right?"

Hey! It was!

He rolled over and pushed up from the floor and announced his approach with a growl. She squealed as he caught her up, seating her on the sink and falling into a kiss he felt he'd been holding back for days. Her fingers tickled at the fine hairs standing above the line of his sleep pants, making his modesty less modest by the heartbeat. How cruel of his best friend to invite him in while she wore so much clothing. The large t-shirt of his she'd slept in was quickly swept away as he kicked free from his pants. She wrapped her legs around his waist and threw her weight forward, necessitating that he support her with hands under her backside. He stumbled into the shower, not exactly caring that the leg of his pajamas made the glass door bounce back open. Oh well, he was too far gone to the urge to have her after all this time to be bothered with trifles like a flood on his bathroom floor.

He nipped her throat, chasing her pulse as it coursed through her, and pressed her back to the wall. He was going to need the leverage.

"You're sure?" Why, oh why did he insist on asking that between mutually needy kisses? He knew why, and it was the crux of the love between them, that forged-in-fire trust.

She pressed his shoulders enough to give him a playful glare. "I am literally wrapped around you and open for the party, Pretty Mouth."

"That better be a private party," he growled.

They'd never made claim over one another, and never demanded anything close to exclusivity so long as everyone consented and stayed healthy and safe. Even as some acts they kept greedily between the two of them only. This was a shift in gravity, a resetting of their center of balance since that fumbling day at fifteen, from the explorations of more base desires of the previous year. If they were choosing one another here and now, he had no interest in sharing her with anyone else. So long as it was what they both wanted.

She scraped her teeth over the join of his jaw behind his ear before answering in a husky, urgency-laced voice. "Exclusive. Only one guest."

That was all he needed.

Until his phone rang in the next room, with that tone assigned to his mentor from school and her parents which was set to bypass his do not disturb function.

"Ignore it," she begged. Oh, sweet hell, it took all his resistance when she begged.

"It could be about your Da." His entire body screamed for him to just shut up and stop thinking for just the few minutes they would need to slake this need, but it was all it took to shift the mood.

She slid to her feet with a small whine. "I know."

Innes trod across the mess of the floor, slinging a towel low over his hips and then answered the phone.

It wasn't her parents, but it was something that needed to be brought up before any of this went further.

Sheer force of will had them on the road to the Quirke farm within the hour, and a familiar quiet settled between them most of the trip.

"So?" she asked. Her patience at being put off from whatever his big news was down to a frayed end, and she curled into her hooded sweatshirt and running tights while she looked at him expectantly.

"I've been offered an opportunity," he started, suddenly not as excited as he'd initially been when it was presented to him. "An internship of sorts, kind of like a Doctors Without Borders situation where I get to learn clinical basics, hands on, in a practical setting."

She let a low, appreciative whistle. "That's amazing."

"It is." Because it was. "We'd travel to places with limited access to basic health care, domestic and abroad."

She beamed, never in their friendship failing to be anything but proud of his achievements. It made his chest squeeze with a certainty their recent decisions required, but also clenched his gut with what he knew was coming.

"So, when?"

"After graduation." No sense in drawing it out. The sooner they both had all the facts, the sooner they could add it to the list of facts to base their decision on.

"Oh." She did an admirable job of not sounding disappointed. She even maintained a strained enthusiasm for what this meant to him. "How long?"

"The summer if I want. A year if I like it."

Quiet. Just the tires on the road as they shifted from pavement to gravel.

"I haven't made any commitments yet." He glanced at her, trying to gauge the expression she wore, which was unsettling in its blankness. "I wanted to talk to you, first. That was before, um, you know."

"You can say sex, Innes. We're not teens anymore." She smiled, a genuine one that eased his cramping belly.

"But it's not just, well, that."

She laughed at him, gently, then started picking at her cuticles. "So..."

"This thing we're doing, thinking of doing? It's big." Sort of. It was new, and they were still feeling out, and up, the parameters.

"It's not a wedding, Pretty Mouth. Almost nothing is changing." He believed she meant that. "And it doesn't have to change."

"I don't want to keep you waiting."

"And I don't want you to stay out of obligation when this means so much to you." She still smiled, but there was a touch of sadness to her eyes.

"It's not an obligation, Kahrin. But it is a long wait."

"I haven't gone anywhere since you've known me. Where am I going to go while you're gone? I'm never leaving this stupid town. I can't even settle on a job." But she seemed to enjoy doing a little of this and a bit of that while it kept her attention. "That doesn't scream opportunity. I'll be around."

"I'm saying that if you want to—"

"I don't. My mind's made up. I don't mind waiting." She poked her tongue at him and added, "I have a lot of stored up memories to get me through any dry spell." She flopped back into her seat. "Besides, I may be needed here. That'll keep me busy."

It should have been that simple, and he let an echo of a chuckle that she instantly recognized. Coinciding with their turning into the driveway of her—and in many ways his—childhood home, the tone shifted even further into somber territory.

He pulled his car into his usual spot, a rutted patch of frozen mud near the exercise pen for the does. He turned off the car, and with the soft electric motor went the last vestiges of keeping things from being heavy and awkward.

"I don't know how to go in there." She stared blankly ahead, her eyes seeming to look through her house rather than at it.

He wanted to make a joke to lift her up. His chest always ached to see her in pain, and this was new to them. A joke wasn't what she needed, and he didn't have it in him, besides.

"Just pretend they're at a co-op meeting."

"If you want to bang one out on the davenport, just ask." She laughed at her own joke with a hollowness that underscored the seriousness of the circumstances.

"It's not off the table," he tried.

"Ohh, the table? Really?"

He shot her a look but squeezed her hand. "He's going to be okay, you know. He was stable when we left, and stable when you called this morning."

"He's my Da." Her voice cracked.

"I know, and the closest I've had to a loving one." That was all he had to say on his own father. "He's your Da, and we know he's a fighter." Though pushing them away did seem incongruous with that statement.

It placated her enough, all the same, and she inhaled courage and got out of the car.

They didn't get to leave the discomfort in the car. Evidence of a life put on pause started at the mud room door. The deck was half shoveled, the shoveled portion dusted with fresh powder that had been hastily scooped away for a quick exit, and an overnight's worth of new snow concealing that trail.

"Where's Pickle?" Innes asked when the Quirke's blue bully didn't bound up to them upon entry.

"Probably the front barn." Which made sense. Who knew how long the family would be in town? It gave Pickle access to the exercise pen to relieve himself, but also the inside where it was snug and heated for the goats and their young when they had them. "We can check on him on the way out."

She kicked her boots off, as did he, and ventured into the dining room. A half-folded willow basket of laundry sat on one of the bench seats, socks hoping for mates laid out over the table. He followed Kahrin into the kitchen which had a view of the goat pen and confirmed Pickle's whereabouts. Dishes were left barely rinsed in the sink—a mortal sin in Ma Quirke's eyes—and the smell of burnt coffee hung around the old percolator.

Kahrin stood frozen in the middle of the room, as if the woven-rag rug had trapped her in an odd stasis. He squeezed her shoulder to snap her out of it.

"How about I clean up down here for your ma while you head up and find what your brother sent you to find?"

"My parents do it in there," she protested.

A fine time to suddenly be squeamish. "Okay, I'll go, and you can wash the crusty dishes."

"My parents had three kids in under three years. I'll get over them having sex."

Which was about what he thought would happen.

With her gone, finishing Ma's chores was a quick process, but also one pregnant with emptiness. The Quirke house had never been silent in all the years he'd been part of it. The quiet became a presence of its own, and an unwelcome one at that.

He gathered up the kitchen rags and towels and dropped them into the washer in the mudroom, after which he sank onto one of the dining benches with a sigh and knuckled tears out of his own eyes.

The Quirkes practically raised him. His mother died during a cesarean following a placental abruption that almost took him, too. Weeks in a NICU had strained his family finances, and by the time Innes' own father had taken ill, there was little hope of getting him proper care. Brodie moved out as soon as he was able, leaving then ten-year-old Innes alone to care for a miserable bastard. He died blaming Innes for all their hardships, and Innes was never sure if his youth and stress hadn't helped him get there.

While Brodie and his wife dutifully took Innes in at twelve, his brother never let him forget what a burden he put upon them. Had it not been for the obligation of family, they might not have and were not shy about saying so.

Meeting the Quirkes at a town meeting changed Innes' life in every way. He'd been a child in need of love, and the Quirkes chose to share their abundance with him. Even as Da Quirke seemed cold and stony, pretending to dislike Innes at times, especially when he and Kahrin became physical, he always made sure Innes knew he was wanted, welcomed, and loved.

Innes did not know if he was ready to let that go. Not after the last few years.

He pulled himself together and began folding socks—the worst of tasks—and by the time Kahrin called his name from the top of the stairs, his face felt cool and no longer tear-swollen. Not that he was ashamed to cry in front of her, but he did not want to turn her grief into his own.

He reached the first landing when the strange tingle from earlier returned like a slice across his forearm. He hissed and shook out his hand to relieve it, but it didn't help, and it didn't pass. Instead, his skin burned from inside. He gritted his teeth, pushing the sleeve of his rusty henley up to see it. By the time his skin began parting, he was screaming.

CHAPTER ELEVEN
KAHRIN

Kahrin was well into her teens when she realized that not everyone's mother had a hope chest. It was such a normalized piece of furniture in the farmhouse, its place at the foot of Ma and Da's bed so established she once thought it was attached to the footboard. She had no idea what had originally been in the large aspen chest, but for as long as she could remember, her mother stored extra quilts for winter within its cedar lining.

When Kahrin asked about it as a younger girl, Ma explained that she'd built it with her own father to store "linens and marriage stuff," whatever that was, and that later Da had done some repairs when they moved into the house. She'd opened it innumerable times, fetching and returning blankets, and could not recall ever finding anything else in it.

She emptied the chest now of all the quilts Ma had made over the years, some out of each child's baby clothes, some out of t-shirts acquired through various activities in high school, some out of fat quarters specifically picked out for the job or scraps of worn-out flannel shirts and denim. She laid each on the end of the bed like it was a sacred relic of a time lost, letting her fingers linger on the top stitching and frayed yarn ties.

She saw nothing of note under them, only tufts of dryer lint and the dog hair that found its way into every crevice of the house. She leaned over, boosted on her knees until she could run her hands over the bottom, finding no latch or handle, even with the aid of the flashlight on her phone. Even the fitting of the boards against one another appeared seamless. Finding nothing, she flopped to her butt, hitting her head on the lid, and dropping her phone inside. It struck the bottom, making a springy sound. She rubbed her head and peered inside. The bottom of the chest had tilted open.

Not needing to be invited anywhere twice, she pried the board up, revealing a packet of papers, envelopes, and photos, tied up with a length of indigo bias tape. A quick thumb through showed her they were mostly vital documents, marking marriage and births, and some photos of Da in regalia from his youth.

She hopped up, hugging the packet to her chest and ran for the stairs. She inhaled to call Innes' name, only to be cut off by his scream. Packet of treasures dropped and forgotten, she dashed down to the switchback where he lay on the carpet, clutching his arm, blood seeping between his fingers.

"Innes!" Too many things needed to be addressed at once. His blood dotting the worn carpet, the smear of it across his arm and chest of his shirt, the way his teeth ground together as he tried to breathe through obvious pain. She wrapped herself around him like she was a protective cloak and he leaned against her, gasping. They stayed that way a moment until she felt his muscles relax, though he trembled, and he moved enough so they could see what the cause of all of it had been.

"What did you do?" she used the hem of her shirt to wipe away the mess.

"Nothing," he whimpered. "The pain just started, as if I was—"

"Being cut?"

"Yes."

Not just a cut. A series of them, clean slashes joining over his pale skin to form rough, geometric letters. "What is this?" Her eyes flicked up to meet his, swollen and red, making the deep brown of his irises appear greener.

He fell back onto his rear, the adrenaline of a moment ago leaving him panting against the wall.

HE'S NEXT.

Innes' head flopped against the wall with a soft thud. She was getting awfully tired of seeing his blood on the outside of his body. "I think it's a message."

No shit, and a grisly one at that. "For who? What does it mean?" she asked, though she already knew the intended recipient. "Someone wants my attention."

"And they can't reach you, directly."

She cradled his head against her chest, combing fingers through his salt and pepper hair as her heart slammed against the pressure building up behind her sternum.

"I don't think Da's illness is a punishment. Not for him, anyhow." Her worst fears became a vise squeezing her chest until she struggled to breathe.

"Me neither."

Once it was cleaned, the wound didn't seem so bad. Oh, it was still a horrible mess, but the cuts already looked softened, the edges even like they weren't as deep as they initially seemed. They slathered it in some of the pungent salve that Da made and bandaged the whole of his arm from wrist to elbow.

"Stop staring at it," Innes scolded her.

"I'm not." She was. She couldn't get the grisly image out of her head. Perhaps Innes was choosing to be with her, but he was certainly not choosing this. She didn't let him out of arm's reach, until he put a firm boundary on using the toilet.

They sat on her old daybed, as if they were still limited to her tiny childhood bedroom for privacy. Strewn in the tight space between them were the letters, newspaper clippings, and even old Polaroids of Da in his dance regalia. All their vital records, shot records, baptismal certificates were kept in a filing cabinet in the dining room area, except one copy of Brecken's birth certificate, and Ma and Da's marriage certificate. That seemed odd, at first.

"Wasn't Brecken born less than a year before Alec?" Innes asked.

"Ten months." Poor Ma. "And then I came along nine months after Alec." And a month early, which no one ever let her forget, as it clearly marked the beginning of her impatient nature. To say her parents were amorous was an understatement for the centuries. "Why?"

Innes tapped the birth certificate. "Look at this date."

She did. "So?" He jerked his head at it, urging her to look again. "Wait, that would make him—"

"A year older," he finished for her.

"That has to be a mistake. I've seen Brecken's birth certificate. It's in the file box downstairs with all of our other documents." Which did not answer why this one was hidden away in a secret compartment in Ma's hope chest.

"It has a state seal on it. An embossed one."

She ran her fingers over the raised pattern, staring like she could change the ink if she was stubborn enough.

"That's not our hospital here," she noted. Her fingers flipped through a few items until she came back to the marriage certificate, the original one signed by the officiant. "That means he was born before they were married." Which was hardly a scandal in modern times, save the few details Kahrin knew about her Ma's very Catholic upbringing.

"That wasn't here, either."

Kahrin's eyes followed Innes' finger to the place noted on the birth certificate, which also did not match the city of Brecken's birth. She also noted that Da's name had not always been Quirke, but Ma's had. She shoved her fingers into her hair, leaning her head into her hands.

"None of this makes sense."

"There is one thing you could try."

Using her fingers, she broke the waterfall of her hair and scooped it back out of her face. "Nuh-uh."

"Kahrin, obviously your Ma knows something."

"Yeah, it looks like she's known a lot of things for a long time now and didn't think any of us would be interested." She flapped her hands at the piles between them. "You know, I always thought my family had this great honesty thing." Her cheeks burned as her temper fanned. "But I find out that Da knew what I am the entire time, and that he's an Adept. Now he and Ma have been lying about how old Brecken is. Even our family name. Why?"

"I don't know," Innes answered as he rubbed his palm over his forearm, "but I think it might be time we find out."

That froze her in place. She tugged her lip between her teeth, ashamed. This was no longer about her, her feelings, or how her family had kept secrets from her and her siblings. She stopped having the right to dig her heels in against her parents' dishonesty when Innes began suffering the physical consequences of their lies. If it were only her, she'd just never talk to them. Well, after she talked to them loudly. But then, no talking to them. She owed it to Innes to at least try and find out who was hurting him, and why.

"I'm sorry."

His lips twitched. "Wow. A whole sorry, just for me, huh?"

She rolled her eyes. "I'm not offering it to anyone else."

"And I'm not asking you to." He leaned forward, resting his brow against hers so they could share breath. "I only want answers, and we only know one way to find them."

She nodded; the motion imperceptible had they not been forehead to forehead. Her heart clenched, wondering when magic would leave them alone. When they would be allowed to live lives of their own choosing, staying well away from the world of magic that she never asked to be a part of. Or apart from, as it stood.

"I will get them." Her fingers curled over the slight bend of the back of his neck, her words murmured like a desperate prayer to a forgotten god. If she stopped touching him, would whoever was after her attack him again? "I don't care what I have to do to get them."

"Don't be so quick to—"

"No, Innes." She broke the contact of their brows but held tight to his other arm. "I mean it. If I have to tear the world of magic apart to do it,

I will find out who is hurting you."

"I know." That infamous mouth of his lingered on the crease of her brow. "But maybe we do this together, hm?"

"You dragged out the 'hm.'" How dare he.

"I'm holding no punches. I learned that from someone."

She didn't say anything else as they gathered up all the papers and mementos or as they drove away from the farm after a visit of playing fetch and cuddle with Pickle. Not until Innes merged them onto the highway did she offer up a soft, "I love you."

"I love you, too," he echoed, as he always did, and she knew he always would.

CHAPTER TWELVE
INNES

Innes unwound the cotton bandaging from his arm, flexing his fingers to test for pain which no longer lingered. Night drew up the edges of the day, tucking it into a neat package and snatching the light from his bedroom. Perhaps the shadows were causing him to see things.

"Kahrin," he called, "come look at this."

"I've already seen all of this," she teased on her way into the bedroom.

"Hilarious." Also, not wrong, and despite the circumstances, it sent a heat through him as he remembered being interrupted this morning. Just two days ago they'd declared a recommencement of their physical relationship, and just the night before a commitment beyond it. They'd yet to act on the former as the latter seemed to entangle them further into something more urgent. Well, certain parts of him would argue about the urgency, but he had to stay clear-headed.

He held his arm out, cut-side-up. "It's healing."

She brushed a single finger over it, tracing the remains of the warning.

"How is that possible?" She looked up, the worry wearing heavily in her expression. "I am definitely not doing this."

"A statement of the obvious." It didn't match up or make sense with anything they knew, or thought they knew so far. "Healing certainly feels like magic."

"So, what's causing this? I doubt whoever did this had a sudden change of heart and decided to patch it back up."

"My thoughts, too." It wasn't like they needed to cover magical tracks. Innes was a pre-med student at the end of his undergrad. Self-harm, even cutting himself, was far too easy a conclusion that anyone who discovered it could jump to. It would discredit any explanation he tried to offer.

"I'm sorry about this," she murmured, ghosting her lips over the angry red skin. The lines were itchy, almost scabbing over already, and all that remained.

"I told you, it's not your fault." He tipped her chin up so she could see the earnestness in his eyes. Despite the warmth, he shivered at the touch of her fingers.

"You could let me make it up to you." Her grin shifted to something a little more predatory. "I know I could use a distraction. I am willing to wager you could, too."

"Wicked woman." He bumped his nose against her cheek. "There is nothing in the world I would like more than to give into that offer right now."

She huffed. "Yet, somehow, I don't think you're going to." While her voice sulked, her face held understanding.

"I just want to give you the attention you deserve. That I deserve. This isn't meant to be a quick one and done." He drew her against him, working his fingers through her loose hair and tickling them down her back as far as he could reach.

"You're attaching a lot of significance to this." She laid her head against his chest. "It's not like we've never done the deed before."

He frowned. "Isn't it significant to you?" His intention wasn't to scold, but he could feel a faint edge to his words.

She planted her chin in the divot of his chest and looked up. "It is, but also, not." He could tell by her expression that whatever face he made just then put a panic in her. "What I mean is, it feels normal. Like an extension of everything to now, and not something completely new."

"It can be both, you know. Isn't that what you're always telling me? That this doesn't have to be an either/or situation?" He stepped back from her enough to keep his hands around her waist but see her pretty eyes. "Let's get this talk with your Ma behind us." He really didn't want that on his mind while he was trying to, well, do other things with Ma's only daughter.

"Okay."

He dropped his mouth to her ear, as if anyone else might be in their house and able to overhear them. "Besides, it's been a while, and I don't plan on you being able to walk straight or sit right for a bit after, hm?"

She laughed, soft and breathy, but he felt the shudder that promise sent through her. "I am going to hold you to that."

He chuckled a groan into the top of her head. Their weekend at the cabin by the lake had been cut short, with so many things left unexplored. While their hunger for it had not lessened, the aftermath of Evangeline's assault on him had put a damper on life for a time. He wanted that back. That carefree feeling they had gone into their curiosities with, and while he wanted it, oh god how he wanted it, it was not something they could, or should, rush.

That didn't mean they didn't have a few minutes to spare. He ducked his head and caught her lips in a light kiss, then deepened it, and for just a brief span of time, lost himself in the feeling of her warm in his arms, of her tongue darting between his lips, of her fingers in his hair, something he did not allow anyone else to do. He luxuriated in that hitch in her breath, the needy little whine she let out, and the sharp inhale as he let his hands slide to her neck, resting the V of his thumb and finger in the place he knew would spike her blood with want.

He pulled her to him with a warm chuckle, and they stayed like that while their pulses settled, listening to one another's hearts in the inky dark.

"Let's go and get back." His words caught over a lump in his throat he'd been unaware of. A subtle grief pushed back against his want of a momentary joy. Also, a startling conflict.

"And then what?" He knew she wasn't asking about the very unfinished trail of thought that hovered between them.

"I'm not going to accept that internship." How could he? Her family upended, their path forward unclear, and the knowledge that any of them could be in danger until they put all of this to rest seemed more pressing than his wants in a career.

And all of that was before he even started to process his own grief over what was happening to his found family.

"But–"

"It's what I want." It even sounded true to him when he said it, so he left it at that. "So, let's go."

CHAPTER THIRTEEN
KAHRIN

Thank the Lord that neither of her brothers were there when Kahrin and Innes returned to the hospital. Kahrin wasn't sure she could handle more of Brecken's barbed words and confronting Ma on Brecken's real age seemed cruel with him there to be blindsided by the knowledge. He deserved to know, but not like this. Not right now.

Ma had set up camp in the room. Da's tray table was lowered so she could use it to hold her scant meal of hospital gelatin and coffee, and she had the foot of the chair kicked out so she could prop her feet up. Someone had brought her a blanket that she draped over her legs, and she flipped through the pages of a feed and supply catalogue, though her eyes seemed to be somewhere other than the lists of seeds and sizing charts of mucking boots.

On the drive over, Innes had cautioned Kahrin to approach this with delicacy. Whatever Ma and Da's reasons for their deceptions, he reasoned, they deserved a chance to explain them. Or, rather, Ma deserved a chance to explain on behalf of her and Da.

"So, does Brecken know he's actually twenty-four, or is he not part of this little family deception?"

Okay, so she worked with a different definition of "delicate" than her best friend.

"Kahrin." It wasn't really scolding, but it was clear that Innes didn't like her brick through a window approach.

She tossed both hands up. "I'm tired of secrets. I don't know how much you know, but you should know what I know. Are we going to wait until someone dies before we all come clean?"

Ma stared at her, and Kahrin could feel the dodge of question forming behind her eyes.

"Don't, Ma. Please. Whatever is happening, we need to get to the bottom of it. This is bigger than whatever you're embarrassed about hiding." Innes didn't stop her when she grabbed his wrist and shoved his sleeve up to show Ma the handiwork of whoever was behind this. "Please. Just tell us what you know."

Ma clasped a hand over her mouth, and Kahrin could see the famed Quirke resolve wither. "We didn't want them to find us."

"It seems they have." Innes kept heat out of his words, but they were edged all the same. That he was hurt by all the secret keeping was obvious. This was his family, too.

"Enough with the cryptic crap, Ma." Kahrin dug the heels of her hands into her eyes, and Innes tugged her into his side.

"I am sure you have your reasons for hiding all of this, but it's affecting all of us," he said, "whether you like it or not."

"Take a seat, kids." Ma gestured to the stiff chairs on the other side of the small room. "This is not a short story."

They did, and Kahrin let Innes hug her against his side, grateful to not need an excuse to be close, just in case whatever was after her tried to attack again.

"I met Iskandar during Powwow season. He was a dancer." A bit of red touched her cheeks, indicating that she'd not learned what type. "I wasn't supposed to be on the reservation, and wasn't exactly welcomed there, either." She looked at her husband in the bed, life being managed by machines. "He's always been so handsome. And funny. He was so full of bravado back then, and I was looking for a rebellion against my father."

While it was cute to see Ma reminisce on their whirlwind romance, one her family did not approve of, Kahrin soon became fidgety, swinging her feet over the floor wishing she'd just get on with it. Some of it—how hot they found one another–she already knew.

"We were young. He was studying sacred medicine with the medicine man. I didn't know he was, ah, magical."

"Are all medicine men Adepts?" she interrupted. Ma paid her a stern look. "Oh, come on, I think we're long past being hush hush about this."

Ma sighed. "No, I don't think so. I never met many others."

"Medicine men or Adepts?"

"Both," Ma answered. "Though I don't think they are always men, either."

"So, all this time, you knew?" Innes asked. "Why go through all the trouble of pretending you didn't?"

"I knew some things." She lifted her shoulders towards her ears. "Some I didn't."

"Didn't want to, it sounds," Kahrin grumbled.

"Look, I didn't know much about your da's culture." Obviously. "Even less about magic, because it was against what my family believed." She looked sadly to Da in the bed. "The two aren't related. Magic isn't an Indigenous thing, as far as I know."

"What about me? Did you know about me?"

"I knew there was something, but I never asked what. We'd run away from that life, and I wanted a clean break behind us."

"Who else knew?" Innes asked.

"About what?" Ma tossed back. "The pre-marital sex that was against my upbringing? My getting pregnant outside of wedlock? The fact that neither of our families were exactly thrilled about our dating, let alone what having a child would mean? Or maybe the fact that I was raised to believe Iskandar's gifts were the world of the devil? My father still used words like 'savage' when describing Iskandar and his friends and family."

"Point taken."

Ma had always been religious, but never levered it against her children, or Innes. Thankfully. They'd been spared strict rules dissuading them from following their curiosities in their teen years, provided safety and respect that meant they'd stayed safe.

"Your da knew it might be possible to pass magic on to our children, though not a guarantee." She took a stuttering breath. "Iskandar's family might have eventually accepted it, especially when his gifts could be used to help the tribe's people, but my family would have fought it with every advantage they had behind them. My father was beloved by the whole parish, and my mother zealous in her support of him. We thought we were protecting Brecken."

"I wonder if he feels protected."

"He doesn't know. We got married in the first town that didn't recognize us. Your da took my name because it was unlikely anyone would look for us under it. We said Brecken was younger than he is because, well because I was embarrassed. And if I ever went home, I didn't want it to hang over his head. We found someone willing to doctor his birth certificate. We were protecting him, but we didn't know from what."

"Me." Kahrin laughed, though she felt no joy in it.

"Perhaps." Ma leaned forward to stroke Kahrin's face, but she leaned out of reach. "His mentor wouldn't have wanted to lose such a promising student, but my parents never would have understood or accepted it."

"The magic?" Kahrin asked.

"Any of it."

She and Innes waited for Ma to expound and realized they would be disappointed.

Had this been anyone else's tale, it might have been the kind of lovey-dovey crap that Innes loved in his storybooks. It had all the markings of the things that put stars in his eyes. But this was no fairy tale, evidenced by the scars on Innes' arm. Not even one of the harsh Brothers Grimm ones meant to scare children into proper behavior.

"It seems it didn't work," Innes said tersely. His jaw tightened.

"Do you think it is his mentor who is attacking us? Who came after us when I was born?"

"What?" Innes looked at her, shocked.

"Later," she muttered, hoping it was good enough.

"It's possible, Kahr. But I really don't know. The less I knew, the better, or so I thought."

"Well, that turned out great, didn't it?" Kahrin slapped her hands down on her lap and stood from her seat. "Then I guess we pay him a visit and tell him to stop."

"Kahrin," Ma started, that warning in her voice that another time would have all three Quirke children and Innes freeze in their tracks, "if someone wants you dead, do you think it's wise to run toward them?"

"We don't know he wants me dead," she said, so matter of fact that she hoped it was true. "And I'm not going to keep guessing while they try to hurt Innes."

That would have been her dramatic exit, but Innes grasped her hand and anchored her to the spot. "I'm not going to let anyone hurt Kahrin, either." She faced him, finding a look in his eyes she knew well. "I don't want a life without her in it." Her heart squeezed, and she thought she might have forgotten to breathe.

If it was possible to find any happiness in the moment, Kahrin could have sworn she saw a spark of it in Ma's dark eyes. "Then you won't come back without her."

"No, ma'am."

Innes had never disobeyed her parents, never broken a promise. Kahrin didn't think he was about to start now. Kahrin didn't think it needed to be said that this particular promise went both ways.

Both together or never ever.

CHAPTER FOURTEEN
INNES

Like most men, and probably many women as well, Innes did not enjoy impotence. Maybe he didn't have it in the usual sense that everyone took it to mean (thank goodness) but the powerlessness he felt in his life right now made even that small mercy seem insignificant. So, while Kahrin blew off steam on her daily run, he hit the gym, letting his thoughts run wild and inspire him to push himself.

He was too old to believe that things always worked out like they did in romance novels and fairy tales. Happily ever afters were often reserved for escapism. But growing up hadn't wiped the hopefulness from him. The part of him that believed that if he just tried hard enough, he could squeeze in one of his own. If he studied enough, if he fought hard enough, if he trained hard enough, even if he loved hard enough, he could find his own little slice of that sought after storybook ending. His own little bit of magic in a life that had started out so bleak. Once upon a time that had included adventure, seeing the world, and going places where people didn't know his sad backstory. It included finding that fair maiden and falling madly in love, maybe seeing the world together.

He'd always counted on Kahrin being part of that, but not in the way that things were opening before them. That was new, and he found he liked it more and more. But he also wanted this opportunity in front of him. A chance to travel and do some good. A chance to be a hero in the way a modern world would let him.

He let a frustrated grunt at his indecision as he did his squats.

Every opportunity seemed to be overgrown with the very magic he once thought would save him from a world where he felt unloved and insignificant. The choices in front of him were being pried away as the tendrils wound between the invisible world and the one where he had to live.

Some hero he was turning out to be.

He cleaned and put his weights away, then went home to clean up and wait for Kahrin.

He couldn't do anything about Da Quirke being ill. He couldn't stop the flood of grief from overcoming Kahrin and her good senses. He couldn't even reckon with his own grief because he had no right to dump more on to everyone else. He needed room to handle his own feelings, but also couldn't bear the thought of separating from the Quirkes at a time like this. Especially not Kahrin.

Kahrin, who seemed so unsure of which way was up at the moment.

She returned from her run and showered (alone), and they went to a pub they liked for a meal. Afterward they sought the advice of the only person who seemed equipped to advise them right now.

"Maybe I should move back home," Kahrin said once they'd relayed the story to Emilia. The woman sat quietly and listened without interruption, at least until that moment.

"Why on earth would you do that, my darling girl?"

"What if Ma needs my help? Brecken and Alec have lives. If Da," she cut off, unable to finish the thought Innes knew was in her head. "If you go on that trip—"

"I said I'm not going."

"If," she emphasized, "you go, what am I going to do in two empty townhouses?"

"If I go, and I already said I'm not," she rolled her eyes, but he kept going, "who's going to feed Emilia?"

His attempt at lightening the mood had at least some desired effect on Kahrin, and the elder woman granted him a droll expression.

"I am choosing to take that in the literal, and remind you she's a grown woman." She turned her head toward Emilia, who inclined her own head in thanks. "And if it's not literal, I'll remind you that I am definitely not her type."

At that, Emilia let a peal of laughter. "More than you think."

Innes winked at Emilia, who traded the private gesture back. Perhaps their own physical relationship had come to an end, but the closeness and intimacy did not. It had even grown with Kahrin, something for which he was grateful. She needed someone as unapologetic in life as Emilia.

"You could go with me," he said. He had no idea where that came from, but it didn't sound entirely absurd.

Emilia tutted before Kahrin could respond. "And do what? Hold your bandages or keep a hotel bed warm?"

Kahrin tilted her head as if that last part was not as unappealing as their fairy godmother tried to make it sound. She waved her hands to scatter the thoughts away. "That's your dream, not mine."

"What is your dream?" Emilia asked, her voice warm and inviting in a way that tended to coax thoughts out of Kahrin. "Some pursuit you could throw yourself into. Perhaps take up your classes again."

Kahrin frowned. "A moot point, because we have to deal with all of this first."

"Is it a moot point?" Emilia leaned her chin on her fist, a finger tapping at her cheek and catching an emerald ring in the light. "This journey might take you to a place you haven't considered. You might find something there." She meant the reservation where Kahrin's da had grown up.

"I doubt it." Kahrin was finished with the conversation, evident by the way she hopped up out of her seat and collected her belongings. She stopped on her way to the door and looked back to the older woman. "Thank you, though. I'll give it some thought." To Innes she said, "I'll be in the car."

Emilia gave Innes a sympathetic look. "I'm happy for this turn in your relationship," she said, pitching her voice for only his ears. "All things considered; you appear happy."

Innes' mouth helplessly turned up at the corner. With everything happening, he'd forgotten to take time to feel happy about it. "I am."

"I originally thought this might be one of her whims. She seemed so out of sorts recently. I'm happy to see I was wrong."

"It's different this time. It makes sense. I've missed, well not her, but her." He felt his face redden and he swallowed hard. "I mean, things about her."

"Her chaos has always called to you. In a good way." A wry twist took her smile. "A way I never would have satisfied for you."

"It's more than that."

"I know, my darling doctor."

"Future doctor."

Emilia waved a hand. "Besides, you're too old for me now."

"Wicked woman."

"Be careful on this trip. I suspect there is more at play here than there seems. I'll be in Europe for the remainder of the season, but I'm only a call away."

"Yes, dear." He got up and leaned to let her brush a kiss to his cheek. "For Kahrin, too."

"She knows. We both still need you."

Emilia walked him out, granting him another kiss before he met

Kahrin in the car. She barely said anything the entire drive back to the townhouse.

"You know," he said as he turned the car off and faced her. "You might find family there. There's a lot you don't know about your family. You could—"

"They are not my family. My family is here." She gestured over her shoulder, indicating people not in the car. "And back in that hospital. Those people didn't want us, so why would I want them?" A dark look of determination crossed her face in the streetlight. "Besides, at least one of them is hurting my actual family. They're not going to want me there when I find out who."

She flung her door open and left the car, her purpose renewed, and energy bolstered by her run and food. He only caught up to her because she bounced back and forth between their respective doors, undecided which house to enter.

"I have to pack." She decided on her door and after a small fight with her keys, they were inside.

Kahrin was not slovenly, really, but she was a person who genuinely believed that some things just belonged on the floor. A couple times a week Innes would insist they hang out on her side, and he'd find a way to trick her into tidying up. Evidently, he'd skipped that routine for a bit longer than he realized. How did she have clothes to wear?

"Do you need to do laundry?" He turned on the lights to find an array of laundry in various degrees of completion around the room, including a semicircle of mismatched socks laid out not unlike the way her Ma had left them at the farmhouse.

"No, why?" She looked around. "I don't subscribe to the clean/dirty dichotomy. There's degrees of wearable."

She was serious. Was she serious? "You know, we're likely to be gone a few days."

"Right." That seemed to click some unspoken direction to her. As if it were the most natural thing in the world, she walked to one end of the room and pulled a few fistfuls of underwear from an empty aquarium that had once housed a toad she'd kept as a pet for a short time. "How do you pack for a revenge trip?"

"Revenge trip?" He wiped his hands over his face.

She pinged around the room, dumping things out of a gym bag and laying it on her davenport before she gathered more items. "Yeah. Is there a dress code? Donning all black seems a little femme fatale for my taste."

Beat them or join them. "Red?" he suggested. "Very sensational."

"Not the sensation I want you associating with it."

"Ha, ha." He stilled her with hands on her shoulders. "How about we sleep before setting off on a rampage?"

"I'm not tired."

He couldn't fault her that, he really wasn't either. "I don't know, we could take a minute to think through our plan."

"Not my forte."

"Believe me, I know."

She dropped the fistfuls of underwear into her bag. "Ma always says clean underwear is the most important part of going anywhere." Her birthday stunt contradicted that wisdom, but this was not the time to bring that up. She ricocheted to a collapsible laundry basket and upended it, methodically sniffing jeans and leggings, and deciding they were clean enough.

He sighed and removed her underwear from the bag and began refolding it into tight little rolls and setting them in a stack. "You want important things on the top, then."

"I know how to pack," she snapped, grabbing each one up and undoing his progress. "Maybe I don't have a lot of need to do it, but I know how."

"Hey." There was no bite in the word, but it had the desired effect of stopping her before she increased in storm category. "I know." He tilted her chin up and used his thumbs to wipe the start of tears away without mentioning them. "And I know you well enough to know you're about to run off, half-cocked, if someone doesn't slow you down to take a breath."

"Not all of us are one-third cock and can wing it." The sharpness of her tone might have been intended as snark, but even she caught herself off guard with a little chuckle at their in-joke. She sighed, her chest shuddering, and plopped onto the davenport. "I'm scared."

Everyone lost their parents eventually, but Kahrin had looked upon her parents' youth with the arrogance of someone who assumed immortality. How could her da, such an enormous presence, ever cease to be? He wasn't ready to lose Da Quirke either, but as he sank onto the sofa beside her, he pulled her against him, and knew that losing her would be worse. He might not survive it.

Both together or never ever.

"I am too." When he trusted himself to speak further without crying, he slipped to his knees in front of her, resting his arms on her lap. "But being a hero doesn't mean never being afraid."

"I know."

"You know a thing or two about being a hero, hm?"

He believed that she did. When he'd been taken captive with Yelena, he knew that the incredibly stupid thing she did as an act of heroism terrified her. She had no guarantee that stabbing herself was something she could survive. She barely passed human physiology. She did know that it was a risk she was willing to take for what she saw to be the greater good. He disagreed, but that was in the past. No more sacrifices, they'd promised. Not if there were other ways.

"I've been watching you for years." She wrapped her arms around his head and curled over him, burying her face in his hair. "You've always been my hero."

He'd not expected the warm feeling that gave him. He was not quite sure he lived up to that admiration, especially given how helpless he felt to do anything useful right now. This problem, none of it was someone he could punch in the face for bringing her tears, and there was no monster to behead with an axe. He was starting to wonder if a hero could survive without heroics to perform.

CHAPTER FIFTEEN
KAHRIN

A grudging night's sleep and a matter of hours later they were on the highway, Innes pretending he didn't love the newest Taylor Swift album, and Kahrin? Kahrin knew that feet on the dashboard annoyed her best friend, but she would spare no sacrifice to keep them from dwelling on the things they couldn't change. Da was sick, Innes was being attacked, and they had a flimsy lead to go on. The two duffels in the trunk were hardly the only luggage they had with them.

When she'd left her brunch with Emilia, giddy with the potential of a plan and high on the confidence of her backless party dress, she'd played out their reunion in her mind. Their trip to the clinic would have been followed by something fizzy and alcoholic to celebrate their bills of health. Then, a frantic shedding of clothes and the sort of frenetic clash of bodies that left red, welted handprints on her rear. That would have been followed up by the slow, rolling, languid coupling Innes expertly drew out the way an artiste might coax curves out of marble over eons of undivided attention. Also, soft shit. So much soft shit.

But everything unraveled with that phone call from Brecken, and here she sat, woefully unfucked with nothing joyful in her brain beyond a vague idea that they were on the same page emotionally. Innes' fingers wound with hers, and that had to be enough to satisfy her need for tactile affection.

Her silence did not go unnoticed. "Where'd you go just now?" Innes' voice scattered her thoughts like shards from a fallen icicle.

"Hm?"

"That's my line," he teased. "A penny for your thoughts?"

"My thoughts are not so cheap."

"I might have a nickel."

"Who carries a nickel?"

"Kahrin." There was a hint of menace to his tone, but no real bite. She was evading, and he'd entertained it long enough.

She huffed a hard breath. "This isn't how I wanted things to be."

He frowned, but not in an unhappy way. In the way that made the little crease between his dark eyebrows form when he was unsure what to say.

"Well, no, I didn't think so." His eyes slid to her, only for a moment, as the visibility outside the windshield was quickly whiting out. She felt a subtle shift of momentum as he eased off the accelerator for caution. It was dark for daylight, even this far north, and a storm was settling around them.

"I thought we'd be able to be normal."

"Says the woman who leaves dates via restaurant bathroom windows." She had to grant him a near-chuckle for that one. "You'd be bored with normal."

"And you'd be bored with a hapless maiden in constant need of defending, so I guess we both have our struggles." She slouched down in her seat. "Now here we are."

He was silent a moment before asking, "Are you trying to pick a fight? Usually, I can hear the bell."

Great. "Does this feel like a fight?" Her stomach gripped tight. She couldn't handle a row just now. Not on top of the delayed gratification of this new twist in their lives, and the shroud of Da's illness behind them.

"Not really. The sun hasn't gone blood red. I've seen no swarms of birds bursting from trees."

"Har, har." She let go of his hand to draw her hair over her shoulder, letting the long braid wind around her hand. "When Emilia encouraged me—"

"You talk to Emilia about me?"

He was joking, right? He had to be. "Who else would I talk to about you? About us?"

"Oh, I don't know. Me?" He clearly noticed her wince, and softened the moment by adding, "I'm more your type."

"Be serious!" She swatted his shoulder, having care not to disrupt his driving in a storm. They'd learned their lesson about winter weather driving the hard way. Twice.

That pretty mouth of his curved into a smugness reserved only for winding her up. "I'll try."

"I was ready." When he didn't ask for one, she continued with her explanation, wondering if it was more for herself than him. Innes had taken everything in remarkable stride; she was still chewing every detail like a dog with a bone. "I thought it would be fun, flitting from person to person, thing to thing. Falling into whatever bed made me happy that night." Just like with her various jobs, she kept them loose and easily exchangeable.

She hadn't realized she'd gone quiet again until the rhythm of tires on the road was interrupted by Innes' query. "And now? What changed?"

"Magic, maybe?" She bobbed her knee up and down, wishing they'd had this conversation in a larger space. "How would I possibly explain this to anyone else I was with?"

"So, I'm convenient." He was teasing, but it still stung.

"No." She let her head drop against the cold glass. "I mean, yes, but not, not in the way you're making it sound."

"How am I making it sound?" He was teasing less now, and she could feel strain twisting like a rubber band.

"When something notable happens, shouldn't you want to share it with your significant other?"

"Ideally, I would think."

Neither of them really knew, because neither of them had actually allowed someone more significant than the other into the close proximity they shared with only each other.

"I don't. The only person I want to share exciting things with is you. The only person I want to have to explain the bad things to, is you."

"Because it's easier?"

"Because we already put in the work. You always said I shouldn't discard the idea of a happily ever after."

"I never expected you to—"

"Let me finish." He inclined his head to give her room for the words to find their way out. "You were right. I do want it, but I don't want to look for it if I already have it. Why would I look elsewhere when what I want is right here?" She swallowed and hastily added, "I mean, if you want it, too."

"Didn't I already say I did?" He glanced at her, and she shrugged. Had he? Maybe not in so many words. The absence of a firm 'no' didn't mean a 'yes.' He'd always said as much. "Did you ever wonder why I stopped sleeping with Emilia?" That might have been the first time he ever said out loud the nature of their relationship, though it was not a secret. He was just allergic to lurid words, she supposed.

"Because of Lizzie?" Or Donna, or Holly, or whatever their names had been. She'd not bothered to learn them or keep track due to their ongoing policy of minding their own damned business about non-magical romantic choices.

He laughed, gentle and affectionate. "When you and I discovered we had, uh, matching tastes," she rolled her eyes at his subterfuge, "it altered how I was with her. I didn't notice right away, but she did." Kahrin drew her knees up to her chest and hugged them. She'd never pried into what he had with Emilia, beyond what he offered, but she'd known. He'd learned it all somewhere, much to Kahrin's personal delight. It added up. "When two people battle for dominance, it can be dangerous." Uh, duh. That was part of the fun of her bratty ways as they explored what some would call the kinkier facet of their relationship: the façade of a battle of wills, even if he was always meant to win it. If their dynamics hadn't been carefully agreed upon, it could hurt either of them. "Our proclivities began to clash, because Emilia is not like me." He flushed with a needlessly nervous chuckle. "Willing to assume either role."

"Oh." She'd not thought of that. Or his switching roles. She was certainly thinking about it now.

"What I mean to say is while I can play either role, there's only one person I trust myself to play that particular role with." He shrugged a shoulder, trying to seem nonchalant about something neither of them were very casual about. She appreciated his effort. "And I don't really want to try it with anyone else."

Now it was her turn to flush, flames climbing up her neck and cheeks. A shiver raced through her, though she realized that he'd not explicitly stated he meant her. Her heart fluttered with it all the same.

She swallowed, gathering her voice. "I've never let anyone else do those things to me." Her hand hovered at her throat over the thrum of her pulse, something he noticed, she guessed, judging how he shifted in his seat. "I never wanted to. I don't want to."

"I know." His throat bobbed. "And it drives me mad."

He didn't have to clarify that it was a good mad. The gravel in his words revealed all of that for him. "Which I think means I've always been yours."

She took that for her answer. "I think I've always been yours."

"No," he corrected. "You've always been your own. You choose to trust me with that part of you, and it's all the more precious to me because of it."

She swiveled her head to the side and gave him a wide grin, though her eyes burned with tears she enjoyed too much to shed. That's what she wanted to hear. That she was more than just some hot woman who was open about enjoying sex. Sex was a transaction, she felt. Sex could happen at any time with anyone if she wanted. What she had with Innes was a specific kind of intimacy that always overrode sex, and a trust she found more erotic than anything she'd experienced with half a dozen other partners. Combined.

"I couldn't do any of this without you."

"Another one for the obvious bank." He smiled, and the heavy snow eased as if it meant to just let the sun cast soft contrast over the sharp cut of his jaw, the slight turn of his nose, and making him dazzle. "Now, rest," he ordered with a familiar command in his tone that gave her need to wiggle her toes in her boots. "I'm not driving the whole trip, and you're not going to get much sleep when we stop for the night." His grin turned wolfish. "Not after that confession."

Exactly how she wanted it.

She did doze, though she couldn't say how long. There was still light in the sky, blush and gold filtering through the trees out the driver's side window, when Innes gave her knee a light squeeze and urged her to consciousness. "Hey, Sleeping Beauty."

"Why didn't you change the music?"

His face tightened, the creases at his eyes a little too dramatic to be genuine ignorance. "Oh, huh. I didn't even notice it."

"I'll expect concert tickets in my Christmas stocking." She pulled the small lever that put her seat upright.

He chuckled. "Noted."

She scrubbed her eyes to move mascara gunk and sleep crust from the corners when she heard him mutter, "Shit."

"What?"

The car shrugged, indifferent to Innes taking his foot off the gas as the largest moose she'd ever seen stepped onto the highway. Her teeth clenched as the massive bull paused. Innes eased his foot onto the brakes, slowing their approach. Until it didn't. Stilled tires giving up purchase on slick ice over macadam had a distinct feel, a surreal sensation of floating.

As it became evident they wouldn't stop in time to avoid collision, Innes jerked the wheel. Kahrin curled her body, arms over her head with an all-too-familiar ending to this scenario feeling inevitable.

They slid off the road into what had looked like a paved shoulder but turned out to be banked snow. The car met little resistance as it sank into the concealed gap between road and woods where it finally came to rest.

Kahrin peeked from behind her arms, certain the impact remained ahead. Instead, she saw the incurious gaze of the black moose. He snuffled, twin spires of steam twirling upward from nostrils so huge she was sure she could fist them. The massive bull, like a black oil slick, dipped his head, expansive rack like hands held out in presentation, conferring some moose message upon her that she had no way of understanding. Because she was not, in fact, a moose. Da always said moose brought with them wisdom, but she couldn't really find it in their current predicament. She flopped against the headrest and shook her head at the moose, as if it had any way of knowing her confusion. It simply turned, one long, knobby limb at a time, and lumbered back into the woods. She followed it with her eyes until it was out of sight.

CHAPTER SIXTEEN

INNES

As Innes' heart made its way back to a normal pace and location, he needed a moment to realize it was a moose, and not a unicorn disappearing across the road. Not that the two creatures held any resemblance outside of a book he once read, but because this felt a little too familiar. So much so that he turned to make sure Kahrin was conscious, and not once again concussed against the window.

It was quiet, apart from a timely Taylor Swift song, flits of low southbound traffic visible on the other side of the trees dividing the highway. And Kahrin. Sobbing.

Kahrin was sobbing.

It was enough to snap him to the present, and he leaned across the center console, wrapping her in the envelope of his arms and hugging her as best he could from his seat. He stroked her hair, keeping himself calm by trying to calm the way she shook from her belly-deep wails.

He didn't need to ask the cause—too many car crashes and head traumas lay behind them. He cooed, one hand smoothing circles over her back as the other sought to release their seatbelts.

Despite the tight fit, she needed very little encouragement to slide over the console and into his lap. He couldn't say how much time flitted by while he waited for the tears to subside, and noticed he'd shed some of his own, too. Three or four songs and several shades of ink brought on by the quickly waning sun.

"We're okay." As far as he could tell. She'd stopped shaking, only soft hiccups remaining. "When you're ready, we'll dig out the tires, and you can press the gas while I push."

Her laugh seemed out of place, but it was better than the way his chest tightened at her tears. "We're half buried."

"Which is better than all buried." He managed that with more confidence than he felt. "Ready?"

"Not yet." Her grip on him tightened, her knuckles white with it. "Just stay a moment longer."

"As long as you need." What an odd thing, he couldn't help but think, this vulnerability that she shared with no one else. It was an intimacy he knew he couldn't live without once he had it, and he couldn't remember a time in their many, many years of friendship when she'd not allowed him to see it. The world got to see defiant Kahrin, who was always sure of herself. He dropped a kiss to the crown of her head, even if she couldn't know the full meaning behind it.

Like most everything else around them, this stretch of highway was remote, far between towns, and without so much as a streetlight to help them once the sun set. Which would be soon. He gave her as long as he dared before whispering into her hair.

"Should we get moving?"

Her breath hitched in that way it did when she was startled awake, but she answered right away.

"Might as well."

They dragged their parkas from the back seat and bundled up against the storm. Using a window scraper as an improvised shovel, they worked to free the tires. When it came to try and back out, however, the rear wheels simply spun, gaining no traction, and every attempt seemed to only make it slicker while the front wheels remained inert. Innes scolded himself for not having kitty litter in his trunk for emergencies like this. By the time Kahrin flopped back into the seat, the dark had overwhelmed them, possibly leaving them worse off than when they started.

She groaned, letting it draw out the full of her lungs. "At least with it this cold, they'll be able to identify our bodies when they find us in spring." She hastily added, "Not to be dramatic."

"Oh, well, we wouldn't want to be dramatic."

Predicting her fuss, he telescoped his intention to wrap her in the blanket from the trunk and caught it around her shoulders.

"Someone will be along. This stretch is rural, not abandoned." He hoped that was true, as he could feel the temperature dropping, and while he thought they had enough gas to get to the next exit, he wasn't sure. Of course, gas didn't matter. with how stuck they were.

"Of course." Innes knew her tone enough to know she was not actually conceding the point. "I bet a car will be coming around that bend any minute now."

If Innes hadn't known that Kahrin was incapable of magic, he might have thought she conjured the bright lights that rounded into view, nearly blinding his vision of a large pickup, the color of which was indiscernible in this light. Seeing the road flares he'd set, the driver slowed enough that the truck only blew past them by about two hundred feet.

In another time, he might have just accepted the coincidence, but the number of times things went wrong in just such a manner froze him to his place, each muscle prepared to react. Bright reverse lights dazzled his vision before the red of the brakes turned everything around them a foreboding green-black. The driver's side window opened.

"Bad spot for star-gazing." A woman popped her head out. Wonderful. A comedian.

"What can I say?" he replied, trying to sound casual, "The spot picked us." He stiffened at the realization of how true that could be.

The rufescent glow gave her grin a startling quality. "Sometimes you can see the Aurora from here." She pointed toward the sky where he could see nothing of the sort. "Looks like you two need a tow." She hopped out of her truck with a small 'oof' and slammed her door shut.

"Nah," Kahrin muttered from the inside of the car, making sure she was heard but trying not to sound like she wanted to be heard. "We're fine freezing to death."

"Not helping." He shot her a sideways glare before returning his attention to the woman. "A hand would be nice, thank you. Is there a tow company nearby?"

"Nah." She tromped to the tailgate in duck boots engulfed by the legs of her Carhartts, which gave her a stout appearance that was incongruous with her face. "I got a hitch and a tow strap. You aren't gonna find a wrecker this far out without trading your firstborn."

"Yeah, I'm a little short," Kahrin added. Really, she was a fount of helpfulness, that best friend of his.

He had no idea if the woman heard her, but she turned on a smile, incandescent in their headlights. "Lucky for you, I'll work for a nice smile, and you got two on-hand." She tossed the tow strap to Innes and knelt by the rear of her truck. "Besides, I'm headed to the rez. The turn off is a doozy, hard to see at night."

Innes tried to keep his face neutral as his heart dropped into his twisting stomach. "How did you know we were going to the reservation?" Despite the bitter wind, a bead of sweat trickled down his back at the reminder of how many people—and not-quite-people—all too conveniently knew where he and Kahrin were at any time.

"Well," the woman started as she dropped to her knees and huffed to get to her back on the ground. She held out her hand for the strap. "Not too many people come out this far on purpose. Usually, they're tourists heading up for dog racing or casinos." She gave the strap a sharp tug, shimmied out from beneath the car, and rolled to her side to push up from the ground. She gave another little huff of air as she braced a foot, then stood. "Rez has both. Grab that kitty litter from the bed and spread it under the tires."

Kahrin clambered out of the car and into snow coming past her knees. "I can hold a light." She tipped her head at him, and he figured she'd come to the same conclusion he had: something felt amiss. What he didn't need her to say to know they both thought it was her plan was to stay close enough to the woman to prevent any use of magic their mystery rescuers might try.

"You don't need to do that." She brushed herself off and held a hand out to Kahrin. "I'm Ena, and we're good to go."

Innes cringed, torn between being on alert and his manners, sure that Kahrin was about to give a reply he would need to apologize for. But Kahrin took the offered hand without ado and gave it a shake her Da would have admired.

"Kahrin. This is Innes."

"Glad to meet you both," Ena replied. She planted both hands on her hips and let out a forceful huff. "Now, who's gonna ride and who's gonna drive?" When they only gave her blank looks, she elaborated. "Tow straps don't stay straight on account of them being straps and not rods." She shrugged and laughed in a way that said she wasn't trying to insult anyone. "Someone needs to steer the car around curves," she zoomed a hand in front of her in an arch to illustrate her point, "put the brake on gently on hills," and did the same to indicate a downward slope. It might have been amusing if he and Kahrin weren't already so tense.

Since Innes' chivalrous nature wouldn't let him ask Kahrin to do something as arguably dangerous as ride in a truck with a stranger and possible magical creature, he was inclined to ask her to drive. But his manners also wouldn't let him volunteer her to do that, either, since it sounded equally dangerous.

Fortunately, Kahrin's manners spun like a weathervane. "I'll ride with you," she announced.

"I guess that settles that, then." He didn't mind she'd volunteered him, but it was unlike her to pass up the risk so easily. Far be it from him to kink shame, but her disregard for her own safety always lit her up in ways he might never understand, even if he often benefitted from it in a, um, bedroom sense. He narrowed an eye at her all the same, a question tugging his mouth.

"Let me grab some things from the trunk," she chirruped, bounding through a path of already broken snow around the car. "Give me a hand, Pretty Mouth?"

Also odd for Miss Independent, but he took it for the signal it had to be and followed.

"What are you up to?" he whispered under cover of the hatchback.

"Keeping our too-convenient rescuer with too much information from getting too magical if she's," Kahrin flapped her hands, "anything extraordinary."

He might have guessed this was Kahrin's purpose if he'd taken ten seconds to think it over. All her actions kept her within arm's reach of Ena.

"And if she's a harmless human, no harm, right?"

"Unless she has a weapon in the car."

Kahrin's eyeroll might not have been clear in the dark, but the dramatic drop of her head was also a tell.

"Very well," he conceded. He ducked his head and stole a kiss. "Can you blame me for not wanting to let you out of my sight?"

She grinned, grabbing her blanket and coffee cup. "Not at all. Have you seen me?"

"Not what I meant!" he called after her.

CHAPTER SEVENTEEN
KAHRIN

Um, Innes had met her, right? In all the years they'd known one another, had she ever let that silly streak of chivalry that overlapped with manners in the Venn diagram of being overprotective of her stop her from being equally as overprotective of him? There was no way in hell that she was going to leave him alone with a complete stranger who turned up out of nowhere and knew just a little too much for her comfort. They'd seen this tree too many times before, in her opinion, and it hadn't improved the view at all. All signs pointed to something magical that wanted either one or both of them for some ill-intended purpose. From the near-miss with the moose to their would-be rescuer, the calculus was funny.

Sure, Ena was nice. She seemed the bubbly sort of friendly that drew Innes in and usually mildly annoyed her. She was also way too willing to help two randos on the side of the road in an isolated part of the highway, in an already rural area. She hitched their car up to her truck without asking anything in return and knew where they were headed. Fine. Like they had many options for getting out of this stupid ditch, and if they made it to a gas station, they could part ways there.

Ena waited while Kahrin got her excuse from the trunk, and they were loaded up and took off.

"So where are you from?" Ena asked. She reached and pointed one of the heat vents at Kahrin, giving her warmth she'd not realized she missed. Then she rested her hand on her stomach.

Kahrin told her, and added, "I won't be surprised if you've never heard of it." No one had. Nothing happened there unless you had a hankering for church potlucks as the cornerstone of your social life. Because no one went there. Probably not on purpose anyway, not until or since her parents decided to put down their lying liar roots, adding farming to the list of life opportunities available to her.

"No! I actually know it!" Even in the dark Kahrin could see Ena's face light up, and not just because of the luminescence of the instrument panel that danced an aurora across her admittedly pretty features in her ridiculously clean pickup that always had a bag of cat litter in the bed. "We drive fish down to a market near there twice a month."

"Really?" Kahrin nodded, unsure what to do with that. Another coincidence? Another unsettling bit of information? "That's a long drive for a market."

"One of our best buyers. When you find one who makes regular, large orders, you do what you can to cater to them." She shrugged, her shoulder bumping into the mess of damp curls that stuck out from under her toque. "Most of our income comes from them. They buy several hundred pounds a month. The rest is community sales. We make most of our money downstate, except this time of year. All the races bring in tourists, and all the tourists know the best fish fry is on the rez."

Wow, she was a chatty one. Not that Kahrin was one to criticize a tendency toward verbosity. "You fish?" She tried to picture this woman with a rod and reel in her hand. "For several hundred pounds a month?"

Ena shook her head. "I helped lift nets on the lake until the little one showed up. Now I mostly mend nets." She patted her middle, and only then did Kahrin realize that the thickness of her middle was a pregnant belly.

That wasn't the detail that distracted her. Cool, she was pregnant. A lot of people were, and thankfully Kahrin never would be. She had no interest in babies, even other peoples'.

"Nets? Like, big commercial nets?"

Ena chuckled, casting her a glance. "You've really never been to the rez before?"

Kahrin's face crumpled into a skeptical frown. Hostility edged her voice when she asked, "Meaning?"

"Ain't you one of the Boushays?" Ena knuckled the end of her nose. "That little thing in the middle of your face is a ringer."

Kahrin held up a hand as if to shield her nose from unwanted attention by a paparazzo. "Nope. My last name's Quirke."

Now it was Ena's turn to frown. "As in Maxen Quirke?" A touch of distrust wound into her words. "Didn't see that coming."

"Didn't see what coming?"

Ena waved at her as if that explained everything. "A relation to that family when you're, you know, brown like me."

Curiouser and curiouser, Alice, Kahrin thought to herself. "I don't know who that is." Or what it had to do with her skin color, but okay.

Whatever tension hung between them evaporated. "You look about my age, maybe a skosh."

"Just turned twenty-one."

"Almost twenty-two," Ena answered, thumbing back toward herself. "Puts you about the age of one of Maxen's..." She trailed off without finishing her thought. "Who're your parents?"

"Are we writing a book?"

She laughed out of nerves, but Ena chuckled along. "I'm told I have a nosy nature. Sorry."

Kahrin nodded and debated not answering. The snow glowed in the headlights as it hurtled at them while speeding down the highway. She looked in the sideview mirror for Innes.

"Grainne. My mother's name is Grainne. My father is Iskandar Quirke."

"No way!" Ena's surprise spread to Kahrin. How much weirder could this conversation get? Ena shook her head with a hiccup of laughter, the kind someone would give when they didn't know what to make of information. "Your Dad took your Ma's name. Wow. It all makes sense now."

"Oh, does it?" Kahrin really did try to keep the sharp edge off her tongue, but her patience for cryptic really was slim to none. "Could you make it make sense to me?" She twisted in her seat to face Ena, drawing one knee sideways on the bench seat. She crossed her arms over her chest.

Ena remained quiet for a stretch of highway, the sound of spinning tires keeping a rhythm of time. "The Boushays only had the one son: Iskandar." It wasn't a common name, for sure. What were the odds that she meant a different Iskandar? "He ran off, a couple of years before I was born, with Deacon Maxen's daughter. It was a huge scandal!"

"What's a deacon?"

"A church elder who can do almost anything a priest can do. Everyone was shocked." When Kahrin's eyebrows shot up, demanding a better explanation, Ena went on. "The Maxen Quirke family is big money. Old money, which you wouldn't know the way they shove a kid off to that cult of Catholics every generation. And they're a pack of racist old cusses, you know? Old manners to go with their old money. Maxen's parish served the rez for years, but he's never been quiet about his feeling on us Ind'ns. Their daughter was meant to go to a convent, not run off with some brown boy."

"My mother was going to be a nun?" That made a weird kind of sense, even considering it made no sense at all.

"That's the part you're hung on?"

"Well, that, and I thought people didn't like the term Indian when referring to Native Americans."

A sly grin curved Ena's generous mouth. "Let you in on a secret: a lot of us don't like being called 'Americans' either." She shrugged. "It's what we know. What we've been called for so long it's hard to get the elders to change their vocabulary."

Ena put on her blinker to indicate a merge off the highway, looking in the rearview to make sure Innes was following. "Cute white boy you got there."

Kahrin blinked. "You mean Innes?"

"You see any other white boys? Cute or otherwise?" She let a low whistle. "All clean cut and pretty. Manners too. Hitched or snagged?"

"What?"

"I saw you smoochin' and assumed."

"Innes is my best friend, since forever."

"That doesn't answer my question, though."

Yes, it did! Kahrin felt her face heat. She'd yet to sort the finer details with Innes, and certainly wasn't going to have this conversation with a stranger. No matter how much more familiar with her family history than Kahrin was.

"We, um, we're not like..." Trailing off in thought, she remembered their conversation that was just that day but felt like ages ago given all that had happened since. "Okay, we're maybe a little like—what's a snag?"

Ena laughed, something Kahrin was surprised to find a lovely sound, if at odds with the conversation. "I'm gonna have to give you an Ind'n primer before I introduce you to anyone respectable." She tapped her hands rhythmically on the steering wheel, alerting Kahrin for the first time that there was no radio to ease the tension. "Your dad didn't teach you things?"

What a rude question! "Of course he did. I can fix a tractor, till a field, impregnate a goat if they won't do it themselves." She flopped back against the seat. "Truth, Love, Courage, something about grandfathers. Protect the Earth, whatever."

"Seven Grandfathers."

"Okay, what's with the pop quiz?" Anger spiked like an icicle. "Is there some kind of sphinx riddle to get onto the reservation? Will an eagle dart from the sky and carry my eyes away? I get it, I'm an outsider, and my Da was a jerk who didn't raise me right."

Ena held up a hand, and as Kahrin gulped a breath to launch into a second wind of a tirade, simply said, "I'm sorry. I wasn't trying to pick on you." Another smile, this one softer and not showing her teeth. "I got excited." She glanced toward Kahrin. "I think a lot of people will." She was quiet a beat before saying, "If you're not here to reconnect, why are you coming here?"

"I never said I didn't want to reconnect." She didn't, but she'd not said it. She just wanted to be in, out, and done, like a bad date. "My Da is sick, and I need to see the medicine man."

Somehow that was enough for Ena. "Oh, okay. That's easy enough. It'll take a few days. He's out teaching wilderness camp. Do you have a place to stay?"

"We reserved a room at the casino." It was all they'd found.

Ena chuckled, then reined it in. "It's peak tourist season, they'll gouge you! The turn indicator blinked as they moved onto a small, poorly maintained road that shot straight through dense forest. "Stay with me and my Noko."

"Your nookoo?"

Ena shook her head and did her best not to laugh. She pronounced the word again, though Kahrin had trouble hearing the difference. "My gramma. My nokomis. We have the space, and, uh," she looked up into the rearview again, indicating Innes, "she'll probably be cool with your snag. You shacking up or whatever she'd call it." She winked. "Noko still goes to mass."

So much information in such a short amount of time. She shook her head, trying to cool the burn in her cheeks. "I'll text him to ask." She held up her phone and frowned.

"Cell reception up here can be spotty, but we'll pull over for gas."

"What?"

"You need gas, right?"

"Oh." Her head was spinning. Ena pulled into a small parking lot and drove past the pump to let Innes steer his way up to one. "Ena, you're not like, a werewolf or something, gonna murder us in grisly ways or drink our blood, are you?"

Ena tipped her head forward. "You're a very strange woman, Kahrin."

"Says the woman who stopped to pull us out of a ditch and knows my entire history."

"Fair point, well made." She patted her belly. "Can we work on trust after I empty my bladder? This little one is relentless."

Kahrin had to admit she was warming up to Ena's candor. "Sure. I need coffee anyway. It's my turn to drive."

CHAPTER EIGHTEEN
INNES

The silent car ride slash drive gave Innes far too much time alone with his thoughts, and only the occasional adjustment of the steering wheel or gentle pressure on the brakes for distraction.

He started reading at age four, if his brother could be believed. Brody had no reason to lie about it, but it wasn't beyond the realm of possibility. He cut his teeth on fairy tales, had growing pains through the Brothers Grimm, and stretched his legs out in magical realism as he merged into adulthood. Magic had been part of his life before he ever saw it for himself. He'd always believed it was there if he could just see it, and that somehow it meant that the world wasn't the bleak and sad thing it seemed when he was very young. The hope that magic might exist gave him optimism that anything was possible. That feeling only grew when he'd met the Quirkes. He was sure that magic had brought them into his life, like Princess Aurora and the fairies.

But that analogy made actual magic, the kind he and Kahrin had proven real, evil.

He was old enough to know that nothing was that black or white. The world existed in shades of grey. He just hadn't counted on magic falling into it.

Magic had betrayed him, as he saw it. Da Quirke, and by proxy Ma Quirke, had betrayed he and Kahrin both. The circle of people he could trust was shrinking by the day. He absently brushed his fingers over Yelena's kiss on his jaw, which he often did when he missed the pure whimsy that magic used to give him.

He wondered where Yelena was now. He wondered if she was safe. He just wondered. Wondered if maybe he'd been wrong this entire time. If magic was real, then the heroic things that happened in stories could happen, and he could be that hero he always fancied himself to be. He'd be able to take this opportunity to travel and bring medical care to underserved people. He'd be able to go out on an adventure and use everything he'd worked to learn and become to be that person who saved someone from certain doom.

Kahrin said he was her hero, and that warmed him in ways he couldn't adequately find words for, but how true could that be? She didn't need him to be her hero. Kahrin was and always had been her own hero. If either of them was able to live apart from the other, it was her. Magic couldn't touch her, and no one would be hunting her for her blood.

Ena pulled them into the gas station, a small two-pump affair with a little shop. Innes filled the gas and checked the car over for damage, then checked the oil for good measure, holding the dip stick under the single flood light. He deemed it safe enough to drive and released Ena from towing duties. It gave them less to worry about. That didn't mean nothing to worry about, given his apprehensions about her. The tension hanging between her and Kahrin didn't help that particular problem. He could sense Kahrin doing her Kahrin best to be the Kahrin version of amicable, and noticed Ena seemed unaware, intentionally, or otherwise, that any problem existed. She chattered at them in the convenience section as Kahrin pulled a cup of watery coffee from the automatic dispenser.

"Having a little coffee with your cream?" he teased, watching her dump her fifth tiny cup of hazelnut creamer into the extra-large cup.

"I need the caffeine and can't risk it tasting like goat crap." She shrugged, using the back of her hand to open the garbage flap so she could dump the rubbish in. "Hazelnut goat crap is better than regular goat crap I'm sure, on account of how much goat crap I've handled in my life."

"Please stop saying 'goat crap'. It doesn't even sound like real words anymore." He ducked his head and kissed her brow, enjoying the feeling of how normal and easy it was to do. No mysteries lay between them. There was no guessing what the other wanted. It was as close to normal as either of them would likely get. Hadn't that always been what he wanted? Someone to settle down with and be normal? Wasn't having that with Kahrin even better?

Yes.

So why did he feel a tug on his heart?

They were back in their car and on the road, Ena's taillights the only thing keeping them from veering off the road in the flurries. Kahrin sat on the very edge of the seat, despite the fact she could have pulled it up further or sat back in it just fine.

"I know how to drive in snow," she said, responding to the actual nothing that he said. "Just not usually this much snow."

"What happened up there between you two?"

"Oh, the better-Indian-than-me know-it-all?" She shrugged, which couldn't be a good sign. "Not much. She's nice enough but thinks she's better than me."

Two things could exist at the same time: Ena could possibly be condescending, and Kahrin could be a touch sensitive to not knowing things. One did not mean the other was not a factor.

"Such as?"

She relayed their conversation to him, or at least her version of it, which he knew to take with a tablespoon of salt.

"Wait, she's pregnant?"

"That's what caught you up?" She shifted in the seat, as if annoying conversation was relaxing her driving. "Yeah, she's all smile and baby bump under those Carhartts." She added a theatrical shudder. "Also, it's weird when people know things about you that you don't know yourself."

"Maybe she's trying to help you connect."

"Why does everyone want me connecting? Maybe she's just hoping I'm a heavy sleeper and that she can off me in her Gran's guest room. Maybe she's hoping to get you alone and nourish her baby with your mystical blood. Like every other damned magical being we've met." Before he could insert it himself, she added, "Besides Yelena." She forced a smile, though he couldn't tell if it was the conversation or the memory of Yelena that made it stiff. It was difficult to know with her sometimes. "And Emilia doesn't count."

"She has been privy to sucking some things." His joke was rewarded with a scowl.

He slipped a hand over her knee, careful not to apply any pressure that might disrupt her control of the car. "We've always survived whatever was thrown at us. This shouldn't be different." He watched her drive, her large mouth in a puckered knot, the tendons in her slender neck taut beneath her skin. Even now, he still marveled at the way irritation and temper made her more lovely. "And we shouldn't be here long."

"God, I hope not."

"If it will cheer you up, I can put Taylor Swift back on." That should get a reaction out of her.

The twitch of her mouth told him he was right, though he already knew he was. "What a heroic gesture, given how much we both know you can't stand her music." That shouldn't have stung, but it felt like a tiny dart struck his heart.

The next hour of the trip passed without incident, their chatter going back and forth over trivial things which were definitely not intended to keep them from the very real knowledge that Da Quirke was possibly going to die before they returned home. Or that they were following a stranger into the unknown.

A sign announcing they'd crossed onto the reservation timed perfectly with a better clearing job of the snow from the roads. They wound through a labyrinth of narrow streets with no road paint until Ena pulled into the yard of a house in a row of reasonably spaced out, identical houses. Most with two stories, almost all of them boasting sharply sloped rooftops.

Ena was out of the truck and to their little car before Kahrin remembered the parking brake. "This is it! Noko will still be up." She pointed with her chin to the lights still on through the curtained window. "If you're hungry, she can whip something up." Ena patted her belly, which Innes could see was obviously round, leaving him feeling a little foolish for not noticing it sooner. "I know I could run down a whole deer if given the chance." She let a laugh that resembled the wooden tones of the wind chimes outside the door to the house.

She hustled to the back of the car to help carry a bag, which Innes was not going to allow under any circumstances, let alone a noticeably pregnant woman. When she tried to insist, he asked and pointed at her belly, then she stepped back, happily letting him take their bags. A hare spooked from near the side of the house and skittered into the woods.

An older woman's face appeared between the curtains as they approached, and Innes braced for a barrage of questions, or even a discussion on unannounced visitors. None came, however, and Ena led them through the unlocked door and directed them to remove their shoes and coats at the entryway.

"Noko?" their host called over a burst of argument laced with laughter.

Kahrin stopped in front of him as they entered a small, spotless kitchen where the woman presumably Ena's grandmother sat with three other people. Innes rested a hand at her back and offered a smile that had a strong record of yielding positive returns when meeting new people.

A woman with iron grey hair held up a finger to stymie any introductions, eyes fixed on a hand of cards. "Fifteen-two, fifteen-four, five, six, seven, and one more for the Jack hand." She laid all the cards out and proceeded to move a small peg around a board drilled with tiny holes and painted with little racetrack-like rings. "I believe that means

I've won, just in time to make a good impression on Ena's friends."

A squat man with a brown, windburned face sat across from her. "How did you get that? That doesn't add up."

"Budge Parker, I've balanced your books for twenty-two years, and for your father fifteen before that. Are you accusing me of a mathematical error?"

"No, ma'am. Just cheating."

"You're not too old to be put over my knee, you know. Show some respect for your elders."

Ena tilted her head to fill Innes and Kahrin in on the scene before them. "She probably didn't cheat, but if she did, Budge would never know it. He's a terrible cribbage player."

"I heard that, missy," the man named Budge said.

"I meant you to." Ena ushered them into the room, which felt cozy rather than congested like Innes might have expected in such a small space. Even smaller than the farmhouse kitchen, it had all the same warmth and welcoming feel to it. "Noko, you be nice to Budge, or we won't have any dinner for Friday."

Another, more slender man, with hair tousled in some places and flattened in others, stood, and pulled out his chair for Ena. "You shouldn't be standing. Sit, sit."

"Uncle, I have been sitting for hours in that truck. This kid isn't going to fall out of me if I stretch my legs. Besides, we have company; offer the seats to them." She gestured to Kahrin and Innes, introducing them in turn.

"Quirke?" Budge noted, exchanging a look with the others at the oblong table. Innes felt Kahrin tense in front of him.

Another woman, sitting across from Ena's uncle and looking close in age, gathered up the cards. "Now, I don't know your faces." She tapped the deck, aligning all the cards until Innes could tell a hole had been punched through the middle of it before twisting a rubber band around them. "Where are you from?"

"Downstate, Auntie Patty," Ena supplied before Innes could answer.

Innes moved closer to the table, offering a hand to shake to Budge, who stood to take it.

"That's a good handshake you've got there."

"Thank you, sir."

Budge returned a firm grip but not an aggressively tight one.

"Rand, check out his handshake."

The man named Rand did so, standing with a low grunt. The woman named Patty added, "You can tell a lot about a guy by his handshake."

"Mm-hm," Ena's Gran agreed. She stood, sweeping around the

kitchen, deftly avoiding bumping into anything as if she knew every inch of the room by memory. She pulled out a Tupperware container from a low cupboard and slid it onto the table before she popped the lid off. "Art had a good handshake. Everyone always said, 'You know Art McKenzie isn't going to cheat you because he's got that good handshake' and they were always right." She waved at the seats. "Sit, sit."

"Are we dogs?" Kahrin muttered to Innes but complied with a smile anyway.

Innes took the seat beside her, and Ena leaned against the counter and crossed her arms over her chest.

"They're here to see Brother Whiteloon."

"Is he doing a sweat tomorrow?"

"Don't think he'll be back from wilderness camp by tomorrow. Probably Monday."

"Oh, yeah, that's right. There's that potluck at the Elder center on Sunday. He'll be busy with it as soon as he gets back." Patty looked at Innes, as if remembering he was in the room. "Do you two have a place to stay, sweetie?"

"Don't you dare, Patty. Look at those strong arms." Innes' cheeks burned, though it was hardly the first compliment paid to him by a woman many years his senior. "If he needs a place to stay, I could use someone to bring in wood."

Ena snorted. "I was hoping you'd say that."

"It doesn't hurt that he's nice to look at."

"Noko!"

"It's not a crime to tell someone the truth. Besides," she set a dish of sandwich cookies in the center of the table, "I can't believe it's a secret." She gestured that Kahrin should help herself to the cookies. "That's not the first you've heard it, is it my dear?"

The latter she addressed to Kahrin, who barked a laugh even though her face looked as though she wished she was anywhere else in the whole world. "No, ma'am. I have good eyes."

Everyone in the room thought that was amusing.

"Now," Noko set cups of hot cocoa in front of them, "what business do you two have with my brother?"

Innes looked to Kahrin to answer, and Kahrin looked to her cuticles to do it for her. Surely, they couldn't offer the truth. Even if it weren't a matter of privacy, he doubted anyone would believe they were there for a magical cure to an unknown malady befallen a prodigal son.

"Family research," he finally said. That was enough truth for their purposes while still easing his conscience. "Kahrin's Da is sick and she's looking for some answers."

She shot him a look. Everyone else at the table exchanged unspoken questions and possibly answers.

Ena propped a foot over the other. "She's one of Senior's grandkids."

The room fell quiet enough that he could hear the moment Kahrin stopped chewing her cookie.

"Patty," Rand said, "we should get going before it's too late. Thanks for the game, Ma."

Budge patted his hands on the table. "You know, I have to run into town tomorrow. I can stop and leave a note for Brother Whiteloon on the way. I bet he'd like to make time sooner rather than later."

"I think that's a good idea, Budge."

Things had gone from uncomfortable to unsettling. Innes looked to Kahrin for guidance on what to do next. If she wanted, they could be on the road and halfway back home before the sun was up.

He didn't think she was going to give up that easily.

"I'd appreciate that, ma'am," Kahrin answered before remembering to swallow her chewed cookie. She flicked her eyes to Innes to reassure him. "But we've been driving all day. I'm not sure I can stay awake much longer."

CHAPTER NINETEEN
KAHRIN

Had there been room to pace, Kahrin would have done so once they were shown to the little spare room in Ena's Gram's house. She had to settle for turning about to flop on the bed, only to get up and dig aimlessly through her duffle.

"I don't feel good about this, Pretty Mouth." This time she flopped face forward to muffle a low scream.

"Would you like to talk through it?"

She felt the mattress shift as he eased onto it. When she turned her face, he was lying on his side, spread the opposite direction so their faces were one in front of the other. He smiled, warmth in his brown eyes, before bumping his nose against hers.

"What's to talk through? We need information, and the only access to it is weirdly nice strangers."

He pushed an errant bit of hair which had escaped her long braid from her forehead, fingertips skimming her cheek as he tucked it behind her ear. "Not every person who is nice to us means us harm," he murmured.

"Do you really believe that?" She held his gaze steady, challenging him to lie to her.

Which he would not do. "I want to. I want to believe that Ena sometimes just stops to help strangers. That she is right, and the only reason we'd be this far out is to come here. That her grandmother is blasé about strangers staying in her house. All of it. I want to think people are good, and not all secretly magical creatures waiting for us to drop our guard."

Just hearing him confess that much helped, and she let out a long breath that had been fighting at her ribs for release. "Do you sense anything?"

He shook his head, silver strands falling in front of his eyes, giving her a chance to return the favor of minutes ago. She let her hand rest there, where her thumb could smooth over the arch of his dark brows, somehow untouched by the premature grey of his hair.

Kahrin dropped her hand and flopped over onto her back, kicking out of her jeans until they could slide to the floor by gravity alone.

"Shirt." She held a hand out to him.

"The one I'm wearing?"

Oh, come on. How did he make it sound like such a weird request? "I don't see any others."

"Maybe the one you packed to sleep in?" Her eyes followed him as he stood, shedding his own clothes and folding them to put on the plain wood dresser.

"But that one smells like you."

"Weirdly, I also smell like me, and you don't have to wear my sweaty shirt to get the effect." Helpfully, he reached into her bag and tossed a shirt she was sure he knew was his anyway. It landed over her face. She heard a jingle announcing the dropping of his jeans.

She laughed into the smudgy darkness of the shirt, practically a Pavlovian response at this point, and was promptly cut off by the feel of his weight as he leaned onto her, pressing her deep into the mattress. She pulled the shirt away from her face and he swiftly caught her arms, pinning them above her head as he leaned down into a kiss. He was heavy atop her, making it hard to draw a full breath, which was not something she disliked. She whimpered into it, curling upward as far as her pinned arms would allow, returning all the heat he gave and more. She was suddenly painfully aware that the thin fabric of underwear was all that remained between them and a joining of bodies they'd been craving since the party.

It seemed almost wrong, drinking in her desire while they were sequestered off in a spare bedroom of strangers. A part of her welcomed the possibility that it was impolite; and hooked her feet over the backs of his calves, eager to pull him closer. His need teased against her, blocked by thin cotton, and she rolled her hips, desperate for some sort of relief from his inexplicable denial.

A clatter of dishes sounded in the distance, which she quickly realized was not so distant. She tensed, stiff beneath him at almost the same instant that he dropped his face into the curve of her neck.

"We can't. Not in here, not right now."

He was right, and she loathed him for half an instant for it. The other half of the instant made clear that even were they free of the tyranny of underwear, she wouldn't have been able to relax enough to enjoy it. She huffed as he released her wrists, inhaled deeply as he freed her from his weight, and whined as he pulled on his sleeping pants.

She held eye contact with him while she slowly changed out of one shirt and into the other and could feel the silent scolding he sent her way to not tease him in such a state. As if he and he alone suffered! He slid into the bed, and she snuggled into him, looking to leech his body heat to counter the cold sheets. He was right: he did smell better than his shirt would have. She pressed her face into the space where his collarbone met his shoulder and inhaled deodorant and that warm musk that always followed him after they'd fooled around. She briefly wondered if anyone else ever noticed it, if they craved it like that first sip of morning coffee when he was near and realized that it didn't matter. She wasn't going to be sharing that private thrill with anyone else, ever again. Only him.

"Thank you for being here with me." The words were muffled against his skin and whispered besides, but he heard her.

"Where else would I be?"

Anywhere. He could be anywhere else, doing anything else he chose. But he wasn't. He was here, with her, because he chose to be. The part of that which warmed her belly and built a pressure behind her eyes drowned out the worry he would resent her for missed opportunities and dampened the feeling of fear that he would consider it settling to be with her. That was disrespectful of his choices, something she always tried to avoid, so she kept those near-thoughts to herself.

The sun was barely creeping into the sky when she woke, dusting the snow outside the window with indigo sparkles between long shadows of the bare birch and full evergreen trees. Already restless, Kahrin carefully withdrew from his embrace and slid out of the bed, biting her tongue to avoid making an undignified shriek as her feet hit the cold floor. As quietly as possible, she fished a change of clothes out of her bag and dressed.

"Another early riser." Ena's grandmother, her noko, stood in front of the stove, her voice calling over the snap and sizzle of bacon. She nodded toward the counter, near the sink. "Coffee just finished. Cream and sugar are on the table. Drop some toast in for me while I finish these eggs, will you?"

Kahrin nodded, unsure what to say, alone with a woman she only knew secondhand through someone she didn't really know and went about completing the task that would earn her a cup. She found bread in the box on the counter and put a slice in each of the four slots of the toaster, then found mugs hanging from hooks near the sink and poured one for Noko and one for herself. The creamer was powdered, and the sugar in a tall canister that she was sure was once a parmesan cheese container with the label scrubbed off. It suited her needs fine, and she let the steam soothe her senses before she took a tentative, scalding sip.

"You look just like him, you know. Senior Boushay." Ena's noko turned and wiggled a pile of scrambled eggs into a large casserole dish before setting it on a potholder on the table. "Your Grandfather Boushay. God rest him." She crossed herself.

Kahrin felt her lips pull tight as she smiled. These were not conversations she'd come prepared to have. When planning their trip, she'd neglected to consider the part where she shared blood with a good number of people here, people who never wanted to know her, and she wasn't sure she wanted to know. But here she was, apparently having these conversations anyway.

"With all due respect, ma'am," she started with a perfect imitation of Innes' manners. The similarities ended there. "I don't know who that is, and I don't have grandparents."

Noko McKenzie laid the bacon on a plate covered with folded paper napkins and sat it down before joining Kahrin at the table. She nodded in thanks for the coffee, and drank a sip, black, without flinching.

"Everyone has grandparents. We all have ancestors. Perhaps you don't know yours, but they exist." She looked at Kahrin over the brim of her cup. "You could know some of them if you wanted."

"I don't." She winced, knowing just how awful she sounded, and took another sip, burning her tongue but buying herself a moment to mull this over. The woman's brown eyes, faded at the outer rims of the iris, drew a shawl of comfort around her. If Kahrin hadn't known she was invisible to magic, she might have thought the ease she was feeling to be some sort of charm. "My da's sick. They don't know what's wrong with him. I'm here to find out if anything in his past can explain it."

That sounded true enough and had the benefit of being pretty true. Da was sick. She did think it was something, or someone, from his past. She didn't think she was going to learn the answer meeting people who never searched out her or her brothers. Perhaps didn't even know they existed.

"Ah." Noko McKenzie set her cup down, then cupped a hand and leaned her narrow chin into it. "So you're looking for medical histories. If you're looking to avoid digging into the past, you won't find your answers." Her words fell somewhere between welcome and caution, and Kahrin didn't know how to proceed.

Noko dished up a plate as she continued. "You might start with the Boushay family, then. They might have answers for you before you find Bill Whiteloon." When Kahrin wrinkled a brow in question, the woman supplied, "One of the Elders. Our medicine man. That's who you're here to see, yes?" She flapped a hand toward the food. "Eat. Eat."

"Something smells incredible." Ena wandered in, the swell of her belly more pronounced in her nightgown and robe. Her hair stood an unruly bramble bush of curls smooshed from what looked like restless sleep. She hauled a pitcher from the refrigerator before sitting, and filled a mug with orange juice before scooping half the bacon onto her plate. "Your snag better wake up before this is all gone," she teased with a smile brighter than her appearance indicated.

"Ena. Manners." To Kahrin, Noko said, "She's right, though. That little one she's carrying loves breakfast meat."

"Don't we all?" Kahrin grabbed a slice off her plate and chewed it. "I'll make sure to save him some."

"No need."

Innes came from the direction of the bedroom, looking rested with his hair in that styled-to-not-look-like-I-woke-up-like-this way. How did he do that? Did he shower? When?

"Smells great, ma'am. Thank you." He kissed Kahrin on the cheek as he slid into the chair beside her. "You left me to fend for myself against the cold. For shame."

"Was it too cold?" Noko asked.

Innes chuckled and shook his head. "No. It was just fine, ma'am."

"He has such manners," she said to Kahrin. "If you have to snag a white boy, one with manners is a must."

"Noko!" Ena's laugh filled the room. "Manners!"

Kahrin watched the red crawl upward from Innes' shirt collar. If he didn't know what snag meant before, he'd definitely put it together now. He cleared his throat and poured a glass of juice for himself.

"What's our plan today?" He'd meant it for Kahrin alone, but addressed it to the whole table, probably on account of them all being there. Those manners.

"Boushay's place isn't far from here. I'd be happy to show you after my errands." Ena had barely swallowed her bacon. "It's a pretty walk."

They weren't going to let this go. Kahrin turned her gaze to Innes. "I guess we're having a pretty walk and a family reunion after errands. You game?"

"Do I have a choice?" The corner of his mouth twitched, hinting at the teasing in his words.

Kahrin smiled. "Always."

CHAPTER TWENTY
INNES

"It will go faster if we split up," Ena said with a wide, pretty grin. The sun had warmed the day up after they left Noko McKenzie's, and she'd forgone her hat, leaving her chin-length curls frizzy and bobbing. "You're a big, strong man."

He noticed a twitch in Kahrin's eye but said nothing about it. "Faster, yes," she said as if she were just making a passing comment, and not a not-so-subtle judgment. "But is it a good idea?"

Innes barely resisted pinching the bridge of his nose. She'd been almost normal before, even given the awkward situation. Now she was twitchy like a small dog might be in front of Pickle, trying to seem intimidating. "It'll be fine, Kahrin."

He looked over the list that Ena gave them, mentally breaking down what he and Kahrin could divide up. If two was faster, three was better than that.

"I'll go with Ena," Kahrin announced. "She can show me around." Kahrin strung her arm through the other woman's. "Since I'm connecting and all that."

Her mind was made up, and whatever happened was between the two women and God now. He gave her a quick kiss and whispered, "Behave," before getting into his car, which had the back seats folded down and a large plastic box of fishing net, frankly, stinking it up.

"Do I usually not?" she asked, with a forced innocence. She was up to something.

"No comment."

He followed the directions Ena gave him, since the smaller twists of roads didn't show up on his GPS. The first stop was apparently the fish market where Ena worked part time, or full time but only part of the time. He couldn't remember. He pulled up, her family name on the sign outside the front of a small shop, and a garage several yards behind that, open with tables and a round barrel-like machine dripping what he hoped was water.

"Sales up front, eh," one of the younger men shouted. He jerked his chin towards a pair of women with a length of net stretched out between them, mending a hole in the top. "Auntie will be right with you."

"Actually," Innes called as he opened the hatch of his car, "Ena McKenzie sent me to drop this off."

"Oh! Ena!" The young man waved at his companion at the table who was wearing chest-high waders and sliding guts from a large fish into a tub. "You the one, then?"

"No, really? She's gonna let us meet him?"

"Meet who?" Innes felt like he was missing some important component to their gentle ribbing.

The man in waders hosed himself off by a large industrial sink and they both washed hands. "I'm Bud, this is James, and you must be the daddy."

Innes coughed, nearly dropping the box. "The who now?" He shook his head. "No, you have to have me confused with someone else. I just got here." Sweat trickled down his neck as if it was possible that he could have impregnated a woman who was late in her pregnancy after having only arrived the night before.

They laughed, and James smacked him on the back. "Well if you're a friend of Ena's, that's good enough for us. Bring the boxes around back."

He did as instructed, piling it up next to a few similar boxes, then stepped back. Everything was set up in a sort of system he could see though he didn't understand, not knowing much about their profession.

"So, how do you know Ena?" Bud asked, as they moved back to the garage. "If you ain't her new snag, I mean. Would Ena snag a white boy?" The last he tossed at one of the women winding the net around a large reel.

"If he ain't clan or cousin, who's to say? Don't you go giving her a hard time." She pointed at Innes. "And you should know how loved that girl is around here, just in case you're thinking of fibbing to me."

He laughed, feeling his face heat. Did everyone just talk so openly about things like that? "My, ah," he tripped over what to call Kahrin in relation to himself now. Best friend always just slid off the tongue out of habit, but was he supposed to call it something else now? "Kahrin has family up here."

"Oh, that's you!" Bud laughed and waved him into the garage. "You ever filet a fish, White Boy?"

"Um," he chuckled, "not lately." Not ever, but he was trying to be casual. He stepped inside and let them put a large rubber apron and gloves on him before showing him around the business end of a fish's innards. Literally.

He left with a bag full of ice and fish that he hoped he'd deboned well, and apparently a measure of respect for his willingness to walk about in the slime. It honestly wasn't any worse than mucking goat pens, except he didn't have a change of shoes to spare his car the fallout.

His next stop, and one that made him wonder if he shouldn't have traded vehicles with Ena, took him to a barn with a converted shop in the front, just off the demarcated reservation line. A few people were milling about outside, and a woman with impossibly long earrings and long black hair sat on a chair inside. There were all kinds of crafts on racks, from beaded jewelry to bags labeled "bannock mix."

"Hey cutie," she said as he walked up to the counter. Her name tag said "Josie" and she had a hoop through her septum. "What brings you this far north?"

"Ena McKenzie sent me to pick something up."

"Oh! Are you the daddy?"

Was everyone going to ask him that? He laughed, his face heating as if he'd not just had this conversation. "No, my, uh," he tried the word out on his tongue, "my girlfriend and I are visiting."

"The Boushay girl?" She grinned, popping on some chewing gum. It was impossible to tell how old she was, but he guessed close enough to his age. "You're the white boy. You are cute. Auntie McKenzie never lies but she undersold you."

Wow, and he thought gossip spread fast in their hometown. "Well, not exactly." He rubbed the back of his head. "I mean yes, I'm the white boy in question, but her name's not Boushay."

She leaned up and whispered. "We don't really use that other name around here, but point taken." She stood and pointed with her nose to the back of the barn. "Sap's this way."

"Sap?"

Josie smiled. "You can't make sugar without sap. Are you boiling sugar tonight?" She led him to where she had several large canisters, similar to what you'd put gasoline or industrial cooking oil in. "Here you go." She indicated three of the large containers and hefted one up. "In that little car of yours, huh? Cute."

Josie helped him load the sap in his car before handing him a paper bag. "This is for Ena. Tell her my Ma had an extra bottle of prenatals from when Jenna had her third back before Christmas." He nodded, filing the information away. "No sense buying a new bottle when she's so close. There's also some of that big underwear for after, just in case we don't make it over for the boil."

"Thanks." The ease with which she shared all of that could have been off-putting, but it had exactly the opposite effect. It felt like a sort of welcoming, like even as an outsider he was being accepted due to his proximity to Ena, if not Kahrin's father's family.

"There's also some tea in there from my noko, for when her boobs start to get sore."

Innes cleared his throat. "Noted."

"Tell her I said hi, White Boy."

"Will do. Nice to meet you, Josie."

Next was a small shopping list from the gas station slash convenience store, including a dozen eggs and windshield washer fluid. The clerk made a joke about that being the worst omelette she'd ever heard of while fishing some Atomic Fire Ball candy out of a jar for a group of 'tweens. He stepped aside to use the only ATM he'd seen since arriving in the small town to take out cash.

He'd finished his list in decent time, if he said so himself, and made his way back to the McKenzie's home. There was a small truck in the driveway that did not belong to Ena, and hers wasn't back yet, so he carried the grocery items inside, intending to ask where to put the sap before he went to all the trouble of lugging it inside. He kicked the snow off his boots at the front steps and knocked before he let himself inside. It seemed odd at first, just walking into her house, but so had walking into the Quirke farmhouse the first time.

"Is that you, Ena?" her grandmother called from beyond the kitchen area.

"Afraid not, ma'am." He set the bag on the counter, put the eggs in the fridge, and took the wiper fluid back to the main entrance.

"Oh, Innes. Come out here and meet my nurse."

Nurse? He followed the voices to the living room, stepping around a woven basket tucked full of yarn and a crocheted project in mid-creation. Ena's grandma sat in a glider chair, one foot in a spa tub, the other propped in the lap of a woman with light blonde hair pulled loosely from her face. She looked to be giving Noko McKenzie a pedicure, clippers angled in her hand as she trimmed her nails.

"Are you all right?" He paused at the entrance to the room.

"Oh, you're right, Mary, he is handsome." The woman shrugged with a sort of apology. "So, you know Ena?"

"Sort of." He chuckled. "A bit better than I did before I left today." He stepped around, offering a handshake, but thinking better of it when the woman had her wet, gloved hands holding onto Noko McKenzie's foot.

"Such a good girl, my Ena. Innes, this is Daisy. She's the diabetic nurse from Indian Health Services."

"Oh, that explains the foot care." He nodded to the foot spa setup. "Any way I can help?" It would pass the time.

"You're helping plenty just sitting here." Ena's grandmother laughed as if she had a secret. "Isn't that right, Daisy? Daisy's single." She looked at Daisy. "This one's been snagged already." Daisy let a soft snort of something close to embarrassment. "But maybe he has a brother." She waved a hand. "Or a sister. Whatever."

"A brother, but he's married." He could hardly imagine Brody here with these warm, effusive people who worked in traded favors and sharing of excess rather than concerning themselves with money.

"You know, I never asked what you do."

He sat on a davenport that was much softer than it looked and sank heavily into the cushions. "I'm in university, actually. Pre-med."

"Handsome and smart. A doctor then?"

"That's the hope, ma'am."

"Don't let them hear that in town," Daisy joked. "They'll try to snatch you up and keep you here. We've been trying to get more hands out here for a while."

"Well, I'm not ready to be recruited," he said amiably. Still, it was flattering. It wasn't too hard to imagine it, living and working in a town like this, a little community that felt collectively like the Quirke farm, the way everyone seemed to know and watch out for one another.

"So what area are you looking to study?" Daisy asked as she toweled off one foot and exchanged it for the other.

"Not sure yet. There's a lot of options. Maybe family medicine."

"Ever think of being a small-town hero? We have internships at the tribe."

He laughed and shook his head. "I should get my undergrad finished, first." Though, it was an interesting thought, at least as interesting as the offer laying before him from his advisor.

"What made you choose medicine when you could just live off your looks?" Noko McKenzie asked.

He cleared his throat. It surprised him, the lump in his throat as he thought of it, despite how long it had been. "My mother died giving birth to me. My father passed when I was twelve." That alone might have inspired many people to a profession in medicine, but Innes' desires ran deeper than that. "We didn't have insurance and I was left taking care of him. I didn't know what I was doing." To this day, he still didn't know, not for sure, if he'd been the cause of his father's death, mixing up medications as he had. All he knew at the end of the nightmare, was that he was free of the man's cruelty.

A stiff quiet settled over the three of them, but it wasn't long lived. Mary McKenzie was ready to change the subject. "Now James called me from the fishery and said you have my dinner."

Her dinner? Innes blinked a few times then realized he'd forgotten. "The fish! It's in my car." He jumped up, his long legs carrying him back to the entrance.

"Put that sap out back too, would you?" Mary yelled after him.

CHAPTER TWENTY-ONE
KAHRIN

"I'm surprised you wanted to ride with me," Ena said. She had such a casual posture behind the wheel, completely at ease. Not at all like the ramrod upright posture Kahrin had when she drove. It had taken her time to get up the nerve to drive before Innes had moved away to go to the university, but even years later she had not learned to relax. Maybe it was because of all the car accidents she and Innes had seen. And been in.

"I'm not." Kahrin didn't bother explaining. Ena didn't ask. Maybe it didn't matter because she was a killer who was waiting to get one of them alone. Maybe it didn't matter because she was a magical creature who did not know what Kahrin was. Whatever Ena's secret was, Kahrin was going to find out, and she was not letting the other woman—if she indeed was human–out of her sight until she did. "I don't know anything about you, and I wasn't going to leave Innes alone with you." There. Blunt. To the point.

If she'd hurt Ena's feelings, it didn't show in her words. "How long have you and Innes known one another?" she asked. As if she didn't have some diabolical scheme behind her pretty, almost black eyes.

"Since forever." She shrugged. "We were ten." Kahrin shot a look out of the side of her eyes. "He's my best friend. I would pretty much die for him." It wasn't exactly Plan A, and she was strictly prohibited from trying it as a Plan B again, but she left that for Ena to deduct what she would.

"It's so sweet, really." Something crossed Ena's face that wasn't quite sadness, but wasn't not sadness, either. "Loving someone for so long. Having someone you can always depend on." She turned her face just long enough to say, "You two are very lucky to have one another."

"I know."

"How long have you been together?"

"We," She paused, testing out the weight of what she was about to say on her tongue. "We've only been a couple for a few days."

"Really?" Ena laughed. "You seem very comfy in it."

"Meaning?"

"You move around each other in tandem. Never in the way. Always aware of the other, even without thinking. It's sweet. People search their whole lives for it."

"Is that how you wound up pregnant? Searching?" As soon as she said it, she realized it was rude, even for her, and she shrank into her seat.

Intentional or not, Kahrin could tell Ena had been stung by her comment, and she pressed her lips together, her smile tight, as they pulled into a small parking lot with a sign that said "Health Center." Ena didn't say anything as she slid out of her truck, only looked to see if Kahrin was going to follow.

Which she did. Even embarrassment wasn't going to keep her in the truck by herself. They crossed a slushy lot to the little center, Kahrin assuming she was now accompanying her on a trip to an OB/GYN, which didn't thrill her, but she reasoned her little outburst indebted her to Ena at least a little.

They turned down a narrow hallway that opened into a small waiting room. Across the room of industrial orange carpet and stiff, molded chairs, was a pharmacy window. Ena didn't take a number, instead she went straight up to the counter with a smile on her face.

"Well look what the cat dragged in," said the woman on the other side of the plexiglass. "Usual pickup?"

"That's right." With a broad grin, Ena gestured to Kahrin. "This is my friend Kahrin. She's helping me with errands today."

"Pleasure to meet you." The pharmacy tech gave Kahrin a look of polite approval before turning her attention back to Ena. "Mrs. Donaldson has a new med this week, so she gets four."

"Mrs. Donaldson, new med. Got it."

The tech disappeared and returned with one of those half-boxes that multiple six packs of pop came in, lined with white waxy paper bags that were stapled shut. Each had a discretely folded label that showed only a name. "It's supposed to drop to freezing tonight. Even if some of these Elders did drive, the roads would be in no shape for it."

"Well, I'm doing meal drop off today anyhow." She picked up the box and slung it against her hip. "Thanks, Truvy."

"She's a good one," Truvy said to Kahrin, obviously meaning Ena. "We don't really have resources for a delivery service, so she's kind of started one of her own."

"That's enough embarrassing me," Ena scolded with a playful tone.

"She also does it for free," Truvy answered.

"We don't want to be late to pick up lunches now. Bye!" She called over her shoulder and Kahrin hustled behind her.

"They just let you pick up other people's medications?" she asked, a little awed.

"Not at first, but I'm related to half of them, and the others have known me since I was knee-high. They all consented."

"What meals are you talking about?"

"You'll see," Ena said with a smile.

They made one more stop in the center, picking up some medical supplies to go with the prescriptions, and were packed back into Ena's truck in just a few minutes. They drove for a small spell in silence before Kahrin cleared her throat.

"I didn't mean to insult you. There's nothing wrong with giving affection freely."

"You didn't." Ena smiled, acknowledging an apology Kahrin hadn't yet given. "We all have love to give and need different ways to give it." Her eyes flicked to Kahrin and back to the reflective road. "I'm not ashamed of my choice."

Kahrin didn't have anything to say to that, especially since she found Ena's lack of shame impressive. Kahrin wondered if she'd have been able to walk so proudly had she been in the same position. Though, she realized just as quickly that she was passing another judgment. "Does the father know?"

"Does it matter?" Ena countered. "If he does, he's not here. If he doesn't?" She rolled a shoulder toward her ear and let it drop. "Well, he still isn't here, is he?"

Kahrin wanted to pry for more, but the way Ena danced around it made her rethink that. "Where are we going now?"

"Lunch." Ena gave her a pleased look, accepting a victory Kahrin had not yet conceded.

"At ten-thirty?"

"I didn't say we are eating it!"

She pulled them into another parking lot, this one cleared with a wheelchair ramp outside leading up to double doors. It might have been a church had it not said "Elder Center" on the sign at the door. Once they parked, Kahrin followed Ena up the ramp to the building. Opening the doors blasted them with a burst of heat, and within a few steps Kahrin had her coat open.

"You can hang that there." Ena pointed to a coat rack full of wire hangers, and hung her own, winding the scarf around the neck of one. "Quick now. Follow me."

Not a small amount of bewilderment took Kahrin as she followed her to a large kitchen, the kind like she used at the catering company. A few women were gathered inside, set up at the counter with a row of large catering-sized pans.

"Well, who's this pretty thing you brought in with you?" one of the ladies asked.

Before Ena or Kahrin could answer, Kahrin recognized one from the previous night's card game. "Oh, Kahrin, I'm so glad you joined us," Auntie Patty greeted her. "Though you could have been on time, missy." The last she directed to Ena with a wagging finger.

Ena produced a large stack of compostable food boxes from a cupboard, and the other women were quick to arrange themselves into an assembly line. "Put this on," Ena instructed her as she handed Kahrin a hairnet and put one on over her own hair.

The meal wasn't anything elaborate: burger patties and gravy over mashed potatoes with a vegetable and fruit side. It took close to an hour for them to assemble all the meals, all the women chattering as they worked.

"Patty tells me you came with your fella."

Her fella? Her face reddened. "That's right."

"He's handling my other errands," Ena explained.

"You shouldn't be hauling all that heavy stuff anyhow," Auntie Patty noted.

"I'm pregnant, not dead." She slid some partially frozen peach slices into the little tray spot for them. Fresh was out of the question, they explained, and the canned stuff was too much sugar for some of the Elders, so bags of frozen normally used by bars were brought in.

"Are you really one of Iskandar Boushay's kids?" one of the other ladies asked.

"He goes by Quirke now," Kahrin said as an answer. "My ma's a Quirke."

Finally, she managed to give that information without a series of glances being exchanged. So she guessed Auntie Patty had verified that fact long before it was a question posed to her. "But yes. Iskandar is my da." She pressed her lips together, taken by surprise by the lump forming in her throat. "He's sick, so I'm here to try and get him some help."

The room became quiet, save the scrapes of spoons against the pans.

"Brother Whiteloon will help you," Ena told her quietly. "I know he will."

Yes. He would. Because Kahrin was not leaving this reservation without making sure he stopped hurting her loved ones. She gave a tight grin. "You do this every week?"

"Day. She's here almost every day, packing lunches and delivering them." Auntie Patty filled a thermal carrier with several boxes and handed it to Kahrin, who understood she was not to let Ena carry it herself. "I heard Mrs. Donaldson is starting a new medication this week, so make sure she drinks her milk at least before you leave."

"This isn't my first day, Auntie Patty." Ena laughed with a shake of her curly head. She leaned toward Kahrin and added, "She'll put the meal away for dinner and take her meds on an empty stomach. She's always sensitive to new medications."

The women all gathered to hug them before Kahrin could protest, and they were on their way to making deliveries minutes later. Each person had genuine delight on their faces when they answered their doors, greeting Kahrin and telling her about all the ways Ena was wonderful. And she was, apparently, very much so. This was hardly the only altruistic activity she filled her days with, just the only one on this particular day.

At two of the houses, they stopped long enough to sort pills into those big pill boxes that had the day and time listed on them, and at three they portioned the meal into two containers so the person could get two dinners out of it.

"So, you just like helping people?" Kahrin asked as they passed.

"We take care of our Elders because they are part of our community. They are our history living among us." Which may have sounded trite from anyone else, but there was a certain genuineness about Ena that Kahrin couldn't even challenge after the few hours together. "They've all had a hand in raising most of my generation. Now it's our turn."

Kahrin thought about this, about the ways that her parents always reached out to help others. Kahrin had assumed it was her mother's gossipy nature that led her to it, and that her father was just miserly and couldn't stand the thought of someone paying to have something done for them. She wondered how much of who they were now had begun right here.

"You know, I don't regret my childhood," Kahrin admitted as they drove back toward Ena's Noko's house, "but I didn't have this. This whole, I don't know."

"Community?" Ena asked.

"No, we have a community. Our town was small." Not this small, but that likely did not need to be said. "Lots of that whole village thing. But I didn't have grandparents. Or aunties and uncles." She left it at that, the thoughts chasing themselves in her mind.

"You know, you probably could, if you wanted."

Kahrin chewed the inside of her mouth. "That's not why I'm here," Kahrin reminded her.

"Maybe not why you came here, but maybe there's a purpose you didn't realize."

Like a magical attack? Kahrin pursed her lips in thought, some of the less charitable thoughts about Ena creeping back as they made the drive back to her house.

This time when they pulled in it was Innes they saw in the kitchen window, which was almost too domestic a sight for Kahrin's stomach. Yet, she didn't quite hate the idea of them in a small, quiet house. Not that she was ready to sell her townhouse back to Emilia and get a place up in this frozen hellscape, but it wasn't the worst thing to imagine. No play bickering over whose name was on what lease or who left whose clothes on whose bathroom floor. As fun as that was, when had she decided some part of her did like that idyllic, quiet life? What happened to her adoration of the unknown?

Once inside, Innes handed over a paper bag of items to Ena that someone had asked him to deliver and relayed half a dozen stories and well-wishes from the locals he'd met during his morning. Kahrin twisted her mouth into what she hoped was a real enough smile, seeing how easily he fit in here, when she did not. Also, that bit about people assuming he was Ena's baby daddy rankled. Why? Who knew? She felt upside-down half the time these days.

"Your Noko is going to let me make a fish dinner." Weirdly when Innes said it, it sounded like boasting. But not in an annoying way. Like he was proud of some privilege. Suddenly he seemed chummy with Ena's grandmother, and she still felt like a suspicious outsider.

"Are you going to use Ma's recipe?" She crossed her arms and gave him a steady look. She had no idea what she expected out of this, but it seemed prudent to remind him that she, and he, had a family back home. A lying family, but still a family.

Concern dominated his expression, his pretty mouth turning downward. "Are you okay?"

"Yeah," she lied. "I could just really use that pretty walk about now. I want to get this visit over with."

CHAPTER TWENTY-TWO

INNES

Even in the town where they lived, Innes would not say he and Kahrin lived in an urban center by any measure. The town where they grew up was known for being a bit of a hick town, which seemed unfair as they weren't playing tractor chicken in the fields. Neither of those places were quite as rural as Ena's reservation, even the Quirke farm. Ena may have undersold the beauty found in their walk, though, and after the morning of errands, it was nice to get to.

While roads were well cleared, that was about all that was. Ena seemed to have some trail etched out in her mind, but the snow in front of them was piled high enough to soak their jeans past their boots. The trees, some of them aged beyond comprehension, grasped the snow in long fingers of shadow as they tried to hold onto the light. Even with the grey overcast, the light left green flashes of dazzle in his vision. Branches swished and scratched as birds traversed them with caws that echoed in the muted day. Just out of his periphery, Innes saw a flash of a hare's tail as it dashed into weather bared bushes. It all sounded both familiar and not. Like what he knew, but amplified.

Innes saw another hare. Maybe it was the same one. If it was, it was following them, which would be odd for a prey animal. It had to be different. He didn't see tracks other than their own, but as they trudged along, he did hear the barely masked crunching of snow.

The third time, he was sure it was the same hare. He paused, certainly wearing a boyish grin on his face as he saw a flit of black, a twitchy nose poking out from a crisscrossing of fallen brush beneath the evergreens. He blinked, curious as to how a hare was black this far north, this time of year. Maybe not every hare turned white in winter? When the hare didn't skitter off again, he crouched.

"Hey there," he said softly, as if he could coax it out. He made kissy sounds as if summoning a cat and felt foolish when the hare didn't move. The others stopped, realizing he wasn't behind them.

"Careful," Ena warned, though the brightness of her smile did not dim even as Innes knelt into the snow. She watched it intently, as if it would sprout horns from the top of its head. She crossed her arms. "That is no rabbit."

When it hopped out from the brush, Innes fell back on his rear. It did have horns. What?

"I'm not a rabbit."

Wait, what? Innes blinked, pushing up to his feet again and backing away, startled.

"Wait, what?" Kahrin echoed Innes' thoughts and answered his unasked question: was he imagining this? She doubled back to him, wrapping arms around him protectively.

"Stand down, Hole," the horned rabbit muttered. "I'm not here to hurt your Believer."

Innes' heart could have given the hare a fair race. He felt it try to launch out of his chest. This couldn't be happening. Well, it could. He knew damned well that it, and many things like it, could. This still felt a mite excessive on top of everything else they were running with right now.

"Charon," Ena scolded, hands on her hips as she stared down at the creature. "What are you doing here?"

"You know that rabbit?" asked Innes.

"Not a rabbit," Charon said.

"Hare, whatever." That was Kahrin, who had no problem arguing with any creature.

"That is no hare. He's a jackalope. Or he is right now. His name's not even Charon."

"Technically, I am not even a him." Charon hopped on muscled back legs a few more feet to the spot cleared by Innes' rump. "I just like this form and thought it would be less alarming."

Innes scrubbed his hands over his face, heels pausing at his eyes before his fingers plowed through his hair. "You didn't think talking would be alarming?" What was he doing? He was talking to a hare. Just when he thought life couldn't get any weirder, a talking fictional creature appears and here he was, talking to it. Instead of getting easier to accept since they'd met Yelena, magical happenstances were getting more complicated.

"Mortals are so fussy."

Ena backed away from the semi-circle of them, only a half-step but enough to underscore the sudden uptick in her nerves. "You did not answer my question." Worry tightened her dark eyes, and Innes noted a hand flutter to her belly.

Charon plopped on his rump and began scratching at one long ear with a heavily clawed back foot. "I'm not here for your child. I'm not sure I could take it if I was. You Holes are a paranoid bunch."

Wait, what?

Everyone looked to Ena, including the not-a-rabbit who hopped up closer—stopping short of the two women—and shook out his coat. Kahrin whipped around and stared, mouth agape.

Charon used his front legs to clean his whiskers, something that might have been normal hare behavior if not for the very real antlers. "They don't know? Interesting."

Innes demanded, "Will someone explain what is going on?"

"I couldn't have known," Ena explained. "How could I have known? It's not like we can sense one another. It doesn't work like— why am I explaining this to you?" Ena's words slashed like razors. "Now, I won't ask again. Why are you here?"

"Call it a curiosity. Call it saving time." Charon hopped forward, pointing with his nose toward the house in the clearing.

"One of the Boushays?"

"Not today." His whiskers twitched. "And not the Medicine Man, either."

Kahrin let out a scream, startling them all, and kicked impotently at the snow with her boot. "What are you talking about?"

"Charon here is what you would call a psychopomp," Ena said, caught somewhere between reverence and annoyance. "And something of a trickster, besides."

"A psycho what?" Kahrin's face crumpled with confusion.

"A guide for the dead," Innes explained. The name made sense now, even if it was a nickname as Ena had suggested. "Sometimes they're reapers."

"We don't actually kill anyone." Despite his tail twitching, Charon managed to sound offended. He wasn't a very convincing hare. Jackalope. Whatever. "We help with the crossover after that die has been cast. Nothing more."

"He also recruits." Ena's lips pulled into a hard line.

What did that mean?

Kahrin wound tighter with confusion beside him. "What, like, come join my multi-level-marketing diet sludge scam team of dead people guides?"

"Not exactly, but I think further explanation may need to wait. I believe you're expected."

The rest of them followed his trail of vision to see a woman standing on the front step of the little house, similar in build to Ena's. She waved.

"You don't expect us to believe that—" Innes turned about, but Charon was gone, tracks and all.

"Come on now, you'll let all my heat out. Come on!" The older woman scooped air with her hand to urge them inside. As they approached, she brushed a featherlight kiss on Ena's cheek and turned to Innes and Kahrin. "And who are your—"

Her eyes widened as they locked onto Kahrin, fingers curling over her mouth as if she'd seen a ghost. A tiny whine of an inhale was all he heard before she spoke again, this time with a warble. "What's your name?"

"Kahrin, ma'am."

Innes slipped an arm around her back, lending whatever strength he could, and lowered his mouth to her ear. "You know what she's asking."

"Kahrin Quirke." A pause hung between them all—Kahrin, reluctant to give the woman in front of them the verification she clearly wanted, and the woman afraid to move in case she spooked Kahrin like the hare she resembled and the one that had vanished. "My da's name is Iskandar."

The woman who was obviously Kahrin's grandmother stared, fingers curled over her mouth.

"They're visiting from downstate. They need to talk to Brother Whiteloon," Ena explained, and added, "I need to see him, too."

"He's not here, I'm afraid." The woman's voice was barely louder than a breeze, her eyes tied to Kahrin. "He's at—"

"Wilderness camp. We know." Ena patted her hand. "Bonnie, can we come inside?" She flashed her pretty smile again. "The heat will get out."

"Oh, of course." She stepped back to allow them to go inside. "Take your boots off and I'll start a pot of coffee for you."

He let Ena go ahead of them and pulled Kahrin aside by the elbow. "We don't have to go in if you don't want to. I'll take you back, we'll pack up, and drive out today. We can forget magic, forget all of it." Even as he said it, even meaning it as intensely as he did, he knew better: there was no outrunning their magical entanglements. The faint scars on his arm proved that. But for her, he would try, because that's what heroes did.

Kahrin's eyes stayed trained on the empty space formerly occupied by the woman who was obviously Da's mother. She had her own heroics in mind. "I think I have to do this. For Da." She huffed a cleansing breath, curling her fingers with his, and added, "I have to do it for us, too."

CHAPTER TWENTY-THREE

KAHRIN

The words came from her mouth, but Kahrin felt detached from them. As if someone else was speaking, someone whose curiosity was about to get the better of them.

"She's definitely Da's ma." She shook her head, smiling when he laughed softly at how weird that sounded. She had the same slight stature shared by all the Quirke siblings, the light copper skin, and the uneven combo of green and brown hazel eyes. She couldn't wrap her mind around it, what it all meant, what it made this woman in relation to her.

The inside of Mrs. Boushay's house was much like that of Ena's Noko's. Decorated differently, but the layout was identical. The entrance opened into a mudroom, and then cornered into a small passage to a cozy kitchen. They didn't make it to the kitchen, though. Curiosity killed the cat, and the cat was definitely named Kahrin, and she drifted along an impressive gallery wall hung with photos and knickknacks and drawings. For someone who wasn't interested in connecting with family, she certainly seemed to be paying it a great deal of attention suddenly. She wondered how many people would be able to do differently, seeing pictures of her da from a completely different life. She was like a runner on a beach, each step slowed by the slip of wet sand beneath her. Her body shifted like she wished to move along, but her eyes stayed fixed to the wall.

"Innes," she called softly to him. She needed someone to tell her she was not imagining this, because it wasn't magic. That much she knew.

"Is that your da?"

She nodded. Her ma had a similar gallery back in the farmhouse, filling the walls that wrapped around the stairs. There was a clear demarcation between the two: Ma's went back to Brecken's baby photos and no further, while this one ended with Da in what appeared to be his late teens or early twenties. The photo Innes asked after was clearly her da, dressed in full dance regalia, bright colored bustles of feathers, and streamer-like fringe on everything. He had bits and pieces of the ensemble still, but only that. A few feathers, various beaded elements in bright colors and patterns, and moccasins. Oh, how she loved those moccasins when she was young, but no amount of pleading would convince him to let her play in them. She'd learned more about Da's youth in the few minutes she'd stood in this house than she had in her twenty-one years with Da. A little further down the wall was a stereotypical tummy time baby picture of Da with eyes almost black and his mouth open in a wide, gummy smile. Someone enjoyed taking photos, as there was evidence of almost every stage of his childhood.

"My Iskandar was a beautiful baby," Mrs. Boushay said. "And a handsome young man." Clearly. It was easy to see what had appealed to Ma, and despite herself Kahrin's frown softened. "You favor him, you know."

Kahrin squeezed Innes' hand until she heard him suck in a breath, drawing any strength he had to offer. "He still is, ma'am. Handsome, I mean."

"Of course." Mrs. Boushay smiled, the creases of her eyes deepening. "You can call me—"

"No," Kahrin interrupted, bracing for a jab in the ribs by Innes' pointy-elbowed manners. "I can't. Not yet." Maybe never, who knew? "I don't know you." It sounded harsh as she said it, even to her own ears, but she saw no good in misleading the woman. "I'm here to try and save my da."

"Bonnie, then. Please." If Kahrin's words had stung, the woman did an impressive job of keeping it from her face. What was there seemed to be a different pain, one she couldn't quite relate to. Bonnie Boushay gestured for them to follow her into her kitchen. Innes cupped Kahrin's elbow, pulling her back toward him until he could speak in a lowered voice. "What's it going to hurt?"

"I can't deal with this, too, right now." She let the gentle pressure guide her into a hug. "It's too much. All of this is just too much." And she was so very small. Seldom had she ever actually felt small, despite her petite stature, but with all of the everything crushing down upon her shoulders, the world just felt too big. "One thing at a time? Please?"

"Of course. Anything you need."

How lucky was she? Being here with her best friend, the person she trusted most in the world, at this moment in her life, was everything. It wasn't that she couldn't do it this alone, because absolutely she could.

She wasn't sure she could do it without him, specifically, and come out the other side whole.

But did he say it because he felt obligated to be there for her? For just a moment she didn't care and clutched his shirt in her fingers for just a heartbeat before pushing away.

"How do you take your coffee?" Bonnie called just before they turned the corner into the kitchen.

"Black," they both echoed, though Innes shot a glance at Kahrin because he knew that wasn't true.

Ena was already in the kitchen, pouring herself a glass of orange juice as if she were in her own house. This did not seem to faze Bonnie at all. In fact, she pulled open the freezer part of her fridge and removed a new can of frozen concentrate and set it on the counter to thaw.

Bonnie then filled mugs with coffee and brought them to the table, along with a cream and sugar service. She didn't sit.

"My Iskandar is sick? Is it bad?"

Apparently, they weren't easing into things. Okay. Kahrin preferred it this way. She nodded. "They don't know what's wrong, but he can't breathe without a machine right now."

Bonnie took this in stride, settling into a familiar stillness, the soft sound of her breath the only indication she'd not turned to stone. By reflex, Kahrin didn't speak while Bonnie held her silence. Finally, the woman sat, rested her face in the web between her thumb and finger, and sighed wearily. There she stayed a few moments, long enough for Kahrin to look to both Innes and Ena in turn, wondering if they should just leave.

Ena asked, "Is there anything in his family history that might help them, Auntie?" She meant well, and didn't know that whatever was happening, it was not hereditary.

Turned out, it didn't matter. "I don't know. My father drank himself into an early grave. My mother went missing and was never found." She delivered these with very little emotion. "My husband," now she swallowed, the sound thick with grief, "he was shot. We never found out who."

Kahrin blinked, and she felt Innes begin to rub a hand up and down her spine. "Any siblings?"

Bonnie shook her head. "A stillborn before Iskandar."

The room seemed hot all of a sudden, the air almost painful to breathe as she felt the strain to draw air in. Pain prickled the backs of her eyes, and a tingle trickled down her cheeks. Not until Innes wiped her cheek with the pad of his thumb did she realize that, like Bonnie, she was crying.

"I'm so sorry. I didn't know."

"How could you, Makoons?"

Kahrin blinked. Innes' hand stilled at her back. Some teachings Da had given her freely and had imparted many of those to Innes as well. But these things? For Da to keep all this family history from her, from her siblings, felt like a betrayal. So, what did she do with that? Did she give in to the petty part of her that wanted to just give up on Da altogether? No, she'd grown too much as a person for that. Nor did she want to go running back to pretend all was well, even if they found a cure.

She took a deep breath and reached for Bonnie's hands. She grasped them in both of hers, noting the similar shape of their thumbs. "I don't know you," she repeated, her words from earlier gentler, "but maybe it wouldn't be so bad to. Just for a couple of days." She puffed her cheeks as she breathed out. "We have to wait for Brother Whiteloon anyway. We have some spare time."

Bonnie's eyes shone, but she lifted her chin, that same stoicism of her son denying her tears their emergence. "I would like that." She looked to Innes and back to Kahrin. "Both of you, please."

CHAPTER TWENTY-FOUR

INNES

It was mid-afternoon when they left Bonnie Boushay's home. They'd chatted and toured the little house long enough that Ena needed a rest. Some of the chipper demeanor she'd wielded the day before was dimmed by fatigue, and Bonnie had sentenced her to a sandwich and a nap.

Kahrin left with a manilla envelope full of photographs, a moderately better attitude, and a promise to consider calling Bonnie her own Noko. They were also invited to the potluck the next day, which Innes suspected was less invitation and more expectation. They had to meet Brother Whiteloon anyhow, though they'd hoped it would be a more private meeting. Kahrin clung to this as her excuse, but Innes was sure he saw a hopeful gleam in her eye. Whether she admitted it or not, Kahrin was enjoying the idea of a possible extended family, though she remained reticent to show it openly.

Ena drove them out to the casino for a late lunch. Not only was it packed as expected for the time of day, but Innes noticed a good deal of trucks with what looked to be campers on the back with little doors. Not until a woman knelt down and unlatched one, did he realize it was essentially a mobile kennel for the packs of huskies who seemed only too eager to be hitched to their harnesses.

After the best fish sandwich he'd had outside of Ma Quirke's kitchen, they meandered the gaming floor, more out of curiosity than any actual desire to play. Innes didn't see the appeal, and even if Kahrin had wanted more than a cursory experience, the first machine she dropped a metal slug into clicked, then broke with a loud grinding sound that did not sound good.

"Coincidence?" she asked.

Innes chuckled. "Are you suggesting slot machines are magic?"

"No. Yes. I don't know."

Ena tapped her chin. "I've never thought about it. Never won much, but I've also never broken a machine."

They left the main floor and were passing the gift shop when Ena grabbed Kahrin by the arm and pulled her over to the side of the hall. She pointed at an older—much older than Emilia—woman being escorted by a familiar looking man whom Innes could not place. "That's Paul and Tippy Quirke."

What? That uneasy feeling knotted up in Innes' belly again at the strange happenstance of yet another estranged relative of Kahrin's being suddenly nearby. Especially given what Ena had told them about Ma Quirke's family and their feelings toward the Native population.

"What do I do?" Kahrin asked him, as if any of those manners she teased him about but also blushed over now and then could decipher this situation.

"What do you want to do?" he turned it around. She didn't like that and threw a desperate look to Ena.

"I've never seen them here, not since Maxen, well, passed."

"Passed?" Kahrin asked, tilting her head. Innes felt his brow pinch. Not because neither of them knew what passed meant, but it was the way Ena said it. As if it wasn't the whole story, and neither of them seemed willing to press her about it.

The decision was taken out of Kahrin's hands then, as Paul Quirke guided his mother toward them, presumably to the women's restroom behind them. As the woman went into the bathroom, her son looked at the three of them, looked away, and then narrowed his eyes at Kahrin. She, in turned, stared at him like a deer in headlights.

"Ena McKenzie," he called to them. "Who are your friends?"

He wandered to them, holding a hand out to shake. "Paul Quirke, Quirke Farms." That was a little too surreal for Innes' liking. "And you are?"

Since Kahrin seemed incapable of answering, Ena took over introductions. "This is Innes and Kahrin." Her eyes flicked to them and back to Paul. "From downstate."

Paul's eyebrows lifted high on his face. He and Ma Quirke shared several similarities in appearance, with dark hair and eyes. He was taller, of course, but they shared a familiar posture. His dark eyes held a glint, like he knew something and hadn't quite put his finger on it. "I know almost everyone around here. Who did you say your family is?"

Kahrin pursed her lips, definitely debating the level of courtesy she wanted to pay the man, and settled on, "I didn't."

Innes' chest stilled in the fleeting moment it took Paul to give a low huff of laughter.

"Of course. That was rude of me. You just look so much like my—"

"Sister," Kahrin filled in. Her eyes widened, like she'd thought she'd said the words in her head and was shocked to hear them out loud. "Your sister, Grainne, is my ma." She swallowed and summoned every last drop of her genetic coding to lift her chin as if daring him to say something about her paternity.

"Well, I'll be damned." Paul shook his head, hand over his heart. Something in his eyes flickered that Innes couldn't place. Not quite sadness, but he didn't seem especially pleased, either. He looked at Kahrin like he was studying her, took a breath and held out his arms, inviting her into a hug. "I can see it. It's there, the Quirke in you."

"I am a Quirke," she corrected him, not accepting his invitation. If she'd been a dog, she'd have been bristling, or Paul might have needed medical attention for his hand.

"Your parents never married?"

Kahrin blinked, and before she could pull a breath to tell him what Innes could only guess was her thoughts on that, he spoke up. "That seems like a very impertinent question for someone you just met."

"You're right," Paul said, though he offered no apology. The hand dryer blared in the bathroom behind them, and then the older woman appeared beside him. "Mother, I need you to meet someone. You'll never guess who this is."

Tippy Quirke's eyes appraised Kahrin in a way that Innes simply did not like. He glanced at Ena, wondering how much of a scene it would make if they dragged Kahrin out of this casino. Then a softness took the older woman's expression, and her eyes watered. "You're going to have to tell me."

"This is Grainne's daughter."

Mrs. Quirke's eyes narrowed just a touch, and her smile puckered like she'd bitten pith inside a sweet orange. Still, when she spoke, there was a shake to her voice. "Well, I suppose I don't need to ask who your father is."

"Excuse me?" Kahrin asked. She crossed her arms over her chest and Innes felt that shift in the tectonic plates of the Earth he knew too well. "What does that mean?"

"Mother," Paul cautioned gently, his smile apologetic even if his words were not. "Perhaps we don't start there just yet. The girl's here. Grainne's daughter, Mother." It didn't take a genius to work out that they had very big feelings about Da Quirke, but there was a marked gentleness at the way he pronounced his sister's name.

Tippy waved a hand and forced a more pleasant expression. "You're just darker than I might have hoped. I suppose that can't be helped." She fished a handkerchief from her handbag and dabbed at her eyes. "Come here." She held her arms out.

Just as she had for Paul, Kahrin refused, and this time even took a step back. "You know something?" Kahrin started. Innes braced. "I've lived quite a while without knowing you, and I have no problem walking away and pretending we never met. I don't need you."

Ena lifted a shoulder and she and Kahrin began to walk toward the main exit.

"Wait, please," Paul called, looking to Innes for help with a canny understanding of the relationship between them. He knew who he had to call on as an ally. "Mother," he scolded. "Wouldn't you like to know more about what became of Grainne?"

"What did I do? I spoke the truth. Grainne made her choices."

"And so did Father. The Lord would want us to embrace this opportunity." He beseeched Innes once more. "Please. Excuse Mother's bad manners and let us make it up to you." He held out a hand to shake. "Mother will be on her best behavior, I promise."

The old woman scoffed but didn't disagree. Whatever challenge Paul had posed seemed to earn him her compliance. "I can't believe it. My girl has been gone for so long."

Innes huffed, hoping he didn't regret this, and loped down the hallway to where the two women waited for him, Kahrin ending a phone call. He lifted a brow.

"Ma, telling me Da's stable." Even though it was a good thing, her face didn't say she felt good about it. Still, they didn't have the information they needed, and were still waiting for Brother Whiteloon.

So, why not do this? "Give Paul a chance?"

"Why?"

Innes threw his hands up. "I don't know. I don't know anything about why any of this is happening, but I know that it is, and I know you. You might pretend you don't want to know anything about them, but we both know you're curious."

"Talk to them?" Ena suggested. "We can walk away whenever you want, but this way you can say, with confidence, you tried."

Innes smiled, grateful for Ena's presence, for her friendliness, and actually regretted how suspicious he'd been of her before. She even seemed to be wearing Kahrin down after their morning together, and that was a feat in and of itself.

"Fine." As grudging as Kahrin's agreement seemed to be, she'd been craning around Innes to see Paul and Tippy the whole time. "You can't keep insulting my da," she called, not sure if they could hear her over the din of the nearby slot machines.

"Or you," Innes reminded her. It was just as much a slight against her. Innes believed she was perfect, in all her messy imperfections. To shun her according to the lovely brown of her skin undermined all the perfectly valid reasons lesser humans than him might have for doing so.

They walked back, Innes' hand firmly at her back so that Paul and Tippy might not forget that she had people who cared about her.

"You have a minute," Kahrin said. She also wasn't wearing a watch, but he chose not to point that out. "After that, I bolt."

"Come out to the farm for dinner. See the family home, maybe learn a bit about your mother's history." He smiled, his dark eyes soft and crinkled at the corners beneath dark brows. The family resemblance was strong, and it didn't surprise him at all to be invited over to a Quirke home for a meal. "Miss McKenzie, you could join us, if you please."

Kahrin looked to Innes, who refused to answer this one for her. He squeezed her to his side, a silent reassurance that he supported whatever she chose to do, or not do, but it was hers to choose, and he would not take that from her.

She lifted and dropped her hands at her sides. "Sure. Why not? Let's have a weird family dinner."

Ena smiled. "I have another obligation, so I'm afraid I'll have to pass." She tilted her head, her tone no less pleasant for the momentary dimming of her expression. "I wouldn't want to intrude. This is a family matter."

"Well, you have surprisingly lovely manners," Tippy noted. Paul frowned and rubbed the bridge of his nose and gave Ena an apologetic look.

"Are you sure you couldn't shuffle it around for us? The three of you seem so close, it would be a pity to exclude you."

Did they? The bond between himself and Kahrin was obvious, but he had only known Ena the better part of a day. Yet, she fell in with them easily. Perhaps Paul was more insightful than Innes.

Ena didn't seem to think so, and while her crooked smile lit up her face, her nearly black eyes showed a wariness he couldn't ignore. "Thank you, but I'm afraid not."

"We'll have to carry on without you." Paul nodded to them in turn. "Seven sharp. Dress is casual." The last he added with a lift of his brow which was clearly a comment of its own.

"You're not some kind of hippy-dippy no meat-eating people, are you?" That came from Tippy, whom Innes reasoned probably put that as kindly as she was capable. This was going to be a long night.

"No, ma'am. My ma raised me on moose meat stew."

Tippy's nose twitched. "Well, I'm afraid we are a little shy on moose meat. You'll have to settle for a good old-fashioned beef pot roast." She addressed her son, then. "Come along now, Paul. I'll have to air out the dining room, and I suppose we could get out that nice china that your father was saving for Grainne's eventual wedding."

Even Innes couldn't hide his cringing at that.

Paul shook their hands. Grasping Kahrin's in both of his and leaning forward, he said quietly. "I adored my sister. My heart broke when she left us. I know why she left, and I don't blame her." A pause, as if he couldn't make his mind and mouth agree on what came next. "Give me a chance to know her child. Please, Kahrin?"

Kahrin nodded in as non-committal a way as she was able. "Okay." Innes almost believed her. First Bonnie, and now Paul?

Kahrin stared after them as they left, the tension in her coiling beneath his arm. "I'm not calling her Gran."

"Understood," Innes said with a grin into her hair.

CHAPTER TWENTY-FIVE

KAHRIN

In the commotion, Innes had forgotten he promised to cook for Noko McKenzie, but she'd shooed them off, insisting that she and Ena would be just fine while they went out to dinner. And since it seemed unlikely that they would be leaving the next day, she'd take a raincheck on Innes' offer.

So, without the last lingering excuse to keep them from going, they changed into their nicest jeans and set out.

Without Ena to guide them, and without reliable cell signal, it took Innes and Kahrin a few roundabout side trips and double backs to find the Quirke Dairy farm. The fact that the property was surrounded by a line of fir trees didn't help them much, as they couldn't see the enormous barn with the name Quirke across in tall, black letters over the doors, until they were well past the point of being able to turn in. Kahrin never thought she'd be grateful to be in a small town smaller than her small-town hometown, but it sure was helpful that there was no traffic around so they could execute a neat three-point turn to go back.

Innes let a low whistle. "That's a barn with your family name on it in great big letters."

"They're not my family," she pointed out. They hated her da. How could she ever be family with someone who hated her da? She could probably swear Brecken off if he developed a strong dislike of Da. Maybe.

The barn was the only building visible from the road, on account of being enormous and white, which was an odd choice for a barn, Kahrin thought, considering it was probably covered in animal crap. Innes stopped the car in the wide, snow-packed driveway and rushed around to open the door for her. She made to protest, but she allowed it, even taking his hand as a help up. It felt very date-like, and she tried not to laugh.

A series of ground lights guided them to and around a narrow, salted sidewalk which led them to an equally white, proportionately large house with concrete steps up to a porch that spanned the entire side. The massive door had leaded glass, which did not look nearly weather resistant enough for a home that took the brunt of nature's cold shoulder two-thirds of the year.

Tippy Quirke met them at the door as if they were selling Girl Scout cookies, inviting them in with a stiff politeness. "There's snacks in the sitting room." She stood aside as they shed their boots and coats. Kahrin's love of old houses had not dimmed since her foray into Evan Greves's house, and while this was less ornate, it still held a startling beauty in an old way quality.

"Three stories?" she asked. "What do you do with a third floor?"

See? She was trying!

"Storage mostly."

Kahrin was disappointed that she didn't say it belonged to the ghost of her dead not-grandfather, but she kept that to herself.

The dark wood floors creaked under their stockinged feet, even when they crossed onto plush rugs. Drapes were drawn against the dark outside, but if she held her breath Kahrin could hear the wind whistling through the double panes. The entirety of the house was lit with dim, antique bulbs made to look like candle flames. The antique wallpaper gave everything a very busy look which Kahrin wasn't sure she liked, and was grateful that Ma had not inherited her mother's taste for interior design. Every room was filled with heavy, dark furniture, and every wall boasted a shelf or cabinet that housed lots of old things, like dishes no one ate with and little porcelain figures that served only to lighten your wallet. Everything was cold, like it had been sucked clean of any warmth and emotion.

"My ma really grew up here?"

"We all did," Paul said as an announcement that he'd arrived on the main floor. He closed the door to the upstairs and offered his hand to Innes to shake again. "We nearly sold it after—"

"After that dreadful family ruined Maxen's life." The Elder Mrs. Quirke genuflected, and Kahrin knew she was going to have to come back to that when she could do so without it being rude.

"Mother," Paul said with weary affection. "It wasn't their fault."

Oh, well, if they were going to dangle it in front of her like that. "What wasn't their fault?" The idea of a family scandal that didn't involve Brecken's unannounced arrival into the world was more appealing than she might have expected.

"We should have drinks." Tippy clapped her hands together and left the room. "Is beer alright? I keep it on hand for the farm hands. I believe it goes with the fun "just in from the fields" look for tonight."

Kahrin's mouth drew into a purse. It's not like she planned on attending any formal dinners when she'd packed for their road trip of justice. She didn't look slovenly, but maybe jeans and a puffy vest weren't doing as much work as she thought.

Paul sighed, lowering his voice for just the three of them. "A child drowned during a baptism Father performed. A terrible tragedy. He was investigated, the family accused him of unseemly things, and it drove him to take his own life." Kahrin had a basic working knowledge of Catholicism, but it didn't answer how a married man was doing a baptism. "In the end it was declared an accident, but the damage had already been done."

"I thought priests couldn't marry." That was Innes, always catching those finer details that she'd not put together until now.

"Ah," Paul started. "They can't. Not without converting in from another denomination." The warmth she was growing accustomed to from Paul's voice stole away at her initial apprehension. "Father was a deacon. Given how remote we are, he was sometimes called upon to perform more time-sensitive baptisms, like for this sick baby. Of course, after the incident, he was removed."

Kahrin meant to question it, the words even bounced up and down on her tongue, searching for room to escape, but she remembered that Maxen Quirke had the kind of money to open almost any door. He could easily have walked away from something like that.

Instead, she went another direction, wanting out of this morbid topic. "So, was my Ma really going to be a nun?"

Paul barked a laugh. "If Father ever thought Grainne would go to a convent and take vows, he did not know my sister. It's why he insisted we save the china." He chuckled, familiar warmth putting Kahrin more at ease. There was a gleam in his eye that reminded her of Ma, reminded her of Alec, even, who always looked more like her than the others. How would Paul Quirke feel about looking like her middle brother?

"My daughter would have come around if she hadn't run off with that man," Tippy said, returning with a tray of beer in fancy stemmed glasses. Innes politely declined, but Kahrin accepted if only to have something to hold in her hands that didn't require assaulting the elderly.

"I assume you mean my da. He has a name."

Paul put an arm around her, under which she stiffened. "You certainly sound like Grainne."

She forced a laugh, hoping they didn't know her well enough to know it was a false laugh.

"I do regret that I never got the chance to welcome him." Paul almost sounded sincere. Or he did, and she was too damned jaded by Tippy to be more generous in her thoughts. She tried to relax into the awkward side-hug.

"I guess you would have avoided the convent, too." Tippy smiled that smile of a rich old woman who believed her age put her beyond reproach, if not her money. "How long have you been married?"

"We're not." Innes put a stop to that one quickly, but Kahrin felt a different tone underneath it. They were being judged by Tippy Quirke's morals. As if she had any room to judge anyone. Kahrin was sure that some places in the Quirke family tree didn't quite branch out. She shuddered.

"Oh, you could have a wedding here. The smaller barn isn't in use right now and it would make a lovely venue for that," she flipped her hand around as she sought the word she wanted, "rustic theme that is so in style now."

"We're not planning on getting married," Kahrin supplied.

Tippy shook her head. "You should make everything nice and legal."

"Mother, I bet the roast is finished by now. Perhaps you should check on it?"

Tippy threw her hands up and walked off again. "Fine! I'm not allowed to have an opinion in my own home. It is dinner time. Some traditions remain, I suppose."

"You have to forgive Mother." Did she? Kahrin wanted to object. Innes squeezed her hand, like he could read her mind. "Grainne leaving was very hard for her, and then Father took his life." A major Catholic sin. "She never quite recovered."

"I don't think racism is an illness fixed with bed rest." Her lips drew into a tight line.

Paul inclined his head but didn't comment. She wanted to believe he was just embarrassed for his mother's behavior.

They took seats at a long table that was very impractical for two people living alone. Paul invited Kahrin to sit near him at the head of the table with Innes across from her and Tippy on her other side. It was bad enough feeling boxed in like that, and then Tippy insisted on leading them in grace. A barrage of questions; pointed, probing, or otherwise followed. It made keeping her irritation in check a challenge. She hoped this wasn't the finest dinnerware that Tippy Quirke owned, as Kahrin certainly took her temper out in every cut of roast and every mash of potato over the ugly flowered pattern. She couldn't imagine her mother ever using these plates, even for company.

At least she could see where her mother had learned the foundations of her cooking, though in her objective opinion, Ma's was superior in every way. The food was good.

And to his credit, Paul was trying. "Innes, what do you do?"

He put on that winsome smile that made people instantly love him and made her want to do things to him out of a very different type of love. Lord she needed to get him alone.

"I'm about to finish my undergraduate work. This time next year I should be in medical school."

"What a respectable profession," Tippy said, pressing her hand to her heart. "And won't you look handsome in a white coat. The hair practically casts you in the role already."

"I guess it's lucky for me it turned so early. Maybe it'll give me a leg up in my medical school interviews." Kahrin adored the way he was so good at keeping things from growing too tense. Despite Tippy's best efforts.

She looked to Kahrin. "Will you be staying home with the children, then?"

"Is someone going to drop children off at my house?" she tried to joke. She wasn't going to get into the ins and outs of her reproductive choices with this abrasive and judgmental woman.

"She means that we don't want children." Kahrin felt her chest flutter at the way he said we. They'd always planned on being part of one another's life, but he was just so casual about this recent change, as if he'd always been ready for it to be a reality and they'd only needed to be open to it.

"Well, you're still young."

"Mother is very traditional." Paul looked to Tippy and lifted a brow. "Some might say judgmental."

"It's not judgmental to want a family." Her eyes softened as they fell upon Innes. "And look at his fine features." Kahrin suspected she knew which features Tippy admired the most. "I'm just saying we could have the family that Grainne so cruelly took from us. I never got to be a proper grandmother. What is an old woman supposed to do in her twilight years?"

"It's not for me," Kahrin said with a tight smile.

"Or for me," Innes reinforced her point. They weren't about to tell these near strangers about how Kahrin wasn't capable of bearing children, having had a hysterectomy at seventeen after her heroics.

"What do you do then, Kahrin?" Paul inquired as he used a shiny roll to sweep gravy across his plate.

Kahrin puffed a laugh of relief. "I was studying sports medicine." She set her fork down. "And now I'm not. I'm not sure what I want to do, since that didn't work out. I enjoy farming, and I'd probably be good at it, but I don't think I want to make it my life."

"It takes a special kind of young lady to do so." Tippy sipped her beer and made a pinched face. "It's a lot of hard work. I worked those fields myself and kept meals on this table until Maxen brought about our success." She lifted her hands. "And now I run this household." She sighed, wistful. "But this large house is too empty."

"I'm trying things out. I was an aerial dancer for a bit, but I never really got the knack for it." Innes nearly choked on his laugh, likely remembering how she'd thought that working in a gentleman's club would be fun. And it was, for about two weeks. No doubt he liked the way she turned the phrase of the job. "Now I work in catering. Probably not forever, just until I figure myself out."

Tippy sniffed but didn't say anything. She didn't need to speak in order to judge Kahrin, and Kahrin looked at her plate with a frown.

"What brings you all the way to our neck of the woods?" Paul abruptly changed the subject, and Kahrin could hardly hide how grateful she was. She didn't try.

"My da is sick." When neither of their faces changed, she added, "We're here to talk to the medicine man and get some family history."

"A bunch of poppycock." So Tippy's feelings on that were clear. She met her son's eyes. "But whatever gets you here at our table." Her entire demeanor shifted, and she rested a hand over Kahrin's on the table. "Please say you'll come back soon. It really is a delight to finally have met you, Kahrin. My Grainne left us so suddenly, and it was just selfish of her to keep you from us all these years. I loved that girl with all my heart, and she broke it." Her eyes shone with tears that she was too proud to allow to spill. "I could love you, too."

"You could have looked for us," Kahrin murmured. She set her roll down. "Did you even try to look for us?"

"I think I'm going to retire for the evening." Tippy stood from her chair. "It was a pleasure to meet you as well, Innes."

Stillness sat heavily in the wake of Tippy's departure. "Please excuse Mother," Paul said quietly, to keep his voice from carrying. "She will warm up to you. My sister was always warm and loving, so you have to believe she got it somewhere."

"Did you try to find us?" This point mattered to her, more than she wanted to admit.

"Your mother clearly did not want to be found, Kahrin. But you've come into our lives for a reason, you, and Innes. I do not intend to waste what the Lord has given us." He smiled, and Kahrin could see herself in his eyes, hear herself in his gentle laugh. "I know it would make Mother happy."

Kahrin swallowed, nodding, because she couldn't argue with his logic. Her parents didn't want to be found. They'd gone to a lot of trouble to make sure they weren't. However, she just was not sure she was ready to open up to these people.

The awkward factor did not ease after that, and as soon as they could do so, the pair of them extricated themselves from the Quirke table.

"Gee, I can't figure out why Ma would run away from home. Knocked up, even."

Innes laughed, the sound manifesting as a puff of fog bright under the moon. He pulled her close and slid his arms around her waist. "It's a true enigma." He bumped his nose against hers. "Don't let them make you question yourself. As long as you're happy with who you are, that's what matters." He pulled his head back and tipped her chin up to meet his gaze. "That's what I love about you. You are you, and you don't try to be anyone else." His face was so handsome backlit by the night sky.

He left it wide open for her to respond with a joke, but something about the moment was magical. The only kind of magic she knew she could hold onto. So, she didn't say anything, and simply tipped up onto her toes to claim a kiss. It felt equal parts familiar and new, warming her belly and easing the knots that this dinner had left in her. He grasped the sides of her face in his hands and made these Quirkes who didn't seem much like Quirkes at all fall out of her mind.

He broke the kiss, his breath heavier. "Let's get back, hm?"

Something hung in that hm, something always hung in the hm, but this held a different kind of something, one that sparked a chain reaction up her spine. When she spoke, her voice drew out husky. "The sooner the better, I think."

CHAPTER TWENTY-SIX
INNES

The barely contained anger that thundered in his ears as he watched that woman—he couldn't bring himself to call her a Quirke—talk to Kahrin as she did was quickly overtaken by a racing pulse that had nothing to do with anger. The cold, crisp air and the bright light of the moon exhilarated him. As if this bizarre dinner and warped would-be family had clarified exactly why his heart ached so much when he thought of the choice he thought he had to make between what he wanted and who he wanted. It had never been an either/or. Kahrin knew all the things about him that others found off-putting or odd, and he knew all the stubbornness she held in her like a bottle rocket ready to blast off into her passionate temper. Their oddities complemented one another. He would go on his trip, he would play the young hero and do good with his hands in the world, and she would be there when he came back. He knew like he knew anything else that she would wait for him.

It was all so clear in his mind, and he couldn't put it into words. But words were never enough for Kahrin. She liked using them, but she preferred to be loved in action. He lost himself in kissing her until kissing was the last thing on his mind, and more insistent parts of his body began speaking a language that was easier between them.

With no small amount of restraint, he pushed them apart, and they got into the car and started the drive back to Ena's. They'd find an excuse when they got there to ensconce themselves in their little room.

Caution wouldn't let him drive as fast as his heart wanted. A bad patch of icy road would put a damper on what they both buzzed with, something that felt too-long denied. They had very few firsts left to share, and yet somehow everything they were doing felt new.

"Innes, look." Kahrin pointed out her window toward the skyline, black and expansive, and off in the distance he could see it: the glimmer of green lights, like a distant fire reflecting off the snow. The passing trees would shut it from view for several seconds and they would find it again when the woods cleared from view.

"The Aurora Borealis," he said. Obviously.

"It's just us," she teased. "You can just say Northern Lights." Her eyes widened and any unpleasant feeling that may have lingered from their dinner was quickly replaced with the curiosity he so adored in her. "Turn here. No-no-no-go-back-go-back-go-back!"

He laughed, applying the brakes, and reversing a few feet to take the nearly concealed turn she instructed. It wasn't as cleared as the other roads, but he followed the winding road through a tunnel of tall trees, trusting her sense of direction. It paid off. In just a few minutes they came out on a clear road that followed the shore of a lake, giving them a wide, clear view. He pulled the car over to what looked like a pull off for a scenic lookout, as if it had been planned that they would wind up on this spot. She was out of the car before he had his seatbelt off, but she only made it a few feet away before she turned her back to the dancing lights and waved for him to hurry. The moon was bright enough to show the opening of a trail that was unlikely to be cleared, but he grabbed her hand and pulled, kicking the snow ahead of him to make a trail she could follow as they worked their way up the incline until it broke open in a spectacular view.

Oh, they'd have to be much further north to see the full show, but the green lights flickered like it was the visual effect of what his heart was feeling, and he wrapped his arms around her and pulled her back to his chest. He held her tight, as if she was the only thing keeping him attached to the here and now. He relished the way her arms felt, wound with his, the way she leaned her head against his shoulder as they just stood there, quietly taking in the breathtaking view in front of them. Breathtaking in more than one way, and Innes squeezed her until she gasped a laugh, wriggling so she could draw a breath to match his once more.

"This would be alright if Da wasn't sick," Kahrin murmured. "It's weird and uncomfortable, but it's new. Different."

"How so?" he asked. He thought he had an idea, but he wanted to hear her say it. As much as Kahrin sometimes balked at breaking free of her hometown in private, the real itch to explore effervesced just beneath her skin.

"This town is smaller than home, but I don't feel suffocated. It doesn't feel too small for me." Her eyes watched the celestial fabric as it wavered like a pennant in the sky. "No one knows me here, not even other

Quirkes. I could find myself." That she would keep her distance from her ma's family didn't need to be said. She swallowed and looked up at him. "But I won't stay without you."

He turned his face into her hair and breathed deep. He knew she was day two between washes of her hair, and it held on to that balance between her light strawberry scented shampoo and her natural scent. The scent he always associated with her. "What if, after your da is better," because he would get better, "you come back and stay while I'm gone?"

"Who taught you to negotiate?" She turned enough to look up to see his face. "I think that means you won't be here."

He bumped his nose against her cheek. "Noticed that, did you?" His hands snaked further until he could wind his fingers with hers, getting as close as public decency would allow, even if the public was only a handful of nocturnal, winter critters. They'd learned a long time ago, that they were possibly always being watched by magical eyes in the woods. It wouldn't do to be caught out by a unicorn while exploring their cravings for one another. "I have to finish school. This place is more for you than for me."

"That's not true," she said softly. "Everyone who's met you adores you already." She grinned and added. "For a white boy snag."

He snorted. "You know what I mean."

"I don't think I could do it without you. Be here."

His thoughts from earlier crept back, making a knot in his belly, the warmer thoughts of earlier taking a back burner. "I think you could. If anyone can, you can. Besides, you're never without me, and it wouldn't be forever. I'll be back and we can decide what we do from there."

It was a compromise, the best he could offer, both to her and to himself. If they were going to do this thing, and he knew beyond a doubt they were, they couldn't sacrifice themselves for it. It went against everything they had between them.

"What if you meet someone while you're out saving the world?"

"I meet lots of someones." He tucked her head beneath his chin, following the ripples of color over the far side of the lake with his eyes. "I choose you. I'm going to come back to you."

"Hm." She stayed quiet, and he wondered if she was actually going to accept it. He dipped his head, brushing strands of hair aside until his lips could find the flutter of her pulse behind her ear and he ghosted an entire haunting of kisses along as much as he could reach before her scarf thwarted him. She shivered. "Maybe."

She guided his hands to very not appropriate for unicorn eyes places, the torment of her warm layers being in the way reignited what their conversation had banked.

"Wicked woman." Even through her jeans he could feel the heat pooled there, something meant for him, for him to notice, for him to indulge in.

Her breath gave a soft hitch which only served to heat his impatience. "We've been screwing our brains out as friends for years but now that we're—"

"A couple?" It felt weird to say, but right.

"A couple, we haven't done it once. That feels wrong."

"Not really." He turned her around. "It was never about the sex, Kahrin. We both know that."

She did and nodded her agreement. "But it's also a little about the sex."

He laughed, almost too loud for the moment. "A little."

He kissed her again, pressing his weight into her to walk her backward until her back found a tree. No, they weren't going to do it out here in the open, as she liked to point out anytime they let hormones take over in inopportune places, but that didn't mean everything was off limits. In the dark, lit by the aurora and bright moon, her fingers found skin beneath his clothes, and before he could get a gasp out at the sensation of her hand slipping past his waistband, she was making her intentions very clear. His teeth expressed how much it pleased him, catching her lips, and tugging until she'd lowered herself too far to maintain the contact, leaving him to lean forward against the trunk of the trunk while she stole all his senses. A bear could have gone trundling past them, angry at his moans waking it, and he would not have noticed. Everything was her mouth, her fingers, his fingers in her hair, and the sounds of her enjoyment in her quest.

He shuddered with a guttural sound, and when she slid back up between him and the tree with her face smug, he grabbed her until he could plunge his tongue past hers and groan at the taste of himself lingering there.

"Let's get back," she murmured against his swollen lips. "I'll drive."

She was going to have to. He was far too drunk on lust and having spent himself to be safe behind a wheel.

"Yes." His chest shook with how low his voice had dipped with need to reciprocate and he growled. "Get us back. Quickly."

The yard light was on, and the door unlocked when they got back to Ena's Noko's house. They slipped in as quietly as they could through the house to their room. Everything past the click of the door lock happened by rote, his fingers knowing every line and curve as he pulled her shirt over her head. Fingertips skimmed over familiar peaks, his tongue followed well-known trails down her sternum, and his teeth nipped at that tender spot high on her inner thigh as he liberated her from her skinny jeans.

For one fleeting moment he remembered this wasn't their house, and that it wasn't strictly polite to carry on like this when guests in someone's home. Everything below his belly screamed for his brain to shut up, and he dismissed the worry as quickly as he could.

Once the earlier favor had been returned, Kahrin was on him like a cat on a kill. He shuddered hard as her nails dragged over his hips, as she straddled him and teased him in the worst, best, way by withholding that last scant space between them until he couldn't take it any longer. He gripped her rear and seated her against him in one motion. He stayed like that as long as he could, luxuriating in the way the reunion felt, giving her a second to catch the breath he apparently knocked out of her, before he felt like not moving would kill him. The first time was over too soon, the entire thing frenetic, like the magnetic field of the distant aurora had crashed them together.

Once wasn't nearly enough, and he flipped them over, this time taking his time, absorbing every sound, every breath until he couldn't hold himself up any longer. He rolled to his side, taking her with him, as if letting go would mean she would vanish from his touch. They curled around one another, arms and legs twisting to find comfortable positions, and fell asleep with no words. Nothing but an overwhelming sense that something, just one thing, had been set to rights.

CHAPTER TWENTY-SEVEN
KAHRIN

A soft knock on the door woke them the next morning, the sun having already risen and proudly lighting the whole room. Kahrin stirred, but gripped ahold of Innes' warm body, afraid she'd dreamed everything that happened the night before. Everything following Tippy and Paul Quirke's driveway wiped that bizarre dinner away from her mind. As long as she didn't move, didn't open her eyes, the only thing that existed in reality was Innes, her, and the life they were choosing. The clashing of bodies felt familiar, safe, and all new at the same time.

The knock repeated, harder this time, and Kahrin realized she'd forgotten to see if it was real.

"Hey, lovebirds," Ena's voice, all too knowing, called to them through the hollow wood door. "Don't rush on my account, but Noko thought you might like to know that Brother Whiteloon is on his way back."

Right. Brother Whiteloon, the whole reason they'd come up here anyhow. The reason they were in this bed and not back in their townhouses. Because Da was sick, and they needed to know why.

"Also, breakfast is getting cold."

Kahrin groaned, but tickled Innes awake, her fingers lingering over the faint scars that marked him. The crescent of a bite at his throat, the shining remains of the writing on his arm. She swallowed, resolving to put an end to this. She'd have skipped breakfast to get on with it if they didn't have their goal in sight.

"Hey you," he murmured just before stealing a closed-mouth kiss to defend her against morning breath. "Still here, I see."

"Only just." She grinned, showing her eyeteeth. "Cold bacon is still bacon, but we both know it's better warm."

She rolled out of the bed before he could launch a tickle assault and jogged in place to wake her body up. She bounced on her toes, hoping it shook away the feeling of wanting to slide right back into the bed and ignore the world around them.

But they'd dallied all she could justify, considering Da's condition. If Brother Whiteloon would be available to confront soon, they needed to be ready.

She stretched, relishing the after-effects that lingered in her muscles and left her suddenly unsatisfied again. She couldn't wait to get to a place where they had more privacy, like their townhouses. Though, as she showered, she remembered the conversation from the night before, the possibility that maybe she could try a new adventure here. She wished she was the kind of person who made pro and con lists, because that might help her narrow down what seemed to be holding her back.

Maybe meeting Brother Whiteloon would send her running back to the city and hating everyone here. That was always a possibility you risked with Kahrin B. Quirke.

She made it to the table first, though Innes wasn't far behind her since he was quick with his showers. At least when he was alone. The bacon was cold, but the coffee was strong, and she didn't complain as he came out and pecked a kiss to her lips before greeting Ena and her noko.

Noko McKenzie grinned over the brim of her mug. Kahrin knew Innes would be flushing to the collar of his shirt before she even asked, "How did you two sleep?"

He almost choked on his bacon, and Kahrin laughed, wondering if he really thought they'd been that sneaky and quiet. She was not a quiet person, at least not without something in her mouth. She stuffed half a long john in her mouth to prove the point he didn't even know she was making.

After three glasses of orange juice, Ena announced they would be off to Bonnie Boushay's to meet Brother Whiteloon. They trekked through the woods again, and at about the two-thirds mark Innes turned on a heel and frowned into the trees.

"I know you're there."

This time when Charon trotted out of the woods he looked like a mangy, black corgi mutt mix. His tail beat against the snow as he gave them all an indifferent look. "I wasn't hiding, Believer."

"I have a name."

"And you had best hope I do not use it anytime soon."

"What does that mean?" Kahrin demanded.

"Think of it like a reservation for an exclusive tour. One way." He leaned his head, batting at his floppy ear with a rear foot. "You're meeting with the Medicine Man today, then."

Ena tilted her head, a brow lifting. "And what business is it of yours?"

"When one Hole is around, all of magic keeps an eye on you. But two? That's unheard of."

Kahrin's eyes met Ena's dark ones. Both women with a single glance communicated that they knew that for true. Both of them should have been drowned in infancy.

She shook the thought from her head same as Charon shook large fluffy flakes from his scraggly coat. "Are we sure Brother Whiteloon is not an Adept?"

"Yes." That was Ena.

"Yes," Charon said at the same time, which earned him a look from Ena.

Bonnie Boushay waved from the window to them.

"He always stops here for coffee on weekends," Ena explained. "It's a little ritual of sorts, ever since Senior walked on."

Kahrin nodded and took a deep breath that lifted her shoulders near her ears. She let it out with a huff. Oh, how it would be nice if she could walk into a house and just have something be familiar, not have to introduce herself to anyone and relay her entire family line as she went.

"What are you waiting for?" Charon flapped his tail against the frozen ground in the rhythm of someone tapping an impatient foot. "This is why you're here, is it not?"

"Don't rush me." A spark of temper warmed her out of her navel-gazing.

"Someone has to. Time is not infinite, Hole. We have work to do."

She did not like the way that sounded. Or that the dog was talking to her directly. "Stop calling me that," she growled. Her irritation had to go somewhere, and the weird demon-death-not-dog was as good a target as any, she supposed.

They found an aged man at Bonnie's round table, well into his seventies, she was sure. It was difficult to tell, the way his face was weather worn with deep fallows creasing his eyes. His eyebrows stood in a storm cloud grey disarray above thin, fading brown eyes. His aquiline nose was just a little crooked, the apple of his throat and cheeks prominent against his gaunt face. Still, with his grey hair thinning and pulled back, and a bolo tie with a buttoned shirt, he had an austerity to him that age would not diminish. Well, being old wasn't going to save him from Kahrin if he was the one hurting her da and Innes.

"Boozhoo, boozhoo," he greeted them with the warmth of close acquaintances.

Ena circled the table and left a peck on his cheek. "Good morning, Uncle." She introduced them, her face back to that saccharine pleasantness that seemed permanently etched there when other people were around. The affection between them was obvious, and Kahrin hoped that Ena could be objective if this was truly the answer to their quandary. "Would it be alright with you if they asked you some questions? I know you've just come home from camp."

"All the way here to see me?" It was phrased as a question, but from the way his eyes fell on her, Kahrin knew it wasn't. Did he know they were coming? If he was the one summoning her via flesh messages, it made sense. Honestly, she didn't know anymore. "I suppose I could make time for the daughter of my best student."

Kahrin nearly flinched but kept her eyes on him. Of course Bonnie would have told him who she was. Still, it unsettled her, and she gripped Innes' hand under the table.

"Thank you," Ena murmured. She set a small red pouch tied off with rough string in front of him. "For your time, then."

He didn't touch it, and Kahrin didn't ask what it was. She was just grateful for whatever Ena had done to make this go faster. The sooner they got their answers and made him stop whatever he was doing, they could get on their way to helping Da.

"Bonnie." Ena rubbed at her belly as Bonnie set mugs of coffee on the table. "This child is restless. Would you mind walking with me to see if I can get some peace?"

Bonnie seemed to take it for the hint it was. Of course, Ena was about as subtle as Kahrin herself, which was not unlike tossing a brick with a note through a storm window to get someone's attention. Whatever worked. The two of them left Kahrin and Innes with this Brother Whiteloon in privacy, which was what they needed.

"Iskandar Boushay's daughter," he said, once they were alone.

"Quirke. His last name is Quirke," Kahrin corrected. She was tired of this thing everyone did where they implied they knew her da better than she did.

Though, given why they were here, maybe it was true.

"So, I'm here," she stated plainly. "You can stop with the invites."

"Kahrin!" Oh, come on. Innes was not surprised that she didn't dance around the point, right? Why would she waste time with niceties when this man was hurting him and Da?

"What are you talking about?" He didn't raise his voice, he didn't even sound offended by the accusations. Only inquisitive.

"I know you're making my Da sick because he didn't kill me, and you're hurting Innes to get me here. I'm here to stop you." She focused her glare, trying to make it as cool as possible despite the tremor of fear working its way up her esophagus.

"I have not seen your father in almost twenty-five years. I don't even know where he is." He drummed thick, dark-stained fingers on the table. "How could I have possibly done this?"

Kahrin blinked. After going to all the trouble to get her here, he was going to play stupid? "Funny how magic works. I know you know what I am, and I know you want me dead, and you're punishing him for not—"

"Young lady, I have no idea what you are talking about. Why would I want you dead?" Still with that even tone, so aggravatingly like Da. Which actually made some things about Da make sense.

"Kahrin, maybe he's telling the truth." Innes didn't try keeping his voice low when he spoke. He knew it had not occurred to her that Brother Whiteloon wouldn't be the solution.

"No." She made less effort to keep her voice down. "How? Da said he's the one who sent the fireball spirit! Why are you defending him after what he's done to you?"

"I just think we—"

"Cinkwun a'bak. Yes. I sent the fireball spirit." His words stopped their impending row and gained him their attention.

Kahrin lifted her hands, shaking her head in short motions in a demand for explanation. Beneath the table, Innes rested a hand on her knee, giving it a gentle squeeze as if to remind her to keep her cool.

"The spirits spoke to me and told me of the danger born into the world." He shook his head, his eyes glazing over as he recalled the memory. "I did my duty to find it."

"Me. You sent it to find me."

"Ah." He nodded as if his head was encased in gelatin, and it required something of an effort. "I thought, when I found Ena, that the danger was no more." His eyes blinked several times as he inspected her face. He reached out a hand, and when he touched beneath her chin with his fingers, she didn't pull away. "I had no way of knowing there were two. It's unheard of."

"Yeah, I keep hearing that." She shook her head, freeing her chin. "If you're not an Adept, why did Da run from you? Are you some kind of magical creature?"

This provoked a harrumph of laughter. "I am no Adept, nor am I of the world of magic." He gave her a wry look. "Not all of us Ind'ns have magic, you know. Some of us merely listen when the manidoo speak." Kahrin flushed, realizing the assumption it sounded like she made. Oops. "So, Iskandar is an Adept." He shook his head nearly imperceptibly as he stroked his chin. "And that's why he left? I thought it was because he was besotted with the white girl he got pregnant." Another chuckle. "He never could resist a pretty face. Considering he's chosen to use her name; he did not wish to be found."

Between Ma's creepy mother and Da's hidden magical powers, it was no wonder.

Brother Whiteloon sighed. "I wish I had answers for you, but I am not the one attacking your family." A twinge of regret shone in his aging eyes. "I loved him like my own son. I would have protected him, as he protected you."

Innes held his arm out and pushed up his sleeve, revealing the faint scarring which was all that remained of the magical assault. Even that was nearly healed. "Would you know anyone capable of this?" A quick flush colored his handsome features. "I didn't do this to myself, sir."

Brother Whiteloon took a pair of glasses from his shirt pocket and balanced them on his prominent nose. He leaned forward, inspecting the scars, then gestured for permission to touch them. Innes consented with an "Mm-hmm." Brother Whiteloon's fingers skimmed over the barely raised skin, a frown pulling at his sagging face. "How long ago did this happen?"

"A few days, sir."

If this surprised the Medicine Man, he revealed nothing in his expression. "It's healed very well, considering." He looked up, regarding Innes with a hard expression. "You are also an Adept?"

Innes shook his head, and Kahrin looked at him, wondering. "No, sir," he answered. Such manners! "I've been referred to as a True Believer."

A soft pang of jealousy still chilled in the bottom of her stomach when she thought of Yelena, whose affection for him had clearly changed him in ways they still didn't fully understand. She hadn't considered that the mark on his jaw where no hair grew might have given him a magical ability, however passive it was. She pushed that feeling deep down and locked it away, knowing that even though there was no competing with a unicorn, she did not need to. It was foolish to feel jealous after all this time.

They never did find out what it meant to be a True Believer. The fact was Kahrin would probably never know, not unless Innes figured it out for himself. She'd never be able to share the part of him that was now magical, just like she'd never be able to share Da's gift with him.

"A True Believer." Brother Whiteloon shook his head, eyes turning wistful. "I never thought I'd see another one." He patted Innes' arm, to let him know the exam was over. "Fortunate for you, it appears the healing gift is doing its job."

"What?!" Kahrin couldn't help herself. Her mind could be considered officially blown. The top of her head miraculously intact, she asked, "Do you mean that Yelena is still protecting him?"

"I don't know who Yelena is," and he didn't press the point, "but that is exactly what I am saying." He looked to Kahrin, the fondness of sharing knowledge shining bright in his face despite the crappy topic. "Perhaps you've had the key to helping Iskandar after all. Come and visit me before you leave, and I will send sacred medicine with you. It will help."

"Thank you." Her chair squealed on the floor as she pushed it back abruptly and hopped up. She pecked a kiss to his cheek as Ena had done. "I'm sorry for accusing you, but I'm glad we found you."

"I've been right here." He took one of her tiny hands in his much larger ones. "You have family here, should you want it, Makoons." She blinked at the use of Da's nickname for her. She pulled her hands back and stepped out of Brother Whiteloon's reach. Who did he think he was? "Only you can decide to accept it, but you may find something you're looking for here."

"And what? Pick up Da's studies where he left off?"

Brother Whiteloon lifted and dropped a hand. "If that is what is meant for you, then I would not say no."

Kahrin pressed her lips together, too many things spinning about her head for her to really express anything on her face. "Who else would know about a Hole in the World? Someone went to a lot of trouble to get me to come here. Someone knows what I am."

"It's hard to say. If we find them at birth, they are often drowned or smothered. Sometimes the parents do not even know what they have." He shrugged and took a sip of his cooling coffee. "The church keeps local records of births, deaths, and baptisms. If a child died, you might find the name there. It's not much, but it's a start."

"It's something. We could use something right now."

The knock of boots against the storm door frame announced Ena's return even before she called, "We're back!"

Kahrin smiled, the skin of her lips aching as it pulled into a tight line. "Thank you again, Brother Whiteloon."

He nodded, understanding their talk was at an end. "Come and see me again. Perhaps at the potluck tonight."

"Perhaps." She wasn't making any promises.

CHAPTER TWENTY-EIGHT
INNES

"I could have told you it wasn't him," Charon said, his little legs working hard to keep up with them as Kahrin set the pace with her furious stomps. Innes was in no mood to slow for him.

"And yet, you didn't." Ena scolded their unwanted companion, who didn't even have the decency to appear sorry.

Kahrin spun about and stepped in front of the dog but not really a dog. Charon skidded to a halt, his feet and claws making furrows in the snow before he backtracked several steps. "Why didn't you tell us?"

Innes watched his best friend put together pieces of the moment like a wooden puzzle for toddlers. She stepped forward again, and Charon back in equal distance.

"It's not my place."

His glib demeanor did nothing to placate Kahrin's bubbling anger, which was in a state of flux since they learned Brother Whiteloon was not the culprit of their troubles. Innes could sense it like one might sense lightning about to strike.

She stamped her foot and moved forward, taking some sadistic pleasure in watching Charon scamper backward once more. "What is your place, then?"

"I'm a guide." He blinked again and stopped ceding ground, calling her bluff to cause him harm when she suspected he knew something. "I guide. I'm not allowed to interfere."

"Enough!" The words startled Innes by tearing his throat raw, and it took the breath from the furthest reaches of his lungs. "Stop being cryptic. People are dying, I'm literally being carved up, and all we are finding are dead ends and weird dogs."

"Not a dog," Charon reminded him.

He could feel the heat reddening his face, and even Kahrin went wide-eyed at his outburst. Her shock did not stymie him, however. "That's right. You're a magical thing. And all that seems to follow magical things is our lives getting torn apart at every turn. I'm tired of it. I'm tired of always looking over my shoulder or having my skin split open. Magic was supposed to be this wonderful thing."

"Innes." Kahrin reached for his hand. He jerked away in reflex, immediately flinching at the obvious hurt in her expression. He moved toward her, and she folded her arms in on herself.

"Like all things, magic is not good or bad," Charon explained in the manner that a professor might a mathematical concept that was second nature to her but which she was unable to break down to those new to it. Bored. Indifferent to his disappointment. Apathetic to his outrage. "It's the whole world around us, woven into," he glanced between Kahrin and Ena, "almost everything in existence. It's the threads of creation. It's a tool for beings who are good or bad in their intention. And yelling at me will not change the consequences of your naïveté. Now, we can continue with this exercise in futility, or we can move along."

Innes tore his hands through his hair, not caring that it went askew. "And then what? What do we move along to, Trickster? More false hopes? More ruined plans? More proof that every time I get two steps forward, magic drags me three back and undoes all my plans."

This time it was Kahrin who flinched. Her fingers curled over her lips and pain iced her eyes. That stopped his rant in its tracks, and he looked at her, brow pinched in confusion trying to track backward through his words to the offense that put the look there.

"You said this was a choice. That I'm not an obligation."

"That's not what I meant."

"Isn't it?" She looked down at her gloved hands, palms turned skyward. "You're here with me because Da is sick." Her eyes searched his.

"No, I'm choosing to be here." Where did she get that out of what he said?

"It's no choice if you feel pulled back into it, though. Magic decided we're safer together, so you really can't leave me when things are like this, can you?"

"That's not—"

"I can't talk about your crisis of conscience right now. We have to figure out who's hurting you and Da."

"Quirke," said Charon.

Kahrin whirled around, tears shining in her eyes and Innes could swear he felt the air itself tremble. Snow shook free of the branches above them. "I said not right now."

Charon rolled his eyes, an impressive feat in the form of a dog. He looked to Ena to help him.

Ena's mouth puckered, expressing exactly what she thought of Charon dragging her into this. "He means the Quirke family. Paul and Tippy."

Innes frowned, his heart feeling too big to be beating in his chest. He didn't want to leave this fight in limbo, but he needed to respect the boundary Kahrin placed between them. "What do they have to do with this?"

Charon began walking, bouncing with every step of his short legs. "Guide, not answer guy."

"That's bullshit and you know it," Kahrin muttered. Still, she followed him, giving Innes and Ena no choice but to fall in behind them.

"Innes." He'd nearly forgotten Ena there until she grasped his arm. "It's in her nature to feel unsteady in the world. She and I, we're not really part of it. We don't fit, and chaos rules our hearts." Her other hand rubbed over the lower slope of her belly. A flit of confusion touched her face and was gone the next moment.

Soon-to-be Med Student Innes pushed away all the other worries, his focus narrowing down to Ena's sudden quiet. "Are you okay? We've been out awhile now. Maybe we should get you home to rest."

Her bright smile returned, making her dark eyes dance. "I'm fine, I promise. We have work to do, and a potluck to get to." She gestured for them to follow Charon and Kahrin.

Something occurred to Innes just then. "Where's the baby's father?" He shook his head, as if to rid the world of the words he'd already spoken. "I'm sorry. That's very personal."

"No, it's fine." She tilted her head, making the dark curls dance away from her jawline. "Who's to say?" She shrugged as if it were a discussion on the merits of cake versus pie.

"He's not in the picture?" He'd had practice keeping pity off his face and out of his voice since he was very young.

"Like I said: chaos." She smiled, clearly unaffected by it.

What kind of man just walked away from that? Unless... "He doesn't know, then."

She shrugged again. "I'm not sure I know." With that cliffhanger, she stepped around him. "We need to catch up with them. It would be unfortunate for all the dead if she unmade Charon."

Wait, what?

He jogged after her on his long strides, his boots thud-crunching on the sun-warmed snow. "Unmade? She wouldn't— do you mean kill him?" He chuckled, slowing to walk beside her. "She's got a temper, and she's also got a slightly crooked moral compass." Chaotic. Like Captain Jack Sparrow's magic compass. "That might be beyond her."

"Not kill." Ena's breathing sounded strained as they walked back toward her house, but he didn't want to anger her, too. "At least not directly. If you fall into a hole, it's not the hole itself that kills you, is it? It's what lies on the other side that impacts if you survive the fall."

"I'm not sure I understand. Is it like a tunnel?"

"Sort of." Ena let a breath and watched the cloud of it rise, blinking against the midmorning sun. "We can't affect magic, and it can't touch us, but our existence can," she paused while trying to figure out how to explain it, "give it another place to go. Like when someone smokes a cigarette in a car with the window cracked."

"I'm still not sure I get it."

"I'm not certain I do, either." Her laugh lilted. "I've never met another one like me. Most of us don't survive because of fear of being unmade."

"Then how did you survive?" His eyes roamed up the trail ahead of them, where Kahrin stomped along, her long hair swishing behind her with each aggravated stride.

"Much like she did, I'm sure."

Innes turned that over in his head. "Brother Whiteloon."

"You are not just a pretty face, are you?" She gave a single nod. "The same."

"Is he your father?"

"You are very obsessed with fathers." She tilted her chin to meet his eyes.

"And you are dodging my question." His lips pulled into a smile, Ena somehow easing the tension that wound through his muscles knowing he'd hurt Kahrin.

She jerked her chin ahead. "She will forgive you, no matter what you choose. We can't survive in the world without our True Believer." Her sigh bubbled out as a sort of laugh. "Not for long, anyway."

"You heard that, did you?" Charon knew too much, and Innes did not like him naming him so openly.

"You bear the mark of a pure immortal." She pointed with her forehead to the place on his jaw where Yelena's kiss prevented his facial hair from growing. "Surely you did not think you were the only one."

"So, who marked Brother Whiteloon?"

"Smart man." Her eyes crinkled as she slowed so they could finish talking before reaching Ena's yard and the others. "When we get back tonight, perhaps Noko will tell you the story of the Thunderbird while we boil sugar. She'll probably make you haul more wood, though."

What else was he going to do? Especially if Kahrin was still angry. "It sounds like we're having a story night. The Holes in the World and their True Believers." He tilted his head and asked, "After the potluck? For a town where not much happens, you sure keep a busy schedule."

"It's our way. Makes the winter pass faster."

As it turned out, Charon was referring to the fact that the Quirkes were waiting at Ena's house when they returned, where he was conveniently absent. Tippy stepped out of the Quirke Farms truck with a fancy basket covered with a towel. Kahrin crossed her arms and looked at the woman, and Innes wondered at the gall that brought them here.

"I feel terribly about how dinner ended the other night." Tippy looked to her son, as if this was not entirely her idea, and stepped forward with the basket in her hands. "I come with an offering of peace. I lost my daughter. It would be terrible to lose you from my life as well. The Lord works in mysterious ways."

Innes stepped behind Kahrin, peering over her shoulder as she moved the towel aside to reveal the contents of the basket. Several tall jars of fruit stewed in a dark liquid.

"Pears?" Kahrin asked. "Spiced, stewed pears?"

Her favorite. And, likely, the recipe she liked best if Innes wagered a guess.

"These were my Grainne's favorite. I took a chance." She sighed, as if her age weighed a pound per year upon her shoulders. "I would make them for her when we would quarrel. Such a headstrong girl." Tippy reached her hand out and tipped Kahrin's chin up. "I see so much of her in you. I'm very old, and it's hard to change my ways."

Innes took the basket and hooked it over his arm. He had a suspicion that Kahrin was going to want hers free.

"You have to try harder," Kahrin said, no room for argument in her words. "I love my da. My ma loves my da. He holds our family together. If you can't accept him, you can't have me."

Something crossed Tippy's face, something he didn't know how to read on this woman. Unlike her son, Tippy didn't have the same warmth in her eyes as Ma Quirke. Perhaps it was acceptance. Perhaps it was a realization of futility of arguing with someone so like her daughter.

"We'd love to take you to dinner." Paul sounded more insistent than seemed appropriate.

"We have plans," he told them.

"We don't know how long we have with you. Please cancel."

Kahrin shook her head, her mind made up before they even asked. "I'm sorry. My answer is no."

Tippy threw her hands up and turned to the truck. "I don't know why I try."

Paul rubbed at the space between his eyes. "She will get over it. Enjoy the pears. Enjoy your plans. Please say you'll visit us tomorrow."

"Actually," Kahrin started, to Innes' surprise, "we'd love it if you took us up to the church."

"Whatever for, dear?" Tippy turned about. "I'd be happy to take you."

"I need to look up some records is all."

"Family records," Innes supplied. Why? He wasn't sure, but it seemed like a moment to be less than forthcoming with information. He was getting an uneasy feeling again.

"Wonderful. Then we can look in my family Bible, too," Tippy added. She reached out for Kahrin, who accepted the hug, in a surprise to everyone.

CHAPTER TWENTY-NINE
INNES

He watched Kahrin plunk the basket of pears down on the table at the community center, as if she'd planned it the whole time, and was happy to give away her favorite treat. Ostensibly, her favorite treat. They wouldn't know without cracking one open if they held a candle to Ma's pears, though they'd never been Innes' favorite dessert. He wouldn't be the best judge.

Unsure what he expected, it was certainly not everyone running to hug him hello, to brush kisses of greeting on Kahrin's cheeks, and overwhelm them with a barrage of joy and fuss. Patty and Budge Parker introduced their son, who turned out to be James from the fishery. Brother Whiteloon sat at the front, leading a group of children in song with a guitar, in a mellow voice and words Innes assumed were the Ojibwe language. Ena ushered several Elders through the food line, filling their plates for them, before joining Brother Whiteloon at the front of the room. She danced with the children, surprisingly light on her feet, as their parents rounded them up to settle them with plates of their own.

Despite the din, and how crowded the hall was, it was nice. Innes and Kahrin crammed at the end of a long banquet table, sharing a single plate. He noticed Kahrin's pears went untouched.

An older woman named Amelia remembered Da Quirke and told them a story about how he had the worst colic and kept half the neighborhood awake with his wails for at least a month of his life. Another uncle talked about how Iskandar was an incredible fancy dancer, and how it fed into his near arrogance in his teen years.

"He was not!" Kahrin laughed, the thought of her Da being very full of himself incongruous with the man she'd grown up knowing.

"It's true. It's how he snagged your ma. She was way out of his weight class."

"Everyone wants to be looked at the way Iskandar looked at Grainne Quirke." Amelia touched Kahrin's hand. "Are they still in love?"

"Yes, and it's disgusting," Kahrin assured them.

They were, very much, and had always been as long as Innes could remember. He had to wonder what life would be like should one half of them no longer be in the world. He had to believe the other would go on, for he'd known them too long to believe either would fall apart, but he couldn't imagine they'd ever be whole again without the other.

He squeezed Kahrin's hand, glad their quarrel from earlier seemed forgotten.

Kahrin was summoned to talk with Brother Whiteloon more while he ate, and Ena plopped down in her chair beside Innes, looking flushed and happy and full of life, no pun intended. "He's fond of her."

"Who?"

"Brother Whiteloon, of Kahrin. He'd be a good teacher for her."

"A teacher?"

"A mentor. He could teach her ancient medicine. He could teach her our history. He could teach her how to control her chaos, and not let her emotions rule creation."

"Well, that's a tall order," Innes chuckled. "She's got emotions to fill someone twice her size, and a temper that is proportionate to her."

"And what better way for her to spend the time while you are away?" Ena touched his hand and leaned forward to share a secret. She was close, but it wasn't inappropriate in its intimacy. "Neither of you has to surrender what you want for the other." She shrugged and sat back, rubbing her belly. "And Daisy tells me that you've agreed to intern here at IHS."

"No, she didn't," he laughed.

"She didn't," Ena confessed, "but that gleam in your eyes says you thought about it."

"I did. But it's too soon to make any decisions."

"Perhaps."

"Where's your noko?" he asked.

"She went home to start the fires for the sugar boil. If you're here long enough, maybe you'll have some fresh syrup to take home with you."

"That man really doesn't know how to take a no." Kahrin stood with her hands on the back of Innes' chair, and he suspected if it were socially acceptable to pee on him, she would, the way she looked at Ena and any other girl who entered his periphery.

She didn't have to worry. He grasped one of her hands and kissed it.

"He sees something in you," Ena said.

"Yeah, my father. And I'm not him."

Ena let that go but stood and indicated it was time for them to get back to Noko's house.

An hour later they actually made it. Apparently, that was an "Ind'n goodbye," making rounds and rounds of farewells until you got close enough to the door to slip out unnoticed.

He had no idea what he expected boiling sugar to look like, but the massive metal barrel stood on cinder blocks over a fire was not it. Noko McKenzie stirred it with a large wooden paddle, and it did, indeed, stay at a boil. Ena brought out a tray of hot chocolate and set it on the patio table nearby, so they might sit around the fire. He sipped as he watched Kahrin give in to the whims of her curiosity, asking nearly endless questions about the process. Noko handed her a bough of basalt to stymie the bubbles from overflowing.

"I was serious, you know," Ena said as they watched Noko show Kahrin how to pour some of the boiled sugar onto the snow to let it cool, then wind it up with a stick to be eaten. "We could use someone like you here. It's hard for people here to trust outsiders, especially medical professionals."

"I'm not a doctor," he reminded her. Why was he always reminding people of this?

"Being trained is only a part of it. You've been here a short time, but the community likes you."

"Do they like me, or do they like that I'm with Iskandar Quirke's daughter?"

"Boushay," Ena corrected, though she had the class to look like she knew she needed to stop doing that. "And does it matter why?"

"It does to me."

"Fair enough." She smiled into her mug and shifted in her seat. "You said yourself, you have time to think on it. If she studies with Brother Whiteloon—"

"That's a very big if," he pointed out.

"If, then you two could build something needed here." She shrugged as if the next words didn't clearly bother her. "And Brother Whiteloon won't be here forever."

"Subtle." He frowned in thought. "This idea wouldn't have anything to do with my being a True Believer, and you possibly losing yours?"

"You don't have to pick apart everything I say." She giggled softly, and Noko McKenzie got a stool for Kahrin to stand on so she could stir the boiling sugar herself. "But please, do think about it. Not just for you, but for her, too."

"She is different here." He smiled, watching her laugh as the bubbles splashed upward and Noko McKenzie shared some funny story or another. "I wasn't sure it was a good different, but it could be."

"It surely could be," Ena agreed. She stayed quiet for a time. "I'm not sure she should trust the Quirkes."

"And why not?"

"Why not what?" Kahrin asked, helping herself to Innes' lap. He wrapped his arms around her and hugged her tight.

"I'm going with you to meet Paul and Tippy tomorrow." If Ena's declaration surprised Kahrin, well it did, because the surprise was all over her face.

"Why?" Realizing how accusing she sounded, Kahrin shook her head like an Etch-a-Sketch and started over. "You don't have to."

Ena smiled, but it wasn't a happy expression. "There's some answers I've been meaning to look for, too. I want to know if there's record of another like us. I need to know if being a Hole is something that can be passed on."

Innes hadn't thought of that, not since Kahrin had brought it up years ago after she'd stabbed herself to defeat Evan Greves.

"Okay. I guess we're a trio then." Kahrin looked at Innes' questioning face. "What? Not like that." She looked back at Ena. "You don't annoy me as much as you used to. It'll be nice to have you along."

CHAPTER THIRTY

KAHRIN

Kahrin knew she was overreacting to what Innes had said before, and she could even tell that she'd interpreted it wrong, but it left a dent in her armor all the same. If Innes saw their relationship as a necessity because of magic, then what did that say about their choices to have one? If he felt like magic was ruining his life, and she was ironically part of that magical world, didn't that make her part of what ruined his life?

She tried not to let it bother her further as they finished up their evening by the fire. Budge and Patty came to tend to the sugar, and after a time they moved it indoors to the stove in two massive pots. When Kahrin got up, Ena was drinking her orange juice by it in a thick bathrobe, her curls still pressed at funny angles from sleeping. Kahrin poured herself a cup of coffee, poured powdered creamer into it, and joined her new acquaintance.

"So, this is kind of an involved process, then?" Kahrin gestured to the tub, the fire, all of it.

"It shouldn't be much longer, really. We'll be able to bottle it today. Noko will have Brother Whiteloon help her while we go up to the church."

"You think they're just going to let us in to look through records like that?"

"I think that Tippy Quirke is the sort of person who can get her way. She'll gain us access to the records."

Kahrin nodded, mulling this over. "So what are you looking for, exactly?"

"Same as you. Signs that someone else like us was born in this parish and died soon after."

"Not every baby who dies will be killed by people afraid of them," Kahrin pointed out.

"True." Ena let a long yawn escape, stretching, and then rubbing her lower back. "But the dates and names might give us a trail to follow."

Kahrin leaned against the counter, letting the smell of maple fill her senses with a sort of homey warmth. She wondered if Da and Ma knew how to do this, and if they'd be interested in adding it to the farm production. In order to do that, though, they had to find out what was hurting Da, and what they wanted with her.

"Do you think Maxen might have known something?" Kahrin asked. She'd been turning it around in her head since Charon had mentioned them the day before, but dismissed it as him foretelling their being at Ena's house. "He was performing a baptism when the baby drowned."

"He wasn't a priest."

Kahrin shrugged. "Does it matter?"

Ena tipped her head in an answer. "Do you ever worry that we might pass this on?"

"Nope." Kahrin shrugged. "I'm missing the equipment."

"Oh." There was a note of pity in Ena's voice.

"It was by choice. I stabbed myself to save Innes and a unicorn."

"Of course."

They laughed.

"What's so funny?"

Innes came out of the spare room looking every bit his Pretty Mouth self. She could have swallowed him whole on the spot if it were appropriate to do so.

"Not having to keep secrets about things. Magic things."

"Oh, of course."

The three of them had a laugh, and Kahrin wondered when they'd turned the corner to Ena being a part of their group. Not a part like that, because Kahrin did not share, especially not her best friend, but still she'd fallen in with them so easily, even if Kahrin was still waiting for a shoe or two to fall.

Mister Chivalry Cameron insisted on driving to the church, which meant Ena sat in the front both for the space and ease of getting in and out, and to give directions. She was also more than happy to show off just what a good Native she was and translated words for Kahrin along the way.

"But if you don't know a word, you can just swing your hands around. Every 'Nish Auntie I know talks with her hands."

The church was not what Kahrin was expecting. The little one that Ma made them go to for Christmas and Easter was considered simple, but this one made it look positively modest. There was none of the pretty stained glass adorning the windows. It was a simple brick building with a bell. More like what she pictured a nunnery to be like. It looked like it had a basement, and definitely had an upper story of some type.

Inside was less dull, and the usual lush colors and materials she was used to seeing lined the floors and pews. There was a woman watering plants around the rectory.

"Can I help you?"

"We're looking for records," Ena started politely.

"For a genealogy project," Kahrin added. "My mother says I'm an Indian Princess so I'm here to prove her wrong."

Ena laughed into a hand and Innes rolled his eyes. Kahrin shrugged as if to ask him what his problem was.

"I'm afraid I can't just let you run around in the records room."

The door opened and Tippy was tapping her shoes off on the front run. "Linda!" she called across the room. She stopped at a bowl near the door, dipped her fingers, and genuflected on her way in. "I see you've met my granddaughter and her friends."

Linda raised a brow. "Oh, I didn't know."

"She's only recently come back into my life. We're hoping you'll let us look at some of the records so I can help her put together her family tree. You know," Tippy waved a hand, "grandmother things."

Linda had no qualms with that, and Kahrin was wondering if some bodysnatcher from one of the horror movies she and Innes enjoyed had taken the woman over. But she wasn't going to argue with greased wheels, and the four of them were given unsupervised access to the records.

"Where do we start?" Innes asked in a hushed whisper. It wasn't a library, for crying out loud.

"Sometime after my mother left." She wondered if Ma even knew that her father had died.

"Great. What year was that?" Ena asked.

Kahrin and Innes bickered over some quick math, her initially forgetting to account for Brecken's missing year, but not wanting to give away that secret to Tippy. The first two years of records yielded nothing, and halfway through the third, Kahrin got an idea.

"Grandma, could you help me?"

It tasted odd on Kahrin's tongue, odd like sushi and not like beer for the first time. It had the desired effect, though, and Tippy came over to where they sat at a small table with chairs.

"Of course, dear. What is it?"

It was a risk, and that risk included Tippy having another fit like she did the other night. "What year did that baby die while Grandpa was baptizing it?"

She guessed right, and Tippy's mouth went into a hard line, just for a moment. The next it was gone, and she looked more sad than angry. She pointed them to the right year, and Innes brought the box over for them to sift through.

They found it easily enough. "The baby wasn't Native," Ena noted. Which was only notable in that they couldn't say Maxen had been careless out of his racist ways that he seemed famous for, at least on the rez.

"No, just poor. It's easy to see what they wanted from us." Tippy's mouth pursed, showing feathery lines of her orangey-red lipstick around the pucker.

"So, we're not related to them. At least not on my Da's side."

"Nor mine," Ena said.

Tippy looked between the three of them. "What sort of genealogy are you looking for, exactly?"

Innes stepped in. "We want to know if there's any genetic issues that might lead to infant mortality." Kahrin saw fear in his eyes as he glanced at her, but the thespian in him made sure he only turned hopeful eyes back to Tippy Quirke. "In case we change our mind."

Oh, he was lucky she loved him and didn't want to live without him. Even as a lie, it made her skin itch over her stomach, giving her an urge to claw out the uterus that was no longer there.

"This is the only reported death around a time Maxen would have been in charge of emergencies here," Ena whispered.

Tippy's eyes narrowed ever so slightly. "I'm not sure what you are implying, dear."

"We're looking for patterns." Innes was too good at this. "Flu outbreaks, any type of illness that killed multiple people in a short time span."

"You won't find anything like that in that year." Her words were clipped, but she took a breath, as if she had a sudden case of the vapors. "But if you would like to see my family Bible, you could come out to the farm. Perhaps you could find out if this child is related to you on our side."

The three of them looked from one to the other, and Kahrin really wished she could read minds, so she knew what the other two were thinking. Instead, they seemed to be watching her, waiting to see if she would guide them.

Why were they always looking to her? Kahrin felt pulled in a dozen directions at once, and here she had family she didn't know who wanted to know her, and her da might be dying, and she'd been counting on

Innes to be the anchor holding her together, but there was that knife hanging above them over what he'd said about magic the previous day. She felt like a thread in a sweater that had caught in the agitator of the washer. Like she was coming apart and there was no way to fix or stop it short of letting her unravel and knitting her back together. She didn't want to be knit back together. Whatever that looked like when you were a person and not a soulless thing like an ugly sweater.

When Innes touched her hand because she'd been quiet much longer than seemed prudent, she grabbed his back, seeking comfort in his bistre eyes, and letting him steady her racing thoughts. "Sure. Let's go. At least we can rule it out. We can always come back here."

Kahrin drove this time, following Tippy as she drove her black luxury sedan, with tires that weren't really functional in this weather back to the farm. They slowed to let Tippy turn into the yard before Kahrin pulled up beside the other car and put the parking brake on.

"So, we're here."

"Shall we all go in?"

"Well, I'm not going in alone," Kahrin insisted. She undid her seatbelt.

Ena nodded, unwinding her seatbelt from under her stomach when she made a pained sound, and let out a hard breath that startled them all. She rubbed her belly near her hips, face crumpled in puzzlement.

Innes' head snapped toward her like a dragon was about to snatch her away. "Are you okay?"

Ena nodded, more insistently than was necessary if she was telling the truth. "Just cramping. It's normal, and too early for anything else." She took a few deep breaths to help it pass.

"Proto-doctor Cameron is jumpy around pretty girls. Thinks they're all damsels."

Innes rolled his eyes. "You're sure? You could stay here in the car."

"I'm fine. It's passed already. Gestation is surprisingly violent to the body." She smiled, lips closed but eyes sparkling.

Innes frowned, but assented with a nod. "If it happens again, let me know." He started up the driveway without them. "I'm not a doctor yet but I know cramping isn't a good sign."

If Kahrin hadn't known his expression of pain so well she might have thought that what Innes did next was a joke. He howled in a way she'd never heard, then doubled over, clutching his middle as if he was now cramping in sympathy.

"Innes." Kahrin sprinted around the car and to his side, hitting her knees and not caring that they quickly soaked through, as she skid the last few inches on snow. She didn't have to ask if it was another magical attack. As soon as she wrapped her arms around him the pain seemed to recede, though it didn't let up entirely. He shook with the aftershock of it, and Kahrin curled forward as if wrapping her body around his head would protect him from anything and everything.

His hands came away from his stomach, smeared with blood, and a splotch of it bloomed over the front of his shirt.

"What's happened?" Ena asked as she joined Kahrin beside him. Her eyes widened as Kahrin pulled his shirt up to reveal his stomach.

"He's been stabbed!" Kahrin cried out. Or maybe surgically opened, judging how clean the wound was. A neat, wide slit. He coughed, a splatter of red dotting his pale skin and the snow around them.

Ena pulled her scarf off, pressing the green fabric to the wound and leaning to put pressure on it. "I don't understand."

Kahrin pushed up onto her knees and looked around them. "Where are you?" she screamed. She climbed to her feet, eyes casting about wildly. Stop being a coward and show yourself!"

"I assume he will heal," Tippy said to them. "If my suspicions are correct."

Kahrin whipped around to face the old woman while Ena kept pressure on Innes' wound. Without words, Ena knew to stay close to him in case the attacker came again.

"I don't agree with my son's methods, but you're here and that's what we wanted. Bring him into the barn. We don't want to make a scene out here for everyone to see." She didn't wait to see if they followed, only called over her shoulder. "Quickly. You don't want him to get too cold."

"Why are you doing this?" Kahrin asked through grinding teeth. Her hands tight in fists, she liked the odds that she could tackle this woman to the ground and even the tables again.

"If you'd just come sooner when we'd asked, we could have avoided this nastiness. Bring him inside and try not to get blood everywhere. We don't want anyone thinking we're slaughtering livestock in the front yard."

"I'm okay," Innes coughed. Already, the blood that had erupted from his mouth was dried on his face. Ena pulled her scarf away when he pushed her hand. "Look."

He was right. Though the wound still gaped, the bleeding had stopped.

Kahrin looked to Ena. "Are you doing that?"

"You know I can't."

"If you let go of me, I think it might heal faster." Shaking on wobbly limbs, he rolled until he could push up onto all fours.

"You could be attacked again," Kahrin pointed out.

"I think that's what they want." Ena gestured to the barn. "If we stay near him, he won't heal, and—"

"If you don't, I'm vulnerable." Some of the color returned to his face and the knots that had formed in Kahrin's gut eased. She'd seen his blood a few too many times, she'd seen him attacked, but this was hitting far differently.

Innes led the way, following Tippy's tracks around the pristinely plowed yard to the concrete slab that served as a doorstep to the barn. They helped him through the side door.

"I'm sorry," Kahrin said, throwing privacy to the wind. "Sorry for getting angry about what you said before. About magic."

"I'm sorry, too, but this isn't really a good time."

"Right, let's see what the bad people want. I'm sure there's room for a heart to heart in their agenda."

"Kahrin." Innes stopped her just inside, the smell of stale urine and straw assaulting her nose. "The last time someone did this, they wanted you to kill someone. Promise me you won't do it."

Kahrin shook her head. "No."

"Kahrin." His face very serious, he said, "I'm invoking unicorn."

"No," she repeated, firmly. "You are not asking me to make a choice like that again." Except that was exactly what he was asking her to do, and she wouldn't give in to it without a fight.

If he had more thoughts on it, they were interrupted by their hostess. "Come in, come in. If you insist on bleeding, do it over in the stall." She gestured to a partitioned space filled with loose straw bedding, a short stack of bales beside it. The pungent sweetness of the straw indicated it was freshly laid out.

"Oh, sure," Kahrin muttered. "We'd hate to inconvenience you by messing up your barn floor."

Their boots squeaked on the painted concrete as they made a somber processional through the dim but open barn. A slim corona of sunlight peeked around the edges of a small, vented window high in the far wall. Honestly it only added to the rather creepy atmosphere, and motes of dust swirled lazily through the light over a backdrop of weathered tools. The only other light came from a set of caged overheads that buzzed and flickered.

They found Paul seated on a large wooden spool, the kind bulk rope came on, with a bloodied towel pressed to his own middle. He looked not unlike he should have been stroking an evil mustache or an evil cat. Or an evil cat with an evil mustache.

Before they reached the scattered straw—which told Kahrin they'd planned this—Tippy grabbed Kahrin by the shoulder and turned her about to face her. Kahrin jerked away, wishing heat could actually be transferred through a glare.

"I almost believed you at that church. Almost believed you wanted to know me, to be my granddaughter. It's a pity you didn't favor my Grainne more, but you have the same lying tells." She shook her head, as if Kahrin had committed the greatest offense. "I guess that will make this easier than I expected."

"Get my mother's name out of your filthy mouth," she spat.

"Kahrin," Innes said quietly. He touched her arm with a shaking hand, the sensation grounding her. "Let's find out what they want."

"What we want?" Paul asked. He laughed, and Kahrin didn't like that he didn't sound more like a cartoon villain with a bad fake accent, and less like that warm embrace of Ma's laugh. "We wanted to be family, but my sister made that difficult."

Kahrin wanted to scream but stood, her entire body shaking. Her fists gripped white knuckle tight. She concentrated on the feel of Innes' skin against hers and breathed deeply, trying to remember that three weeks of yoga she tried, and quickly remembered why she'd chucked the mat into a dumpster after finishing her free trial at Innes' gym.

Paul looked weak, from what she guessed was his spell outside. And before.

"It was you. You're the one attacking my da, and Innes."

"My sister ran away, married an Adept, an Indian one at that, and gave birth to a Hole in the World. She didn't make it easy to find her. What your father couldn't hide, you certainly did. Someone had to get your attention."

"Gee, I can't imagine why she'd want to hide from you." Metal siding rattled somewhere just at the edge of her notice. "You had no right to attack us."

Tippy wound her fingers together, hands clasped in front of her like a child in prayer. It was completely at odds with the covered mucking boots she wore now under a heavy flannel and rubber apron. "Did she at least have you baptized?"

"Mother, this is not the time." Paul tilted his head and regarded Kahrin. "I'm not sure something like her can benefit from baptism."

"What do you want?" Innes growled, the color having returned to him as his temper joined hers on the edge. He glanced in the direction of the sliding main doors.

"Kahrin," Ena murmured, breaking her out of her rage stupor. She held out a hand. "Look at me? We have to stay calm." Kahrin blinked, not understanding. "Holes can tear under pressure. Get wider."

On the other side of her, Innes squeezed her hand until the fine bones ground together, and she breathed out, hard. The room went silent.

"You got us gussied up and here. Just tell us why." She squeezed Innes' hand back.

Paul stood. "I want you to fetch me a soul."

Wait, what?

CHAPTER THIRTY-ONE

INNES

Wait, what?

Innes stared at Kahrin's biological uncle. The same effusive energy of his sister exuded from him, charm animating his features. No wonder Innes hadn't suspected him of anything before. He almost expected to be offered pie, not a painful stomach wound.

Instead, Paul wanted a soul. Huh? How did that involve him or Kahrin? How was Ena part of it? Or was she just collateral damage at this point?

A whirl of black mist spiraled into the room, glittering like mica even in the lack of light, then coalescing until it filled in the form of a ragged, black dog in front of him.

Charon.

"I assume this was my entrance?" The indifferent trickster sat on the concrete floor and sighed.

"Must you be a dog?" Tippy groused.

"You!" Innes' jaw clenched as blood rushed to his ears and thundered. He whipped his head around to face Ena. "Did you know?"

"I swear I didn't. I told you, he is something of a trickster."

Charon grinned in that weird way dogs did, showing his teeth. The effect was always more menacing than cute. Doubly so on their would-be guide. "The Quirkes and I are of a common purpose, in a way." He rolled onto the floor, scratching his back on the scattered straw, setting Tippy into shooing him. "They want something I have; I want it out of my realm." He vanished and reappeared out of Tippy's reach and focused on her as he dragged his crotch across the floor. "They can't come get it, and I can't free it on my own."

"But," Paul pointed to Kahrin and Ena, "you can."

Innes did not like where this was going, even more than when it had gotten him carved and stabbed. "From where?"

"The Land of Souls," Ena murmured. Kahrin sucked in a breath, as if she knew the term.

"Savage rubbish." Tippy Quirke waved her hands in front of her face like she could clear it from air. "Purgatory."

Charon rolled his eyes as if it was him who should be weary of all this back and forth. "Yes, yes. Everyone has a different name for it. Purgatory. Land of Souls. The Deeper Well. The Underworld."

"The Dwelling of All Souls," Kahrin said, low and uncertain. "That's what Da called it in his stories." She narrowed her eyes, trying to pull information from somewhere in her memory.

"Whatever you want to call it, we need to get on our way to it."

"We?" Ena barked an incredulous laugh. "Why would we trust you now?"

"Well, not you." He nodded his snout at Ena. "Unless you want to surrender that child of yours." He tilted his head and sniffed the air as Ena whimpered with a cramp. "At least not yet."

"No," Ena pleaded. "Don't do this."

"I'm not a reaper, Hole. Only a guide."

Ena cried out, then doubled over the round of her stomach with a pained gasp.

"What's happening?" Kahrin, clearly thinking she was missing some magical element, looked around, bewildered. It wasn't magic, only inconvenient timing.

Innes let go of Kahrin's hand and guided Ena to the stall of straw. She let a terrible screech as he helped her lower her weight onto it. "Someone get pillows."

"Well, at least we don't have to depend on the other one," Tippy muttered as she disappeared around the far side of the stall.

Paul heaved a sigh. Clearly, the medical emergency wasn't part of his plan, but he was taking this strangely in stride. "Bring me the soul my father sent to Purgatory, and we will tend to your friend until you return."

"Why do you think she's a bargaining chip in this?" Kahrin demanded. "We barely know her."

"Kahrin?" Innes couldn't believe she would be that cold.

"I'm saying, they couldn't have counted on this." She lifted her chin and challenged Paul to argue. "I'm not a monster, I don't want her or her baby to die, but they didn't know this would happen."

"No, we didn't." He looked to Charon. "But that thing did."

Of course he did. Innes sucked air through his teeth and shot daggers with his eyes to Charon. His attention was quickly shifted as Paul reopened the wound in his arm, blood floating up like smoke from it as he wound it with power. Before he could react, the rope of power shot across the room, jarring into the still-healing wound in Innes' belly, gripping tight and giving a jarring tug that dragged him toward Paul. He could feel something being drawn out of him, or into him. A barely noticeable ebb and flow. Still weakened from the attack outside, he wheezed while trying to push through this new disorientation.

Kahrin lunged at Paul who stymied her with a palm-out hand. "Ah, ah, ah. If you hurt me, you hurt him, and vice versa."

"What?" She stopped, even her chest going stone still.

"We're connected," Innes breathed. "I can feel it."

"Indeed," Paul nodded at Innes as if it were a reward for cleverness. "We didn't know the convenience of timing of Ms. McKenzie's premature labor, but we did count that Kahrin wouldn't come without her True Believer." He smiled, as if he were capable of doting on his niece. "And imagine the delight when we realized the nature of your relationship."

"What did you do?" Kahrin now sounded on the verge of tears.

"An umbilical spell."

"What's that?" Innes suspected he knew but needed to hear Paul say it to believe it.

"An insurance policy."

Charon explained. "We assumed the Hole would not travel without the Believer. You can't go into the realm of the dead with a living soul, or you forfeit it." He laid down, resting his chin on his front paws. "The umbilical spell will anchor you to the realm of the living, guaranteeing you can return. It also guarantees Paul will not be attacked by you."

"If anyone but me breaks the spell," Paul made sure to give Kahrin a significant look, so she understood what he was saying, "we both die. If you don't value my life, my dear niece, I know you cherish his."

Even suspecting this was the case, cold rushed through Innes. He was bound to this man, Paul, who was so ruthless he was willing to kill anyone Kahrin loved to get her to do this for him. What was so important about this soul?

"How am I supposed to go in, then?" Kahrin's voice pitched in panic. "You want me to leave my soul there?"

Paul huffed as if this was the most obvious thing ever. "You really know nothing about yourself, do you?"

"Meaning?"

Innes' brows drew together as the answer snapped into place in his mind. "You're wrong."

"Wrong about what?" Kahrin's temper was warring with her panic for dominance, and Innes knew they were risking her losing control again.

Tippy returned with a stack of dusty saddle blankets and set them down as she looked around the room, distaste clear in the drawn set of her mouth. She genuflected and murmured something Innes couldn't hear before she started propping Ena into a more comfortable position.

"On your side, dear. It's better for the baby." Ena moaned as Tippy urged her to roll. Tippy glanced at her son. "We should have plenty of time, just as the mongrel told us."

"Time for what?" Ena's voice warbled as if she suspected what the answer was.

"Hush now," Tippy brushed a hand over Ena's forehead before she jerked her face away. "Getting riled up will only make this worse. We can't undo what God has decided for your bastard, but we can make the best of it."

They meant to trade the lost soul for that of Ena's still unborn baby. But something didn't add up.

"If you think a Hole has no soul, then why do you think one can be brought back from the Land of Souls?"

Paul snorted. "Even if it were possible, I'd do no such thing. There are reasons they aren't supposed to live."

"Cursed things," Tippy spat.

"What my father condemned to Purgatory was far more useful, and he was far too short-sighted to see the usefulness of sparing it." He tilted his head. "Though we wouldn't have been able to contain it as we can now."

"If Grainne hadn't run off, we could have put it in that bastard of hers." Brecken. "She thought we didn't know. A mother knows."

He and Kahrin exchanged a look. He wondered how she was still standing, learning all they were about her blood relatives—they certainly were not family—and wondering how much more she could take.

"You wanted Kahrin to get pregnant so she could carry it."

"Well, I wasn't exactly going to put her in the squeeze chute to do it," Tippy said. Kahrin pressed a hand to her own mouth. "But yes. I had hoped your lifestyle would do nature's work for us."

"Maxen Quirke was an Adept?" Kahrin's voice shook, and Innes' chest squeezed with the urge to go to her, to comfort her. To hold her against his chest and feel the fear leave her.

"Of course not!" Tippy Quirke clearly did not approve of Adepts. "He was a man of God, and he did what he was called to do. Drowning that child in the baptismal font was a blessing."

"He murdered a baby." Innes felt like he was standing in the pages of one of his darker storybooks. The kind where villains were obviously evil. Evil enough to thoughtlessly kill babies. Though he supposed that wasn't exclusively the province of fantasy stories.

"Yes, and its parents did not know what they had. But we do," Tippy said.

Paul waved a hand, deeming all of this a trifle. "It doesn't matter. I am an Adept. I want the soul back. I hold your Believer's life in my hands. That's what you should focus on."

"I'll do it." Kahrin scrubbed her hands over her face and screamed into the cups of her palms. "I'll do it. Leave my Da alone, let Innes go. I'll do it." She looked up between her fingers.

"As soon as you bring me the soul."

Tippy added, "Once we have the baby in our possession, we will all get what we want."

"How do I even get a soul out of the Underworld or whatever?"

"If I knew, I wouldn't need you, would I?" Paul said. "An abomination to magic, a stain on our family. At least you can serve a purpose. Getting the soul back is for you to figure out."

Innes knelt beside Ena, an impulse to stroke her hair from her sweaty face stopped just before he could act on it. "Hang on, okay? We're going to fix this." He didn't know how, or if it was even the truth, but part of being a hero was instilling hope in others. Even if they failed, he needed Ena to believe they would succeed. "We'll save your baby."

She nodded, and if she didn't believe him, he couldn't tell. He moved out of the way for Kahrin to crouch near her next.

"I'm sorry I yelled at you for trying to teach me things. And for calling you names."

"You didn't," Ena said with a soft, strained laugh.

"Well, not out loud, but trust me. I did." She grasped Ena's hand in her own. "I need you to teach me more things, so you have to hold on."

Ena gestured for Kahrin to lean closer that she might share something only for her. The consequences of breaking the spell kept him at a safe distance for their secret, and his own pang of jealousy twisted like an ugly knot in his stomach. She and Ena shared something he would never understand. Was this what Kahrin felt, he wondered, when she thought he would prefer to be elsewhere? Without her?

The conflict that had been tearing him in half seemed far less dire, and far more foolish. The things they wanted and needed were not at a cross purpose. But maybe he was the one holding her back?

"We need to reach the realm before the sun sets," Charon said, reminding him that the time for pondering their relationship was not now. "And it's quite a journey. Do hurry." Charon dissipated into a sparkling cloud once more, his words echoing in Innes' head.

CHAPTER THIRTY-TWO

KAHRIN

Kahrin shook, though it was anyone's guess which emotion was doing it. Anger. Terror. Grief. She felt all of it at once, in a hot tangle of agitation vying for attention. If she tried to tease it apart, she got that unsteady feeling again, and the one place she usually turned for comfort and strength when she didn't have enough of her own was unavailable.

So afraid of undoing the umbilical spell, she stayed well away from Innes as they walked down the wide driveway. The need for casual reassurances that were so foundational to their friendship, their love, made her wonder how sexual frustration over the past few days had felt unbearable. That was nothing compared to this, and she had in fact, until last night, been very, very horny.

"You can stay here." She knew Innes would never hear of it, but she suggested it anyway. "I have Charon guiding me. It's safer if you stay, and you'll heal faster."

He didn't even dignify it with a lecture or a grunt. "I don't trust Charon, and I won't trust him to bring you back."

"And I don't trust anyone not to harm you." The shaking gave way to stinging bits of glass, in the form of tears behind her eyes. "Who's to say they won't kill you as soon as I deliver it?"

For all the confidence he tried to exude, a falter cracked his face. "I thought of that."

"And?"

She saw his muscles twitch as he leaned toward her, then jammed his hands in his pockets and straightened his posture. "Kahrin, what I said earlier? About magic ruining my life?"

"I know, Pretty Mouth."

"Please, let me say it."

She nodded, noting a shine in his eyes, knowing him enough to know it meant this was important for him to get out, even though her stomach froze in glaciers of worry at what he might be about to say.

"I meant it." That was not how she'd expected him to put it. "But I think that's because my expectations were naïve. Magic seemed like a dream that would lead to something better, and when we met Yelena, I thought that meant that I had been right, and that magic would always feel, well, magical." He grunted at the impulse to reach out. "The truth is that life isn't a fairy tale. Magic isn't going to fix everything that ever hurt me in the past. Magic isn't going to hand me dreams." He shrugged. "Maybe it was just trying to get me to see that my vision was incomplete."

"How so?" she whispered. She didn't know how long they had before Charon appeared and led them on this impossible mission, and she needed this resolved before they went, wherever the damned trickster not-hare not-dog whatever was taking them.

"Because it didn't have you in it. Not— not like I've seen it could be these past few days. These past few years. I don't want a hapless maiden who needs me to rescue her. I want my best friend, who might let me, one day, because she chooses to believe I can."

"Always looking to be the hero." Her lips pressed tightly together as she breathed deeply through her nose. Snot was plugging things up as she fought the waterworks. "Even though you've always been mine."

He flushed. She grinned.

"I wasn't sure what that meant until now. Magic ruined my life plan, but it was a stupid life plan."

"Obviously, if I wasn't in it."

"You were always in it. Just, just different."

"I wish I could kiss you right now."

He chuckled, the sound low and familiar in the most enticing way. "I'm still mad we didn't make it to a hotel." His eyes darkened. "I was ready to split you in half."

Now she flushed. "Well, I won't be getting that out of my head anytime soon." The night they'd passed last night was nothing short of wonderful, but they both knew they had cravings beyond it. Things only the other could be trusted with.

"I'd settle for that kiss."

A soft 'pop' was the only warning they had that everyone's favorite haggard not-a-dog had appeared. "If you two are finished with whatever this is?"

"Shut up," they yelled in unison.

"Mortals are so testy." He trotted off, expecting them to follow. "Stay close." He looked behind him, directly to Kahrin. "Not you, Hole. Stay well away from us until you're needed."

"How are we supposed to drive anywhere if I can't touch anyone?"

With a weary sigh, Charon sat and began scratching at his ragged ear. "We are not driving, of course. You don't get to the Underworld by car."

Her nostrils flared as she thought of several ways she would be willing to try sending him to the Underworld. "My b. It's been a while since I've gone."

"Kahrin," Innes murmured. "This won't help."

Fine. She smiled, tight and tense. "Dearest Charon, how does one get to the Underworld?"

Innes rubbed at his eyes with finger and thumb. Apparently, that wasn't what he had in mind, either.

"I am trying to show you." Charon took off running on stubby legs and leapt over a snow-covered fallen tree. One moment a dog, the next a raven, wings wide and shadow almost blocking the sun ahead of them.

Charon swooped, circling around and around as if in a funnel. Beside her Innes winced at something she couldn't see or hear. He shielded his eyes, but when Kahrin looked ahead she saw only the wooded trail, and the setting sun.

"We go through that?" Innes sounded unsure, which she could relate to, on account of not being able to see whatever it was he was referring to.

"Yes." Charon turned his head to the side with the twitchy sort of movements that birds used to examine their curiosities. "Mind the step."

"What step?" Kahrin asked. Her heart felt too big for her ribs as it pounded faster and faster.

"Take my hand," Innes said, offering it before they both remembered the spell. He stepped back, thoughts flitting through his expressions as he chewed over the bone of their problem. He unwound his flannel scarf, knotting it to form a loop at both ends. "If we keep it taut, we won't touch, and we won't get separated."

"Are you sure? I mean, this isn't exactly the kind of situation where we can just go on a hunch."

He nodded. "So far, it appears you have to actually touch something to unmake it." Every word except "unmake" made sense, but she wasn't in the mood for a magical vocabulary lesson. Innes set the end on a stump and backed away until the scarf didn't give him any more room to go.

Kahrin took a breath and held it as she moved only as close as needed to slip her hand through the other loop. She exhaled her relief.

"See?" He waggled fingers at her. "Still here. Just follow me through the portal."

"There's portals now?" She tried to laugh, but not seeing whatever they were moving toward made it far less funny and left her more unsettled than a situation where she was already afraid for both of their lives already did. She swallowed. "Why not?"

"Trust me?" Innes asked.

The most needless question ever uttered by such a pretty mouth. "Of course I do."

"You understand that time is finite, yes?" Charon clacked his beak to get their attention. "We can only go through it on the 'tween. As neither of you are on the cusp of death, it must be twilight or break of dawn." He jerked a wing in the direction of the quickly setting sun. "Tick, tock."

She watched Innes' chest rise and fall before he stepped forward. She let the scarf take up the slack before she followed, but two steps later, he was gone, and she staggered. "Innes? What happened?"

"It's okay, Kahrin," he called from nowhere. "Follow the scarf."

"Follow the scarf," she muttered in echo. The fabric pulled taut, urging her forward, so forward she went. A few steps further and her foot disappeared in front of her. She nearly toppled over in surprise, though why anything surprised her anymore, she wasn't sure.

"Step down," he coaxed. "It's quite a drop, but you can do it."

"Sure, sure." With another deep breath, she pushed herself forward through whatever she couldn't see.

CHAPTER THIRTY-THREE
INNES

Sometimes Innes wondered what the world looked like through the blinders that came with Kahrin's particular existence. From where he stood in the dark, cold tunnel, she was lit with the golds and blushes of the setting sun back in the world of the living. Vibrant and alive, even with the utter terror that gripped her. Letting her stumble into the realm of the dead on her own went against all his manners, and the ingrained ways of their friendship besides. If he thought not being able to reignite their physical relationship had been unbearable until the previous night, this was much worse.

Once her eyes met his in the green glow, she gained confidence and finished her descent without further falter.

"So, this place is cheery." She reached out ahead of her, marveling at the shifting light that somehow left them in an eerie darkness. The walls around them shifted from green to pink and purple and back again. "Some curtains, a rug. Warm it right up." She turned about as much as the scarf joining them would let her. "Are we in the aurora?"

He'd not thought of that, but he looked around with that in his mind.

A loud caw warned them to duck as Charon soared through the opening, pulling it closed like a drawstring purse behind him. "How else would you get to the Land of Souls, Ojibwe?"

Here they stood, sealed into the realm of the dead, the Dwelling of All Souls, as Kahrin referred to it. Hopefully that was not the last they would see of the sun.

Charon landed on the floor and unfurled, rising like an umbrella opening until he stood tall. He didn't exactly have a form, but what Innes could see was largely anthropomorphic. There were no defining features, no stereotypical markers of gender in any variant. Even his face didn't seem to settle in shape, resembling both skull and plague doctor mask at once, and yet neither of those things seemed to be right. A glittering black cloud with two deep holes of nothing stared blankly at them.

"That's better." Charon shuddered himself out like a sheet on a line snapping in a breeze. "Shall we walk?"

Innes and Kahrin gazed around the room, what he thought were walls before, were more of the mica cloud, glittering to a chilling and breathtaking effect all around them. What he didn't see was any discernible path.

"Where?" Kahrin asked his question for him.

Charon waved an arm-like appendage and a trail appeared before them, the walls of variegated light towering into infinity. "This way." He looked to Kahrin. "Have care, Hole. You are unseen here, but you will destroy anything you touch."

"I get it. No fingerprints on the walls. Can we get this over with?"

Charon led the way, the cavern widening enough for Innes and Kahrin to walk abreast with the scarf stretched between them to remind them to keep distance. The road ahead of them seemed to wind, but it never felt as if they were turning. Rather, the path moved to accommodate their steps, even as it sloped sharply up or downward.

He gripped the fabric between them, relying on it to sate the need to curl Kahrin's fingers with his own, if only to have something solid beside him. The light tug back served as a mockery of the squeeze of her hand back in his. But it was what they had.

"What did Paul mean back there?" she asked.

"Paul." His stomach dropped. He'd hoped her often flighty attention span would have left that bit behind all the other thoughts that had to be zipping around in her mind. He knew better than to underestimate her curiosity. "He thinks you don't have a soul. So, you can't trade one, or lose one."

"I'm sorry, but huh?" She looked to Charon as if he were going to provide her insight.

"Do you understand what a hole is, Hole?" Charon sighed, shifting the chilled air around them. "An empty space. Things can pass through it, but there is nothing to disrupt it. There's nothing in it. It's hollowed. A nothing carved out where something should have been."

"What does that have to do with anything?" she asked.

"If you're an empty, vacant space, there's nothing connecting you to anything. No spirit can touch you. No cosmic connection. No magical tether."

"So, I'm not even a real person? Is that what you're saying?"

"Yes," said Charon even as Innes shouted, "No!"

"Of course you're a person." It hurt even having to say it. It hurt that they had to be here, in a situation that made her doubt even her own humanity.

"Were you even listening?" Charon grumbled, the sound vibrating in Innes' chest. Combined with the persistent tugging of the umbilical spell, the discomfort was becoming nauseating every step they took.

"You can't know that." The tendons of Innes' jaw tightened.

"You're right. I am unfamiliar with the dealings of souls." He gestured his vague shape around them vaguely. "Having no experience."

"You can't even touch her. How would you know what she is?"

"Stop talking about me like I'm not here." A tremble in her words shattered his heart.

"I'm sorry," he whispered, his impotence to comfort her fueling an already short temper.

"On the bright side," Charon added, "you will not be making any Faustian deals."

"Great silver lining there." With one arm anchored to Innes by the scarf, she could only wrap the other around herself as she curled inward.

He couldn't, wouldn't believe that what Charon and Paul thought was true. Of course Kahrin had a soul. No one could be driven by such passions as she was without one. She liked to think she flitted from one thing to the next, because she liked being unsettled. In reality, she barreled between points with purpose. Kahrin saw what she wanted and chased it, even if she found she didn't want it as soon as she caught it. Yes, his best friend might be chaos incarnate, but that didn't mean she had no soul. Did it?

Of course not. And he wasn't going to let her spend a moment thinking she was anything but a whole person.

"You have a soul." He said it with enough finality that he hoped it stuck.

They continued in a stiff silence after that, only the faint wind-like sound in the distance and all around them. They walked for what could have been minutes or hours, or maybe it was simply the passing of a heartbeat as the sound grew louder, and the ground beneath them sloped. The path in front of them opened wide into another room, and Charon stopped them with a wave of a wispy appendage.

"You're joking," Kahrin said. "Is that an actual river? Of the dead?"

"Not exactly," Charon explained. "It's a barrier, rather."

Innes opened his mouth to explain further, but she beat him to it. "Spirits won't cross moving water."

For the first time since all of this started, Innes beamed. The knowledge gained over their misadventures stuck with her and solidified the stories they'd read together. She didn't need things fed to her as often as she thought, but Kahrin did often dismiss her own intelligence. A blessing really. For her.

Maybe for him, as well.

"You'll need to stay here, Believer."

"Wait, what?" Kahrin stomped toward Charon, yanking the scarf tight and making the tattered ends of what looked like his robes scatter. "What do you mean he has to stay here? That wasn't the deal. I'm not leaving him alone here."

"Why will you not listen to me?" Charon turned his hollowed nothing eyes to her. "He has a living soul. The tether to Paul will only do so much. If the other souls see him, they will grasp ahold, and keep him. Do you want him stranded on the other side of the river?"

Innes heard Kahrin swallow and could feel her determination to keep control of this situation as much as possible. Her eyes shone in the glow of the aurora as they met his. "I can't leave you here."

"I can't go with you." Just saying it was like a kick that knocked the air from his chest. He smiled all the same and added, "I'll be fine. Right here." He unwound the scarf from around his wrist and let his end drop to the ground. "Wrap it around you. Pretend it's my hug."

She laughed, tears cracking through it. "It feels like good-bye."

He grinned, giving as much reassurance as he could. "It's not. Our story isn't done, Kahrin. Now, you have a soul to steal."

"Okay, Charlie Daniels."

"You know, the Devil really did win that match." He had better backup. Naturally, she conceded. No one could deny that.

She blinked, a dawning on her face. She spun about as she wrapped his scarf loosely around her. "How do I even catch a soul? Paul said I have to figure it out, but obviously I don't know how any of this works." She knew more than she realized, but this was not the moment to interject. "If I can't touch a soul without destroying it, then how?"

"You'll need a vessel. And a way to hide it."

Her face wrinkled with an annoyed confusion. "Sure. I forgot my vessel at the house of horrors back there. Anyone got a spare?"

"Wait," Innes said. "If Ena can carry a baby, does that mean you could, you know," he motioned with two fingers toward his mouth to indicate swallowing. When she looked at him blankly, he nearly choked. He knew damned well that she knew how to swallow things.

"You want me to eat a soul? I don't think that's how it works."

"It could work with a barrier between you, but you can't touch it, and eating it would definitely count." Charon, helpful as always.

But Kahrin's face lit up. "But you can!"

With the tone of the truly aggrieved, Charon explained, "If I could bring a soul out of this realm myself, do you think I would risk bringing you here?"

She turned to Innes. "Give me a condom." She held her palm out flat in front of her. "The one in your wallet."

He frowned, trying not to groan. "You know I don't keep them in my wallet. It could damage them."

"If you keep them a long time, yes. I put a plum flavored one in there at the clinic." She shrugged. "I thought it would be funny."

Because of course she did. He pulled out his wallet and sure enough, slipped into the space behind his ID was a foil package.

"Probably not great for preventing pregnancy, but that's not a problem we have. I bet it's tough enough to hold a soul."

"What?"

Even Charon looked at her with whatever could pass for confusion on his shimmering, empty face.

"It works for drugs, right?" Uh, no. No, it did not. "We put the soul in, down the hatch it goes, and smuggle it out."

"That," Charon started, as if he was ready to deliver another explanation on how she did not know how being a Hole in the World worked. Which she did not, and neither did he. "That might work, Hole."

Innes flipped it clumsily through the air, and Kahrin deftly caught it mid-flight. "Good job being prepared, I guess."

Kahrin was not someone he would ever call stupid, even if she sometimes believed it of herself. There was something genius in the moment that warmed him. He grinned. "I love you."

She blinked as if she'd never heard him say it before. "I already let you in my pants, Pretty Mouth. You don't have to say that." Her nose wrinkled and he puffed a laugh. "I mean, I love you, too."

"Go," he whispered. The sooner she left, the sooner she'd be back. The sooner they could get out of the realm of the dead. But... then what? Were they going to just hand this soul over to a man with obviously ill intentions? And what did Paul want with it? He added, "Come back for me."

She turned and walked backward, smiling at him. "I'll always come back for you. Just like you would for me."

Innes wrapped his arms around himself and watched as Charon led his best friend, his lover, his partner in every way, down the slope and toward the water's edge.

Then, from behind him, Charon's ethereal voice said, "It's time for us to talk, Believer."

CHAPTER THIRTY-FOUR

KAHRIN

Kahrin shivered as the mutable tunnel enshrouded her, even as the cavern widened. A fog that stayed fluidly out of reach closed off the path of sight behind her, cutting Innes out of her view, only allowing her to see what lay ahead: the banks for the river, and as she moved closer, what first appeared to be a wall of millions of parts.

The ground rose into stairs to meet her feet as she walked downward, ripples of aurora light arcing around the room from the reflection of the water. Maybe it was downward. There was no way to tell what was up or down, or if she was moving at all rather than walking in place. Even the river seemed to move through the room like a rope, looking the same from all angles. Given that she was possibly not a real person, and for all intents and purposes did not exist in this realm, any of it could have been true.

Charon said nothing as they reached the bank, only waved an appendage, summoning a flimsy raft in front of them. He or it or whatever nodded that she should board the raft. If she couldn't touch anything, how was she to know that she could stand upon it? If she didn't exist, if she was a nothing where something should have been, did it even matter? She held a breath of nothing as even the air seemed to evade her and leaned into the weight of her lifted foot. Forward she fell, braced for the unknown, and startled as her foot hit the shaky surface of the raft.

Pushing from the shore with one of those big poles used to move boats, Charon remained quiet. The river appeared vast, infinite, though she could see across it clearly, and the trip itself seemed to only last a few speeding heartbeats. Barely an inhale and exhale of nothing. She looked upon the wall she'd spied from the other bank, which was no longer visible to her. The wall was not in fact a structure, but a crowded space flowing with mostly white puffs. They moved around and slithered over one another, occasionally leaving peeks of indiscernible colors, making them stand against the others.

They ebbed and retreated, pushing up against an invisible barrier that refused to let them cross. An endless belt of motion, those in the front retreated only to have their positions taken up by those behind them.

A wall of souls, gathered in place by walls that were the river she could now see formed a ring around them.

"How do I know which one it is?"

Charon, helpful as usual, shrugged his wispy shoulders as if to remind her that it was not his problem.

"I can't just wade through them." The knowledge that she could destroy anything she touched sent a trickle of ice down her spine. Bad enough to die, but possibly worse to have the essence of your being unmade, swept into an abyss of oblivion. It weighed upon her, sitting on her shoulders like a pile of Ma's carefully crafted quilts. A responsibility she never asked for but was helpless to refuse.

She retraced steps of the conversation, Paul's demands frightening her to a point that she may have missed a few vital details in the very few details he gave. A soul condemned by a grandfather she never knew, a holy man as opposed to a magical being. But wasn't the ritual and the workings of the faith of her mother rooted in magic? A baptism was a protection charm. A rosary a talisman, like Emilia's embroidered hanky.

Paul wanted a soul of a being who was not wanted by the trickster guide who guarded the realm of souls. This Dwelling of All Souls. In the same way she couldn't feel the bewitching of André, or the protection provided by the snowdrop hanky, then she would not be able to see a soul banished by the magic of faith.

And that's when it became obvious: a flit of nothing between the barrage of something. Where the other souls collided and pressed together, a single place remained where the others moved easily like millions of silver fish in a stream. Something that wasn't supposed to be here. Like her.

"That one." She pointed a single finger and looked to Charon. "That's the one."

So, what to do now? She tore the foil wrapper away from the condom and unrolled it. "I assume it's not just going to willingly swim in. I can't push it in, so," she dropped the rest of the thought into silence and spun about, extending her arm and offering the rubber to Charon. "But you can guide it in."

Charon heaved a sigh but did not argue. A hand morphed out of the mist that made up the demigod's body and turned palm up for her to drop it into. He moved, oscillating, shimmering shadow giving the impression of feet as he glided into the swarm.

"Further left," she called. "No, my left." Charon wove through the chain link of souls, letting her direct him to the correct one. The one that likely fought against the current of its kin, struggling to stay ahead and visible.

Featherlike fingers pulled wide the thick band of rubber at the top, and she watched the shape of the condom writhe in ways that she hoped to never witness in the living world. Then, it settled, and nothing but a slight bulge remained.

"Knot the top," she directed as Charon returned to her. He did as she asked, setting it on the floor of the cavern and backing away, to allow her room to retrieve it.

It pulsed in her hand, heavier than she expected. She couldn't help but puff a laugh through her nose at knowing, objectively, the weight of a soul.

"I'm not swallowing this," she announced, as if Charon gave a single care. The indifferent cavern around them didn't care, it didn't even know she was here.

"If you wish to take it across the river, or through the portal, you won't have any other choice." Of course Charon couldn't give her solutions! Only problems! "Once a soul is here, it is the ward of the afterlife. You would have to outsmart Death itself." He shrugged. "The only way to do that is to stay beyond Death's notice."

She huffed. "That doesn't mean I have to swallow it. I can just hold it in my mouth." Not at all excited about what was about to happen, she stuffed it into her mouth with an exaggerated motion and clamped her teeth shut. Even with the artificial plum flavoring, the latex tasted horrid against her tongue, which should not have surprised her. She resisted gagging, but only just.

They turned back to the raft, the return faster than the approach, Kahrin moving with the confidence of experience. Saliva pooled in her mouth at the tartness and bitterness of the condom, threatening to escape, and as she tried to swallow the spit down, she gagged, coughed, and nearly spat it out in the middle of the river. Overcorrecting, she gulped, and the condom disappeared down her throat.

She fell to her knees, rocking the raft until she was certain it would capsize. She shifted her weight, Charon providing a counterpoint using the pole, and they made it across. Kahrin crawled off the raft, and flopped onto the bank, staring at the green and purple, ever-moving ceiling.

"That did not go according to plan." She felt sick, and she had no idea how she was going to get the soul and hand it over to Paul soon enough to help Ena and save Innes, but at least now she didn't need to worry about how to smuggle a soul out of the Underworld.

"We should make haste." Charon floated along on the semblance of limbs that was his true form. "I am unsure what happens when one goes missing."

"You don't keep track of them?" Her brows knit together, and eyes narrowed.

Charon gestured to himself. Itself. Who knew? "Again. Guide. I'm no accountant."

She didn't need to be told twice to hurry back. The sooner she got back to Innes, the sooner they could leave, and the sooner he would be set free of the umbilical spell.

She sprinted, light on the balls of her feet over a ground that moved at her pace. The fog shrouded around her once more as she took the flowing stairs two at a time and skidded to a stop.

"Pretty Mouth," she panted. "We've got it. Let's go."

Innes, hair disheveled, let out a hard sigh. "Kahrin, we have to talk about something." He took her blinking for the question it was. "You can't give that soul to Paul."

CHAPTER THIRTY-FIVE

INNES

"It's time for us to talk, Believer."

Innes knew he wasn't going to like the topic. "Now what? What could you possibly have to say?"

"The Hole doesn't know what she's retrieving. If she knew, she might not have agreed to come at all."

"And that would ruin your perfect plan," Innes growled.

"It would certainly ruin all of yours. Are you familiar with a korrigan?"

Innes shook his head. The word didn't ring a bell.

"A korrigan is like a siren," Charon explained, his voice hovering all around as his physical form and Kahrin disappeared from view, and presumably, earshot. "But not restricted to the seas. The Uncle intends to raise it inside the body of a child to be loyal to him. The Grandmother hopes to use to control her family."

"What are you telling me?" Innes frowned, a molten flare of temper threatening to move him, to find out if you could actually punch a demigod, or at least its disembodied voice. "That this was all for nothing?"

"I wish it were that simple."

"Then we tell Kahrin to leave it here. You're still out there with her, you can stop her now."

The very cavern heaved with Charon's weary sigh. "If she doesn't come back with the soul, Paul will end your life via the spell, possibly end hers, and the other Hole's as well."

And knowing his best friend the way he did, she would not let that happen if given the power to decide. So, the soul would not be willingly left behind.

"He will not be the only one to try and claim it. They are fortunately rare, but extremely dangerous." Charon's voice circled Innes, booming from all sides and then traveling like sound in an IMAX theater, until it was in front of him. "Others will find out about the Hole's existence and will try to manipulate her into helping them gain this creature. Every trip she makes here threatens the threads of existence. The soul of the korrigan must leave this realm, and it must be now. It has to be put somewhere it can be guarded and controlled."

Innes tried to squint through the fog that cut him off from sight of Kahrin and Charon, traveling away. He was certain the fog helped Charon be in two places at once and was sure their conversation was not for Kahrin's ears. Not yet. And Charon knew it.

"She can unmake existence. How does that work?"

"The world is made of magic, is it not?"

Cold ran through him until it felt like his blood had frozen solid. "You double-crossing piece of—"

"And what choice did I have, Believer?"

"There's always a choice," he snarled through gritted teeth. "And you chose to trick me. To trick all of us. How are you any different than Paul and Tippy?"

"I couldn't have predicted the spell, but neither could I let it stop us."

Tears stung Innes' eyes, but they were not for Charon. He turned his back to their trail away from him, swallowing the full weight of what Charon was telling him. What it meant.

But as Charon said: what choice did he have? "Go do your job, trickster. Leave me alone to think about mine."

Just like that, the voice was gone, and a suffocating silence fell around him. Even his grunts and screams as he tore hands through his hair and knuckled tears out of his eyes seemed swallowed by it. No doubt the mist around him helped with that.

He crouched down, resting on his heels, and let his face drop into his lap. For a few minutes he allowed himself to weep. He let himself heave and sob over what this meant.

Had he brought this on himself? This moment of decision where he knew the right answer because it was the heroic thing to do? Had he not spent time wondering if a hero could survive a world where he had no heroic deed to perform? What he'd failed to consider in those previous moments of navel-gazing was that being a hero was often not survivable.

With everything that awaited him back in the world, he allowed an utterance of "It's not fair," before he heard sounds of Charon and Kahrin returning.

"Pretty Mouth. We've got it. Let's go."

"Kahrin, we have to talk about something." He trembled, hoping he had the strength to explain. "You can't give that soul to Paul."

CHAPTER THIRTY-SIX

INNES

"What do you mean we can't give it to him?" Denial. On the Kahrin scale of acceptance, this tended to be the longest step. "If we don't, he'll—"

"I know."

"And if we leave it here?"

"Yes." Innes shook, trying desperately not to let his mind wander past this moment. He had to take each moment at a time, or he'd never get through it.

"Releasing a korrigan into his possession will bring disaster, and not just for your family." His family. "There's no telling what it will enable him to do."

"I don't even know what a korrigan is."

"I don't think that matters. It's like a siren, can control people with its voice. The only thing we need to understand is that we can't let Paul have it."

Kahrin rounded on Charon, her voice leaping to a pitch that bounced around the walls. "You lied to me! To us!"

Anger. They were right on track.

"I do what I have to do for the safety of the world."

"I don't care about the world!" She rammed knuckles into her eyes and looked back to Innes. "I won't do it."

"Kahrin."

"How can I do that? Both together, or never ever. You promised." Tears glassed over her eyes, brimming at the lid line and snagging momentarily in her thick lashes, before trickling down her cheeks. "You made me promise, and now you want to break it."

"I know. But you have to listen to me." She shook her head, but he moved, not letting her break line of sight. "This is my choice."

"What?" She froze. "Your choice is to leave me? To leave me alone?" She shook her head, slicing her hands through the air between them, and he was sure he was being twisted in half. "You said you choose me. Chose us."

"You think I'm choosing to leave you?"

"Aren't you?"

"He'll use the korrigan to control who knows how many people? Maybe even your family."

"I know. But what about my choice? I choose you!"

"Your choice could end the world," Charon said.

Kahrin spun toward their guide. "Shut up. You did this. This is all you. You knew from the beginning."

Charon made whatever the demigod version of a sigh was, heaving it out hard. "I did not know the how."

"I don't believe you. I won't do it," Kahrin insisted. She stamped her foot. "I'm not leaving without Innes."

"You'd choose one man over countless other souls?"

"Yes!" Her voice echoed everywhere, and the walls trembled. "And I always will."

"Kahrin." Innes' own voice warbled now. "If I stay here, if we break the spell, it will kill him, too. All of this will end with us."

"I know!" The last she screamed in a way he'd never heard from her before, severing his heart into pieces, and nearly his resolve. He never could stand to see her in pain, not any that was not of her choosing, and he never thought it would be him who was causing it. "I know."

"So you know there's no other way."

She crumpled to the floor; face buried in her knees drawn to her chest. "I know." She sobbed, bitter and open and loud enough to shatter the restraint he had on his own tears. "But I can't do it, Innes."

"You have to."

The damned spell. Even now, as they knew the inevitable, he couldn't hold her, couldn't comfort her. If they wanted to say good-bye, it had to be like this. He let her cry it out for a time, however long it was he had no way to know. She clutched at his scarf tied around her, pressing her face into it.

"Why does it have to be you?" She looked up, the wavering green light not able to obscure the color of her mismatched eyes, enhanced by the puffiness of the brown skin around them.

He knelt in front of her, aching to reach for her in any and every way. Soon, he thought.

"We're heroes, Kahrin. That's what we do."

The cavern lurched, tossing him sideways and then back without the ground beneath them ever really moving. Kahrin stayed planted, Charon remained still, floating in his usual incurious manner, but Innes was sent sprawling.

Charon, in his bored tone, offered an explanation. "The missing soul has been noticed, I believe."

Innes felt a jerk from inside his navel, pulling tight and then releasing hard enough that it snapped him back across the floor again.

"The realm will fight to lock down any souls it detects. I do not believe that tether to Paul will last long."

Dammit. It was too soon. Of all the things that just could not, should not be rushed, this moment, this point of their story was at the top. And yet, here they were.

He grabbed the ends of the scarf, unwinding it from her throat until he could just hold her facing him in it. "Listen to me, Kahrin. You have to go, and you have to keep going. You're the strongest person I know, and you cannot give up."

"How? How do I keep going?" Her voice cracked beneath her sobs.

"Because you're not going to let this all be for nothing. Because you chose me and respect my choices." He swallowed, feeling his throat close with a lump. "Because your story is still in the middle, and someone has to tell mine."

That's when he knew he had her. All the stories, all the books, all the whimsy of childish stories. No hero would allow a story to stop in the middle. Her chin stopped quivering, and she wiped the sleeve of her coat across her face to clear it of tears. Her pretty eyes searched his face, and acceptance began to rule. And, god, she was beautiful, even now, stained with tears and breaking his heart. This was supposed to be the beginning of their story together, their journey as a couple.

"And you choose me."

"If I had to do it again, I would have done it sooner." He laughed a bitter sound. "I wouldn't have let anything stop us from," his face warmed, even now at the worst time, "you know."

"Sex, Innes. Good lord, you can say it." She looked up as the cavern rattled somewhere beyond the flourishes of mica and green. "I wish we could, just once more."

He did as well, the feel of her in his arms, her muscles clenching around him, her bratting ways and teasing touches. Or even just the soft shit she pretended to hate. The softness and surety of always knowing she was there. The warmth and silliness and sometimes chaos of her unfailing love.

"I'd settle for that kiss."

"Me too."

"You ready?"

She shook her head. "How could I ever be ready?"

"It has to be a mutual choice." The reality was exactly the opposite, but he knew she'd understand. She'd do the right thing.

She laughed, tears streaming down her cheeks and wetting the front of her coat. "Just like everything we do."

They both knew there was only one way to make it true, then.

He tugged the scarf, pulling her to him, and caught her tight in an embrace. In the same motion, his mouth clashed with hers, and he drank of her, loving her like a dying man.

Because, well, he was.

The tug in his belly snapped, he felt a chill charge through him, lightning quick and too brief. His hands gripped onto her as if she could stop the inevitable.

CHAPTER THIRTY-SEVEN

KAHRIN

There was only one way for this to truly be a mutual choice, and honestly, if this was the truth she had to live, it was also the only way she would choose it.

Innes yanked her to him, wrapping her in his arms as if they were out of time.

Because, well, they were.

She clutched to him, greedily taking the kiss he offered, knuckles as white as if she could hold him to the world. As if she could stop all of this, if only she was strong enough.

But she wasn't.

She felt him go cold, the chill so fast it took some of the warmth from her body. Stiff and still under her hands, against her body, full of life one moment, and gone the next.

Gone.

He was just gone. She thought there would have been a body to carry back, but there was nothing as the room shifted around her and Charon. The Dwelling of All Souls seemed to accept Innes in trade. She turned to Charon, shaking, her tears spilling to the ground and causing parts of it to scatter into tufts of smoke.

"What time is it?" she demanded.

"Does it matter?"

"It does to me." She needed to know. She needed to be able to count every minute she had to be in the world without him.

"Just past midnight in your world."

She swallowed. "You knew."

Charon nodded.

"Take me back." She choked, gasping for breath and drawing in the dry nothing offered by the realm. Grief roiled in her stomach and gorge rose in her throat. Afraid to lose the soul, to make all this a horrible, awful waste, she swallowed again, hard enough to hurt

"It will still be true when we return to the world of the living."

"I said get me out of here!" She shrieked, stamped her foot, waiting for Innes to touch her shoulder or elbow and calm her. But it wasn't going to happen. He would never again lay a hand on her. His voice would never dip low and rumble reassurances only for her ears. "I will tear this place apart if you don't take me back now."

Challenging a bluff Charon never called, she screamed and smashed both fists against the nearest thing that looked like a wall, watching it shatter, cracks forming down the walls and across the floor. She'd not thought it through, of course, not thought about what would happen next when her weight and mass that was not welcome in the realm of the dead was suddenly testing it. She skittered back away from what she'd done, the gaping holes of nothing she'd left behind her.

"Move," Charon ordered, which she was already doing. She took to her toes in whatever direction the room chose.

"If this place is all magic bullshit anyway, can't you just open it anywhere?"

Charon snapped to the form of a raven once more. He beat his wings to get a lead on her, then looping in wide circles. She didn't see anything, but she never saw anything. On the way in, Innes had promised her it was there. She had no reason not to trust him now.

She gained the distance between them, closed her eyes, held her breath and leapt.

She hit the ground on the other side, her head tucked, but landing her full weight on one shoulder, pain exploding through her elbow and fingers. She slid across newly refrozen snow, scraping across it with that wretched sound things made against ice. She came to a stop, looked up to see the first glimpse of dawn between the trees.

Every sense faded to numbness. Light didn't pierce her eyes, and the ache in her joints didn't reach her thoughts. Lying still on the ground, she refused to move. Refused to believe it was the start of a day without Innes in it. If she didn't move, maybe the sun wouldn't keep rising, and none of this had to be real.

Of course, life did not work like that, even in the wake of the loss of it. Kahrin clenched her eyes tight, grit her teeth against the painful pull behind her jaw as she fought to not cry again.

This can't all be for nothing, she told herself, lying as still as she could. She had to see this through. She had to finish what they'd started, what Innes had literally given his life for.

She stood, trying to get her bearings, but nothing was familiar. Even the shadows were different in unfamiliar trees. She buried her hands in her hair, gripping near her scalp, and screamed.

"Are you trying to attract the entire town?" Charon, a black dog once more, sat in front of her, tail flapping against the packed, frozen snow.

"I don't know the way back."

Charon sighed, and if he had any scolding on his lolling tongue, he held it. Instead, he jumped to his feet, trotting off. "Guide, remember?" he barked over his shoulder.

As if summoned, sirens wailed somewhere outside the woods, and they broke into a clearing as police and ambulance lights blurred past, leaving green trails in her vision.

Kahrin followed because what else was she supposed to do? She veered between hurrying to get this all over with and slowing to put off facing the truth for as long as possible.

He was gone.

Innes was gone.

Not since she was very, very young had she needed to live in the world without him. Did she even know how?

I can't think about that right now, she told herself firmly.

Charon led her back to the car, though she could follow the familiar sound of emergency vehicles ahead. From there it would have been impossible not to find the Quirke Dairy farm. She paused at the end of the driveway, the bright flashes of an ambulance and floods of blue and red from the police car stunning her into indecision. She stared at the sidewalk that wrapped around the house, a pair of paramedics rolling a stretcher with a zipped black bag on it. Her heart sped up, choking her, and pushing her into a run.

In all of this, she'd nearly forgotten about Ena.

She found Ena lying in the back of the ambulance, vitals being taken and a mask over her face to help her breathe. She turned her head to see Kahrin, smiling as if her life and that of her unborn weren't hanging on the line. There was sadness in her eyes, but Kahrin sensed it was unrelated, and her acknowledgement that if Paul had died, then Innes' fate was obvious.

Kahrin nodded, chin trembling, eyes burning. She inhaled deep and let it out in a shaky huff.

"Is she going to be okay?" Kahrin asked the paramedic.

"Right now, they're both stable, but we have to hurry."

Ena reached out for her hand, and Kahrin took it, squeezing.

"Is it done?"

Kahrin closed her eyes and nodded, a shudder threatening to break her facade of false calm. "Yeah."

"Bring Brother Whiteloon to the hospital," Ena said with a lift of her mask.

The paramedic pressed it gently back in place and helped Kahrin down off the back of the rig. He closed the doors behind her, and the ambulance turned about, and pulled out of the driveway with sirens wailing.

"You did this," Tippy Quirke screamed, her voice splitting into a rattle. "You killed my boy."

Kahrin's eyes cast about for Tippy, who was fighting off any attempt by police or EMTs to calm her. They walked with her, holding her back from lunging at Kahrin. They paid little attention to Kahrin, almost as if she wasn't there. As if she wasn't a person. For a moment she thought about what Paul had said, about how she had no soul of her own. She couldn't think about that now, either, but she knew she was going to have to find out what that meant for her. For the things she'd done, the people she'd helped kill, with Innes included in that now.

The police helped a wailing Tippy into the back of the police cruiser, wailing. Kahrin wanted to but couldn't spare any pity for the woman who had helped bring about this situation. The loss of Innes rested as much on the older woman's shoulders as they did on her son's.

There would be no forgiving that.

Kahrin looked at her through the window, across the yard, and felt nothing. Not anger. Nothing but the bottomless nothing that was the world with Innes yanked out of it. Taken out of it by her, in a terrible choice she had no good alternative but to take.

Tippy banged on the window, and Kahrin could hear her screaming at her with several choice words about herself and her parentage that she would not repeat. Paul's demise would only go so far to comfort her, to make her own loss more tolerable.

"We're not even close to even, you old bag," Kahrin muttered.

She wasn't sure how she'd climbed into Innes' car, or how she found the way back to the reservation. Moving in a fog, she barely paid attention to the turns, but surprised herself in the end. Noko McKenzie met her at the door, and with one look at her face, pulled her into a hug. Noko McKenzie didn't ask for an explanation, only held her while Kahrin struggled against a sob. And sob she did, with devastating, shaking wails. Without words, Noko McKenzie knew that Brother Whiteloon needed to be called. He arrived right away, knowing almost immediately what was amiss.

"One minute," Kahrin yelled as he helped Noko McKenzie into his car. From the back of Innes' car, she retrieved his medical kit and dug around in it, hoping her incredibly anal-retentive best friend really was as extra about planning as she always teased him for being. Ipecac. Sport drink. She gulped a slug of one and downed the other. It didn't take long, and she doubled over, emptying the contents of her stomach in a vaguely purple puddle onto the yard.

"Is that it?" Brother Whiteloon knelt beside her, and she didn't even question how he knew. It seemed right that he would, even if she couldn't explain it.

He offered her the handkerchief from his shirt pocket, which she took, but wiped her mouth across her sleeve, unthinkingly, instead. Using the hanky, she picked up the tied-off condom and wrapped it, cradling it like it was the most precious thing in the world, and not a regurgitated condom covered in vomit.

"Hopefully you know what to do with this."

Brother Whiteloon produced a small leather pouch from his coat, slid the drawstrings loose, and put the soul inside. "I do, but we need to hurry. The window to make it work is small."

CHAPTER THIRTY-EIGHT

KAHRIN

Kahrin spent too much time in hospitals, but at least today she wasn't the patient. She stared at the chipped tile of the polished waiting room floor and kicked at a scuff with the toe of her boot. "Twinkle Twinkle, Little Star" had played at least three times. She didn't know how long she stared at that scuff mark. She glanced at the clock behind her, focused on the black mark on the white linoleum, and when she looked up again, hours had passed. At least one meal's worth, but she didn't feel hungry. The ipecac still upset her stomach, and grief was a destructive force to appetites besides. Food seemed like a petty thing in the wake of Ena's emergency birth and the loss of Innes.

"You look like you need this more than I do," Brother Whiteloon said, appearing out of nowhere and handing her a doubled paper cup of coffee.

She smiled her thanks and took the cup, contemplating the reflective surface, swirling with the oil slick like colors of coffee that sat too long in a pot. "How's Ena?"

"Recovering, but she'll be fine."

Kahrin bobbed her head up and down, relieved but not having the energy to express it. "The baby?"

"Stillborn," he answered. "But fine now."

Kahrin looked up, an eyebrow cocked high. "So, it worked."

It was his turn to nod, dipping his chin. "Just barely."

"Just barely is better than not." She took a deep breath and sighed it out. "I guess we'll take it." She paused, wondering if she wanted to know. "How?"

"Are you familiar with doulas?" She didn't know or care what a doula was, so she nodded rather than ask what it had to do with anything. "Part of my calling is to introduce new souls into the world as well as guide them out."

"Out. Right." Her breath shook, and she rolled her eyes to the ceiling, hoping those traitorous tears would go back where they came from.

"You can see her if you like."

"Maybe in a minute." How could she go into the room and see what Innes had traded his life to protect? Because he'd want her to. She swallowed.

"Your friend—"

Kahrin waved a hand to stop him. "Don't. Don't tell me whatever you're going to say about him. Not yet. Please." Her chin shook.

"As you wish. If you need anything, just holler."

An uncomfortable silence settled in the room. She didn't know what to say to Brother Whiteloon, and she'd stymied the only conversation he seemed capable of right now. She sat, listening to the sounds of everything around them, the way everything was so alive. The scratching of staff signing things, coffee machines brewing, carts and equipment being rolled back and forth. She tolerated it as long as she could, and when she felt every muscle in her coil up in agitated energy, she pushed up from the chair. She pointed down the hall, and Brother Whiteloon told her which room to look for.

It was a double room, but Ena was the only occupant. The curtain to the other side was tied back. Ena lay in the bed, eyes closed and breathing softly. When Kahrin stepped in, she opened her large, nearly black eyes.

"There you are."

"Here I am." Kahrin's smile flickered and faltered. "I don't really know where else to go." She shoved her hands in her pockets and walked slowly to the side of the bed. No matter where she walked, she felt unsteady, lost, and alone.

She pulled the small armchair close to the side of the hospital bed, chewing on her lip as she tried to think of something to say. "How is she?"

"Beautiful. In an incubator." She smiled, but this time it didn't reach her eyes. "But she's not mine."

Kahrin hadn't expected that. Her mouth gaped as she searched for words. "I mean, kinda."

Ena sighed, seeming to shrink into the mattress and crappy pillow. When she opened her eyes again, Kahrin noticed the bruises of fatigue rimming them. "Don't worry, I'm going to love her, I'm sure." She looked at the ceiling. "She's a stranger to me right now."

"She would have been before, too." That sounded kind of smart.

Ena mulled this over. Whether she believed it or not, Kahrin wasn't sure, but she seemed to accept it with a tight smile.

"Does she have a name?"

Ena let a huff of laughter. "Kerrigan."

"That's funny," she answered, and meant it. She tried to find enough pieces of her heart to give it the laugh it deserved.

"I thought, maybe Innes as a middle name." Kahrin blinked. "If that's alright with you."

"Free world," she said. "I don't own the name."

Ena reached for her hand, and Kahrin allowed it. "I'm asking for your permission to honor your lost love for his sacrifice."

Kahrin squeezed her hand but didn't answer right away. He always was the sappy one of them, and if she thought on it, it seemed like something he'd like. It made sense. He'd blush and try to demur from it, but she was pretty sure he'd be touched. Maybe, somewhere, he was. If his soul still existed. If she hadn't destroyed it.

"I think he'd like that." Her eyes fluttered and she looked down at the floor between her knees again. It began to waver in her vision. "It doesn't feel real."

"It will. Once you accept it, you can begin to heal."

Kahrin scoffed. "I don't want to heal. Nothing will ever make this feel better." She shook her head, determined to change the subject. "She'll be safe with you? You know, from people?" She hoped Ena knew what she meant.

"Her gift won't work on me, and when she comes into it, I'll be able to protect others while she learns to control it." She shook her head as if that didn't exactly thrill her, but she was trying to convince them both that it did. "It's a calling. Brother Whiteloon says he can't think of anyone better for the responsibility. Something to ground me, to focus me. Maybe he's right."

"Maybe." Kahrin took her hand back and tapped both on her lap. Out of small talk. Out of questions. "I--" she stopped to swallow. "Need to call my parents." She shook her head. That was the last thing she wanted to do, and if Ena said anything else, Kahrin only gave a small grunt as if she heard her, preoccupied with how she might get out of telling them just yet.

She pulled her phone out, holding it up and wandering around, looking for a place where she would get a signal inside the building. Having to go outside and freeze to get one would be the wonderful cherry on this crap day. She found a seat crammed up against a large window in the waiting room and found enough signal to check her voicemail.

"Kahrin, it's Ma. Call me."

"Hey Kahr, it's Alec. When you get this, call me."

"Kahr. Brecken. Where the hell are you? Unlock your face from Innes' and call us back. Da's awake."

She dialed Ma. She kept as many details vague as possible, and pushed the conversation to stay on Da, and his sudden upturn of health.

"They gave him a transfusion from what Innes donated. That seemed to turn the corner. Isn't that weird? Considering there was no match for Innes when you two were in that accident?"

"Yeah, Ma. It is." She pulled her leg up and hugged it to her. It seemed that particular blessing of Yelena's extended beyond Innes' demise. He'd saved her Da's life, but he'd never know it.

"When will you two be heading back?"

Kahrin fought the lump forming in her throat and laid on the false cheer. "Oh, well, you know. There are some things to take care of. Lots of people to talk to."

"Be safe, Makoons. Both of you."

She disconnected without telling Ma goodbye. She stared out the window, having no idea what to do now. There was no body. Nothing for any sort of service. She wasn't sure she could handle it anyhow. God, she was lonely. And alone. What she wouldn't give for some of that soft shit right now.

A shiver ran over her, like icy fingers along her arms that raised goosebumps. Some of the tension eased, and for just a moment, she thought she could smell Innes' aftershave. For a moment she could swear he was solid, beside her, and she could almost feel the warmth of his hand in hers. Memory was a powerful thing. A cruel thing.

CHAPTER THIRTY-NINE

INNES

If he focused, if he tried, he was sure he could wrap his arms around her. Maybe he could comfort her. He could reach out, feel her warmth, smell her hair, her tears.

At first, he thought he'd dreamed all of it, because there she was. There was Ena, giving birth. There was Brother Whiteloon, waving a feather and discretely releasing the korrigan soul as the doctor caught the slick, still newborn. He heard the child's lungs burst into life. It was startling in its beauty to see and followed a logic he'd not considered before.

It didn't make a lick of sense, his predicament, though. He sat in the chair beside Kahrin. Even though everything was slightly muted, he could smell her coffee. Was he a ghost?

No, ghosts couldn't touch. Couldn't feel. Couldn't smell. They couldn't bury their nose in the hair of their lover, their best friend, and inhale the familiar tang of sweat-salted skin and strawberry conditioner. And yet, he could do all of that. But even with his arms around her, she stood. She was able to walk away. Able to leave the room. Leave his sight.

He hurried to get into the car when Brother Whiteloon drove her back to Noko McKenzie's. He rode beside her, fingers curled over hers. Palpable waves of her grief pressed against him, and he tried to reassure her. Tried to tell her he hadn't left her. Perhaps this was not hell, but it was near enough to it for him.

"I'm right here, Kahrin. Please. Please see me. Look at me."

She didn't, but for a moment, Brother Whiteloon looked in the rearview mirror, then back to the road.

Innes turned to facing her, a knee pulled up the way she so often did in their car. He couldn't lift her hand, couldn't pull her wrist to his lips, so he rested both of his hands on her knee. Over the little tear in her jeans from where she'd fallen out of the Underworld. The Dwelling of All Souls. "I didn't leave you, but I don't know how to get back." He didn't know where he was, or how he was. "I need you to find me."

He brushed a knuckle slowly over the apple of her cheek, and she blinked. Her eyes flicked to him, just a flutter until she decided there was nothing there. She touched her face, following the trail of his fingers. She could feel him, he could tell, just not immediately. Like he'd slipped into some lapse of time that put the slightest fraction of a moment between them.

"I'm going crazy," she muttered.

"You okay?" Brother Whiteloon asked.

"No." Kahrin was nothing if not honest, even if she didn't elaborate.

"I'm sorry 'bout your friend," he said for about the fourth time tonight.

"Me too," she finally answered. She rubbed at her eyes. She was tired, had to be exhausted. "I can't believe he's gone."

"I'm not gone," Innes insisted. "Kahrin, I need you to hear me."

Brother Whiteloon looked up once more, his aged mouth tugged into a frown with deep creases at the corners. He pulled up to the house and Kahrin and Noko McKenzie got out of the car. Innes hustled to slide out before they could shut the door. What would happen if they shut it before he could get out? Would he cross through it?

He didn't want to find out.

He left no tracks in the snow as he hurried to the door ahead of them, or at least none that remained. They scattered smooth as soon as he lifted his foot. Noko McKenzie unlocked the door and the warmth from inside washed over him as he slipped through ahead of them. He kicked off his boots, not sure if he could track in mud or snow.

"Can I get you anything to eat?" Noko asked.

"No, ma'am. I think I just want to sleep."

"You can call me Auntie, if you like."

She wouldn't, at least not right away, Innes knew. Kahrin was stubborn, and she would resist help, sympathy, and was likely to take this out on these near strangers.

"I'll try," she promised.

That one he knew she could keep. She would try, if only because they had welcomed her so warmly.

He followed her to the bedroom. He turned around as she undressed to give her privacy. It only seemed right, since she didn't know he was here.

"Take the shirt," he said over his shoulder. A moment later he heard her dig into his bag.

She wrapped his orange sweatshirt around herself, drawing her knees up inside it as she slid into the bed. His heart squeezed, like a vise pressing all his ribs together, as he heard her go from quiet tears to wracking sobs.

"How could you leave me?" she hiccuped. "I'll never forgive you for leaving me."

Innes slid up behind her, molding his body to her back, and draping his arm around her middle. He ducked his head, resting his nose at the join of neck and shoulder. "I know."

She stiffened, held her breath. "Innes?"

A hope flickered in his heart, a tingle of excitement surging through him.

"Don't be stupid," she scolded herself. She took a deep breath, and repeated the words, as if to cement them in her mind.

"I'm here." He swallowed. "And I'm staying with you until you find me." He pressed his lips to the ball of her shoulder. "You have to find me."

CHAPTER FORTY
KAHRIN

The sky was impossibly clear, filled with indifferent stars, the moon all but blacked out. She could smell the sweetgrass and tobacco, and the weirdly gentle drumming didn't bother her as much as she thought it would. In fact, she found something soothing in the unfamiliar rhythm.

Kahrin looked across Auntie Mary's backyard, where a group of these near strangers, this would-be family, circled a fire pit. The flames danced high, sparks leaping until they seemed to take a place among the stars, swallowed by the sky. Despite the cold, she had to guess there were at least thirty people gathered around, some with plates of potluck food, others talking, enjoying the night.

Innes wasn't Ojibwe. Brother Whiteloon had offered to hold the ceremonial fires all the same. For her. She couldn't think of a reason to decline, so she accepted. Honestly, being surrounded by people helped, even people she didn't know well. Maybe she didn't want to know them. Maybe she didn't want to call anyone Auntie or Uncle or Noko, but there was a balm she'd not expected in seeing how they came together, how they just folded her into their life and held her up while she passed the worst of the first storm of losing Innes.

"I found these, but don't let Noko see you with them," Ena said, handing a heavy pair of shears to her. "I'm only mostly sure that I can't be put over her knee now that I have a baby of my own, even for using her sewing scissors for non-sewing purposes."

Kahrin took them, watching as Ena's arm went right back to holding up the sleeping girl wound up in a large scarf made for fastening babies to her body. Baby Kerrigan slept as if nothing in the world was wrong. Kahrin envied her. She'd not been sleeping well, sometimes swearing she could hear Innes every time she went still and quiet. She could almost feel his fingers in her hair as she would drift off, only to jerk awake and discover she'd imagined it all.

"You sure you want to do this?" Ena asked.

"Brother Whiteloon says it's tradition." She ran her fingers over her long braid, looping the end of it around her hand.

"And you are beholden to tradition now?"

"I don't know, but this feels right." A sad smile touched her lips, but she didn't feel the squeeze of tears behind her eyes. Perhaps she'd spent them all. "And Da's still in the hospital. He won't be able to do," she gestured to the fire, "this." He would, she knew, if she asked. But that would require asking, and she didn't even know how she was going to face him with this.

"When are you leaving?" Ena had settled into motherhood quickly, bouncing lightly on her feet, swishing the baby back and forth slowly. Her worries over not loving her new daughter seemed to vanish when she'd brought her home to cheers and applause of so many loved ones. So many members of a loving extended family. A family that was ready to include Kahrin, too.

"I don't know." An honest answer. It had been a few days. She could have left any time. She'd even tried getting in the car. She made it as far as starting the engine but couldn't make herself drive. "I feel this odd tether. I'm sure it'll pass. As I get used to it."

"You could stay."

She swung her head to look at Ena. "How?"

She laughed softly. "You already have a room, and if you don't want to stay with us and a new baby, you know Bonnie would be happy to have you."

"I'm not ready for that. Yet."

Stay. A week ago, she and Innes had talked about it. She'd laughed. A few days ago, she would have laughed, maybe thrown out a sarcastic comment about not needing any of them. But right now, standing here, watching the fire dance, and hearing the sounds of life as all the people paid respects to a wonderful man they didn't know, it didn't seem so crazy.

"What would I do?"

"Learn" Ena said easily. As if she'd planned it. How did she make it sound so simple? "Learn your history. Learn your culture. Learn who you are, alone." Ena rested her nose against her daughter's head a moment, then added, "Learn medicine with Brother Whiteloon."

Kahrin made a face. "I'm sure everyone would love that."

"Why not?" Was she serious? "You're Iskandar's daughter. Brother Whiteloon knows your secret as he knows mine. He could help you like he's helped me. At least talk to him, before you reject the idea altogether."

Kahrin's eyes fell on the Elder in question. He sat in a chair, a drum in his hand, beating it with a leather wrapped mallet of some type. She didn't understand the words he chanted. She didn't know the purpose of the song, but she knew he was doing it for her. For Innes. And somehow, that made her want to understand.

"Okay," she said, before she really knew she was talking. "I'll talk to him, but I'm not making promises."

"Of course not."

The breeze was bitter and dry, the early hints of spring creeping in, but a warmth ghosted over her side, like the brush of a shoulder. Like someone standing behind her. Her hand twitched, fingers curling over air. Pain pierced her heart as she remembered there were no fingers to grasp. No warm, solid chest to lean into. How would she go home? How would she tell Emilia? Or Ma and Da? Or anyone? How would she sit in her little townhouse when everything around her reminded her of Innes? Of Innes being gone?

"Maybe."

"Maybe?" Ena echoed in question.

"Maybe it would be okay for now. Just," her throat squeezed, and she swallowed the lump, "until I figure things out."

Ena wrapped her hand around Kahrin's and squeezed. "You'll have all the time you need." Kahrin looked up and met her dark eyes, the firelight dancing in the shiny surfaces. "And a friend, if you'll allow one."

Kahrin swallowed, letting her eyes drop to their joined hands. "That might not be so bad."

She pulled her hand free of Ena's and took up the shears.

"It's so pretty. Are you really ready to part with it?"

"Brother Whiteloon says it can help. And..." She trailed off and touched her braid where she could have sworn she felt something, and decided it was a wistful imagination. "And I need to let go."

A soft sound, like a gentle 'no' whispered across dried leaves and grazed the small hairs of her ears. She shivered. She was in her own head again, arguing circles about how to grieve, how to accept this absence, this hole in her life. She had to start somewhere, and removing this reminder of the intimacy she lost, of the could-have-been that would have been, seemed as good a place to start as any. If only Innes hadn't needed to be so damned heroic.

Would she have loved him if he was anything other than himself? No. She was certain of that.

The shears sawed through the braid with only a few pumps of the handles, and before she could overthink it again, her braid lay in her hand, and the remaining hair tickled at her neck, like a feather light brush of lips.

"I should have used a mirror," she murmured. She shook her head, feeling the uneven strands bob.

"I can fix it," Ena assured her. "It's kind of cute."

"Of course it is. I'm adorable." Was it too soon to begin finding something to joke about?

"I can't argue with that." She tilted her head, rubbing her hand over Kerrigan's back. "I'm glad I've met you. You've given me Kerrigan, and with her, it's a small spark of good in all this."

Kahrin breathed deeply. "I'm glad to have met you, too." And meant it. She looked at the hair in her hand again. "No sense putting this off."

"When you're ready."

"I'll never be ready."

Ena tucked Noko's shears into her back jeans pocket and covered the handles with her sweater, then took Kahrin's hand again. "I'm here."

The way it echoed in her mind in Innes' warm baritone squeezed her chest, and she stepped off the porch, approaching the fire. She stared into the flames, letting the heat sting her eyes so that any tears at all might join her in this moment.

She tossed her braid into the red coals and watched the strands curl in on themselves. She closed her eyes, lifted her chin, and let the chanting and beat of the drum caress her.

"Goodbye, Innes," she whispered.

"It's not goodbye," the night whispered back.

AUTHOR'S NOTE:

Thank you, from the bottom of my heart for reading *The Dwelling of All Souls*, and following Innes and Kahrin in their adventures. If you have time and are so inclined, please leave a rated review on Amazon, Goodreads, Barnes and Noble, BookBub, or your favorite place to review books.

Reviews are so important to authors, and more so for indie authors. Reviews help keep us going, encourage us, and get word of our great stories to new readers.

For more of my work, you can visit my website brhillmann.com, or follow me on Instagram @brandann.r.hillmann, and Twitter @OuyangDan. I would love to hear from readers because these stories are for you as much as they are for me.

ACKNOWLEDGEMENTS:

The Hole in the World series began as a platonic love letter to a dear friend. None of this could be possible without her support and generosity in trusting me to care for Innes as I do Kahrin. Lucky her, she gets Kahrin if anything happens to me. So, Caraine, this is for you, first and always.

To my family. Thanks for putting up with me when the story has to come out, or when the story won't come out, and all the in-betweens that can make me a monster to live with. Your encouragement, support, and faith in me keeps me flying.

To my beta readers, Claire, Jada, Jessica, and Ryann. You are awesome, and the first ones to stand between me and some of the silliest nonsense ever committed to page.

To my editor, Cathy, who understands my work and makes these stories better. To my proofreader, R. Pincus, because my fingers have minds of their own. You both take this book from good to awesome.

To Cami and Stephanie, my socially distanced writing group. Thank you for your wisdom and support as well as the laughs. Thanks to all the wonderful Bookstagrammers and authors I've met in the Writing Community. Thanks to the Romanstagram chat for taking in this genre outsider and cheering her on like one of your own.

Finally, thank you to every reader who let Kahrin and Innes into their heart. Without readers, a book is just words on a page, and not a living world.

ABOUT THE AUTHOR:

Brandann R. Hill-Mann is an Anishinaabekwe speculative fiction author, stage manager, puppeteer, and podcaster. Her short stories have appeared in *Anathema: Spec from the Margins* and *Page and Spine*. Her debut novel, *The Hole in the World* released in October of 2019, and the follow-up, *Blood of the True Believer* in August of 2020. *The Dwelling of All Souls* is the third book in *The Hole in the World* series. Brandann is a citizen of the Sault Sainte Marie Tribe of Chippewa Indians and graduate of the University of Hawai'i at Mānoa's department of Theatre and Dance. She is currently on the island of O'ahu in Hawai'i where she drinks too much coffee and lives with her family.

www.ingramcontent.com/pod-product-compliance
Lightning Source LLC
Chambersburg PA
CBHW021142190726
48288CB00008B/2775